100 HOURS

RACHEL VINCENT

 KATHERINE TEGEN BOOKS
An Imprint of HarperCollins Publishers

Katherine Tegen Books is an imprint of HarperCollins Publishers.

ISBN 978-0-06-241156-3

Typography by Carla Weise
17 18 19 20 21   PC/LSCH   10 9 8 7 6 5 4 3 2 1
❖
First Edition

To every girl out there who's ever discovered
her true strength under terrible circumstances.
You are my inspiration.

NOW

"She's getting closer!"

I glance over my shoulder, and the movement throws me off balance. My cousin grabs my arm before I can fall, then she's in the lead, clutching the cell phone in one hand.

Footsteps pound behind us. Silvana huffs, as if each step drives more air from her lungs. But her pace is steady. She's strong and fast.

She's almost caught us.

"There it is!" My cousin points at a break in the jungle trail, and ahead, I see moonlight gleaming on dark water.

The beach. The boats.

We're almost free.

100 HOURS EARLIER

GENESIS

"You really came here on a private jet?"

Samuel's mouth is so close to Neda's that they're practically kissing, and that obviously makes her happy. No one in this tiny Cartagena dive bar knows she's five pounds too heavy and four inches too short to ever have anything more than her face appear in *Teen Vogue*, even if her father did design the latest Hermès handbag. In Cartagena, she's just another hot American tourist. Where everyone else sees anonymity, Neda thinks she's projecting mystery.

Neda only sees what she wants to see. Cheerful delusion is part of her charm.

The rest of her charm is money.

"There's no other way to travel." Her lips brush Samuel's cheek, and he's so into it he's breathing hard. His hand is on her thigh. She's high on the power she has over him—I can see it in her eyes. "Commercial is so . . . common."

In the chair to my right, Nico stiffens. He grew up in a five-hundred-square-foot bungalow just outside my grandmother's neighborhood with his mother and three younger sisters.

As usual, Neda has no clue, but Samuel doesn't care what she's saying. He's probably not even listening. He tugs her into the middle of the bar to join three other couples dancing to the strong, fast beat and brass notes of the cumbia-reggae fusion video playing on a small television mounted over the bar. She stumbles, but steadies herself without his help. She's okay, for now. But just in case, I finish off her margarita. I'm doing her a favor. She can't afford the calories and she can't handle her liquor.

"That's a tourist drink. Try this." Nico pushes his bottle across the table toward me. Most of the locals are drinking rum, but he likes *aguardiente*, an anise-flavored liquor. He thinks I've never had it because my dress is expensive, my nails are perfect, and I call my grandmother Nana instead of *abuela*. But Nico has only seen what I've let him see.

He was surprised when I asked him to show my friends and me something outside the touristy Cartagena party scene. But that was the point. People can't assume they know you if you keep them guessing.

I grab Nico's bottle and pour an inch of *aguardiente* into my empty glass, then throw it back in one gulp.

His brows rise. "Not your first time?"

I sweep my long, dark hair over my shoulder, and I know he can't look away. "Nana sends my dad a case every Christmas. He doesn't count the bottles." My dad only sees what I let him see too.

We drink half the bottle while Nico tells me about the hike he's leading next week, to the ruins of an ancient city in Colombia's Sierra Nevada. He moonlights as a tour guide because helping my grandmother around the house pays the bills, but it doesn't pay for college.

"Come on." Nico leans closer, and his eyes shine in the glow of colored lights strung over the bar. "You wanted to see the *real* Colombia. Let me take you to Ciudad Perdida."

"We're not going to be here that long." And I am *not* taking a generic tour with a dozen budget-traveling tourists, even if Nico is the guide. "But maybe I'll let you show me something special tomorrow. Something . . . secluded."

He leans back in his chair and gives me a slow smile. Now he gets it.

I take another sip of *aguardiente* and glance around the bar. The local guys in the corner booth are still watching us, but that's no surprise. People watch my friends and me everywhere we go.

What *is* strange is that they're watching Maddie, in her eco-friendly dress and "vintage" sandals that actually came from Goodwill.

"Your cousin is having fun," Nico says.

She's dancing with one of the local guys. The pretty one with bright hazel eyes and a scruffy, square jaw.

Paola, the bartender, pours with a heavy hand, and her generosity has miraculously dislodged the stick from my cousin's ass. Really, it's about time. Maddie was uptight before her father died, and since then, she's elevated the role of buzzkill from a hobby to an art.

Fortunately, I don't have to watch out for Maddie like I do Neda, because her brother, Ryan, would never let anything happen to her.

"You're bored," Nico says, drawing me out of my thoughts.

I cross my arms and lean back in my chair. "Is that your best guess?"

His gaze narrows as he studies me, trying to read my mood. "Is this a game?"

"Isn't everything?" My glass is empty, so I take a sip from his, watching him over the rim as he tries to make sense of the puzzle that is me and my friends dropping cash in his neighborhood dive bar.

He nods at the dance floor, where Neda and Maddie are now dancing in a sloppy group with three guys. "I thought your friend and your cousin didn't get along."

"They don't." I raise his glass. "This particular social discrepancy is brought to you by the miracle of tequila."

"And that one?" His focus settles on the end of the bar, where Ryan and Holden are laughing at some story the bartender is telling them, as she refills my cousin's glass with straight soda. Every time Paola bends over to grab a glass, they look down her shirt. My cousin is subtle. My boyfriend is not. "Is that also the tequila?"

I watch for a minute. Then I look away. *That's nothing. That's Holden.* I stand and take Nico's hand. "That's . . . not what I came here to see."

MADDIE

The fast, heavy rhythm of the cumbia beat pounds through me, driving every spin and little kick, and each connection with Sebastián. His hands find my waist and I smile at the reckless thrill his touch sends through me.

The floor swells around me, then it begins to spin. I stumble. Sebastián laughs and pulls me in closer. Then we're dancing again.

I am drunk for the second time in my life.

The first time, I almost died.

This bar isn't the kind of place I expected Genesis to drag us to. There are no bright lights or throngs of international tourists. The bartender isn't swamped and the local crowd doesn't care what I'm wearing or how well I move. They just want to have a good time.

For the first time in nearly a year, I'm actually having fun. But Genesis doesn't get credit for that.

In the pause between songs, I catch my breath, and movement from one of the tables catches my eye. My cousin tugs Nico out of his chair, her predatory gaze locked onto him like some kind of laser target.

He probably doesn't even know he's caught.

My phone buzzes, and I pull it from my pocket, but Genesis plucks it from my hand on her way past with Nico. "Do you really think you should be drunk-texting your mommy? I promise she'll survive without hearing from you for a few hours."

She drops my phone into her purse, and as the next song begins, I frown as I watch Genesis and Nico disappear into the back of the bar. But I can't really say I'm surprised. The problem with being given everything in life is that you grow up thinking you can take whatever you want, whenever you want it. Even if your boyfriend is sitting half a room away.

Holden looks from me to Genesis's empty table, and his jaw clenches. He slides off his stool.

It's *possible* that my staring wasn't as subtle as I thought.

"*¿Qué pasa, hermosa?*" Sebastián runs one warm hand up my arm.

"*Nada. Lo siento,*" I tell him.

"*¿Quieres otra copa?*"

"*No, gracias.*" I would *love* another drink. But unlike my cousin, I know better than to take something just because it's offered.

Sebastián shrugs as the music changes. This is a slower song, without the familiar cumbia moves.

I must look lost, because he smiles and dances closer. His hands find my hips, and I'm moving again. Then he kisses me, right there on the dance floor, and suddenly I'm kissing and dancing simultaneously. Even though my brother thinks I can't walk and chew gum at the same time.

My head feels light. The rest of the bar has lost focus, and I don't even care. I feel like anything could happen here, and all I have to do is let it.

GENESIS

The *aguardiente* has done its job, and Nico takes over where the alcohol has left off. I am drunk on him. I am drunk on the cumbia beat, and dark hallways, and calloused fingers. I am intoxicated by the way he presses me against the wall. By the way his lips trail from my mouth toward my ear, then down my neck. He's not gentle. He is not hesitant, or apologetic, or so eager that the moment threatens brevity.

Nico is twenty. His problems are as substantial as his passions, and he knows what he wants.

He knows what *I* want.

"Take me somewhere tomorrow," I whisper as his hand glides up from my waist, over my dress, and his tongue leaves a hot trail on my neck. "Show me something beautiful. Something real."

His hand slides into my hair. "Parque Tayrona," he suggests, his lips skimming my skin.

I frown and push him back. "It's spring break. I'm *over* crowded beaches."

"I know some secluded spots." He leans into me again, and his breath brushes my ear. "*Vistas exclusivas.*"

I smile and run my hands over his chest. That's what I

want. The real Colombia. Places not listed on travel web-sites.

I'm not supposed to be in this bar. I'm not supposed to be in this country. But "supposed to" means less to me with every passing second. This is my life. This is my spring break.

There are no limits but those *I* set.

Nico tugs my head back with a loose handful of my hair. Our kiss is shameless and reckless and scandalous and all those other adventurous things that taste sweeter in the shadows.

I am breathing hard. My head is barely tethered to my shoulders. Then—

Nico is suddenly gone, and his absence throws me off balance. A hand grabs my shoulder, pinning me against the wall and I open my eyes. Holden has a handful of Nico's shirt in his right fist, while his left digs into my skin. His brown eyes burn into me. "Do your pleas for attention always have to be so pedestrian? Or is this some kind of ironic social commentary?"

Nico pulls his shirt from my boyfriend's grip. "Jealousy is an ugly emotion, *mono. ¿Cierto?*"

Holden's pale face flushes. At home, insulting him is grounds for a fight. But at home, his father can make legal charges and public scandals disappear.

Holden is the right guy for Miami. There, he knows all the right people and says all the right things.

But we're not in Miami.

"Let go, Holden." He has no high ground to stand on. This is how we are.

He turns on me, and blond hair falls over his forehead. He's so mad that for a second, he forgets I'm not someone he can push around. "Don't make this worse, Gen." He turns back to Nico.

Anger blazes up my spine and muscle memory kicks in. I grab his hand and twist, and the pressure on his wrist, elbow, and shoulder force him forward, bent at the waist. Holden clearly thought the Krav Maga black belt rolled up in my top drawer was just an accessory—another bullet point on my college applications.

Now he knows better.

Satisfaction warms me from the inside. Then I realize I can't take it back. He won't underestimate me anymore.

"Damn it, Genesis!" he snaps, and I let him go.

Nico laughs, and I silently curse myself for caving to such a revealing impulse. "*Tu novio es un tonto.*"

But he's wrong. My boyfriend isn't a fool. He's just drunk.

"What did he say?" Holden demands, his cheeks still flaming. He stretches his arm to ease the pain, and I know I will have to do damage control. So I lie.

"He said you drink too much."

Nico glances at me in surprise. "She is too hot for you, *gringo.*" He grins at me.

Holden's fists clench and he looks at Nico as if he's large game fit for nothing but sport shooting.

I tug my boyfriend toward the front of the bar. "Come

remind me what I see in you." When I look back, I see Nico watching me, grinning. He thinks we've gotten away with something. That I might come back for more.

He's the fool.

Holden and I get a dark booth near the door. His hands are everywhere. He needs to be in control of this moment, so I let him think he is, and the making up is so good I almost want to pick another fight, just so we can do it all over again.

This is what I like best about him. Holden's temper runs hot, but so does the rest of him. When I have his full attention, it's like we're on fire. Nico was added fuel for the flames.

"Why do you push my buttons?" Holden murmurs against my neck.

I tilt my head back to give him better access. "What are buttons for, if not to be pushed?"

Holden groans, and his mouth trails lower.

Over his shoulder I watch Ryan coax the bartender out from behind the bar.

"*Corazón*, you don't drink and you can't dance!" Paola calls as she follows him, hips swaying. "What do you have to offer a woman?"

"Come find out . . ." My cousin backs onto the dance floor, his hips twitching in his best imitation of salsa dancing. I laugh. He actually has rhythm—he plays the drums—but his body doesn't seem to know that.

Holden works his way up my neck again, and I'm

breathing hard by the time he gets to my mouth. "I didn't get a very good look at that back hall," he murmurs against my lips as his hand slides up my leg. "Why don't you show me what I've been missing?"

Before I can answer, my phone buzzes from my purse. I pull it out and glance at the text on my screen.

Why aren't you in the Bahamas? Call me THIS INSTANT.

Holden frowns while I type. "Who's that?"

Don't worry. No pasa nada. Besos.

"I'll show you my texts when you show me yours." He doesn't need to know it's just my dad checking up on me.

Holden's brows rise, as if I've just laid down a challenge. He reaches for my phone, but then Maddie slides into the booth across the table, saving us both from a scene I was almost looking forward to making.

"We need to get Neda out of here," my cousin says. "She's drunk."

"We're all drunk," Holden points out.

"But the rest of us haven't decided to parade stunning cultural ignorance and a shockingly thick wad of cash down Cartagena's unlit back streets in the middle of the night." Maddie's disgusted huff hints at reemerging sobriety. "But that's no surprise, considering Neda still thinks she's in Cart-a-gee-na."

I follow her pointed gaze to see Neda stagger as Samuel leads her toward the exit. She doesn't even notice when she drips tequila on her twelve-hundred-dollar sandals.

I wave at Ryan and nod in their direction. He says a polite farewell to Paola and joins us. "I'll take her, you take him," I whisper as I slide across the patched and sticky booth.

"Hey, does Paola work tomorrow night?" Ryan says as we sandwich them. When Samuel turns to answer, I ease Neda from his grip with one hand and take her drink from her with the other.

"Where are we going?" she asks as Holden opens the door for us.

"Home." I set her glass on an empty table.

Neda looks confused. "Back to Miami?"

Maddie grabs Neda's purse and rolls her eyes. "Yes. Click your heels together and say, 'There's no place like my ten-bedroom beachfront estate.'"

Outside, the lights are few and far between, and the street is nearly empty. There are no tourists here. No street vendors. I turn to ask Holden to call for a car, but he already has his phone pressed to his ear, giving our location to the car service. "*Aquí en cinco minutos, extra de cien.*" In his sad, broken Spanish, he's offered the driver an extra hundred if he's here in five minutes. He doesn't like Nico's neighborhood.

"I wanna stay." Neda's speech is slurred and her steps are the slushy scrape of sandals against pavement. "Samuel and I were—"

"Don't run out on me, Neda." Ryan slides one arm around her waist, taking most of the burden off me. "It's not every day I get to walk with a gorgeous model on my arm, *mi corazón*. I'm drunk on your beauty."

Neda giggles and I hang back to let Ryan work his charm.

As we walk toward the corner, Holden slides his arm around my shoulders. "Is the rest of spring break going to be so full of local color?"

"Why else would you come?"

"I came because you said Nassau was dull and Cancún was 'obvious.' And because you promised me nude beaches."

"Admit it." I slide my hand up his chest as we walk down the cracked sidewalk, and the heat in his eyes resurges. "You haven't been bored for a second since we stepped off the plane."

93 HOURS EARLIER

MADDIE

I wake up at dawn and find Abuelita alone in the kitchen, pouring Masarepa cornmeal into a glass mixing bowl. A canister of salt and a small bowl of melted butter sit on the counter. The scents of black coffee and fresh mango trigger memories of childhood visits. Though Uncle Hernán flies her to Miami for most holidays, I haven't been in my grandmother's house since I was a small child.

"*¡Buenos días*, Madalena!" She pulls me into a hug as soon as I step into the room, the brightly colored tiles cold against my bare feet. "You're up early for a Saturday."

"*¿Arepas con huevo?*" I guess.

Abuelita smiles. "*Sí.* Are they still your brother's favorite?"

"*¡Por supuesto!*" Anything edible qualifies as Ryan's favorite, but Abuelita's egg-stuffed corn cakes hold a special place in his heart. And in his stomach.

"*¡Qué triste que tu madre* never mastered the art!" She says it with a smile, but she means every word. My mom is second-generation Cuban American, and in Abuelita's eyes, Cuban food cannot compare.

"*¿Van otra vez a la playa con tus amigos?*" my grandmother asks as she forms small cakes from the cornmeal mixture.

"They aren't *my* friends, Abuelita. Genesis and the Dior divas have appointments at some spa this morning, but they'll probably want to party tonight. I doubt I'll go." Not after the fool I made of myself in the bar last night.

"Your cheeks are pink, *flaquita*." My grandmother's eyes brighten as she smiles. "Did you meet a boy?"

"Their tongues certainly met." My brother pads into the kitchen on bare feet and slides onto the bar stool next to mine.

Yes, I kissed Sebastián on the dance floor. But Genesis went into a dark hallway with Abuelita's handyman, right in front of her asshole boyfriend, and no one seems to think *that's* worthy of public broadcast.

The double standard in my family never seems to work in my favor.

"You're such a pretty girl." My grandmother smiles at me over a growing collection of *arepas*. "A little too thin, maybe. You deserve some fun. You've been through so much . . ."

"I'm so sorry for your loss." The man gives my shoulder an awkward pat, and his words play on in my head as the sentiment echoes down the receiving line. I stare at his dress shirt. There's a stain on the

underside of his belly. He shuffles to my left to shake Ryan's hand.

My brother smells like whiskey, and our mother hasn't even noticed.

"Maddie, please let us know if there's anything we can do." The woman next in line takes my hand, but I hardly feel her grip. I've hardly felt anything in days. I stare at her shoes until she moves on.

The coffin is closed, and if I can't see my father's face, I don't want to see anyone else's either.

"Are you taking care of yourselves?" Abuelita slides the first corn patty into the hot oil with a gentle expertise perfected by fifty years' experience. The cornmeal sizzles, but the oil does not pop.

"¡Desde luego! Which is why I can't have many of those." I nod at the carb-heavy fried corn cakes, which would wreak havoc on my blood sugar.

"Uncle Hernán gave her an insulin pump." Ryan glances at my stomach, where a slight bump at my waist betrays my most obvious concession to my illness. "So she doesn't have to mess with needles anymore."

Abuelita nods. "Hernán has always taken care of us."

I bite my tongue to keep my thoughts from spilling out. The truth is that every time my father came to Colombia with the nonprofit organization he worked for, he spent as much time with his mother as he could.

My uncle hasn't set foot in Colombia since he left as a teenager. He just sends money.

When he found out our insurance wouldn't cover my insulin pump, he threw money at the problem. Not that I'm not grateful. But I was just another issue he could resolve by writing a check. Like he did for Ryan's rehab.

"*Buenos días*, Nana." Genesis strides into the room in running shorts and a sports bra, tightening the ponytail cinched high on her head. There's a sheen of sweat on her face and her hair is damp.

"*¡Buenos días!*" Abuelita steps back from the stove to accept a kiss on the cheek from the oldest and least culturally aware of her granddaughters.

"My phone," I demand.

Genesis plucks it from a hidden pocket at her waist and tosses it to me. There's a text from my mother.

Hope you're having fun! How are the Bahamas? Take a snorkeling class for me!

"Genesis!" My cousin's name sounds like an expletive as it explodes from my mouth. "Why does my mother think we're in *the Bahamas*?"

"Because she doesn't know how to track your phone?" Her casual shrug makes me want to choke her. "My dad figured it out before we even landed."

"You said you cleared the change of plans with everyone who mattered!"

"Yeah." She gives me another careless shrug as she pours a glass of juice. "Nana and the pilot."

"You didn't tell me your father hadn't agreed," Abuelita scolds. Yet she sounds more embarrassed than angry about the lie. "He called last night, and he was very upset."

"Do Neda's and Holden's parents know?" I demand. "Do they even care?"

Ryan puts one hand on my shoulder. "Maddie, calm—"

I turn on him. "She's never the one who has to deal with the fallout from the crazy, reckless way she barrels through life." Practically kidnapping her own cousins and dragging them to Colombia. Letting Ryan party with her friends during the height of his addiction, even when she *knew* he had a problem.

"You're overreacting," Genesis insists as she plucks a slice of mango from the tray. "Nana called me a couple of weeks ago to ask when we could come see her, and I seized the opportunity." Meaning she bribed the pilot.

"Did you even ask your dad?"

"Of course not. He would have said no. But we're here now, and he'll get on board once Nana calls and asks why he's trying to keep her grandchildren away from her." She hugs Abuelita from behind. "He won't say no to his mother."

"You probably got that poor pilot fired."

Genesis shrugs again, and I want to punch her. "He made his own choice."

"I'm going home." Anger burns in my chest; I feel like I'm breathing fire. "Are you going to make my mom go into debt for a last-minute ticket, or will your dad send his pilot?"

"The jet lands in an hour. But if you get on it, you'll miss Parque Tayrona. Nico's going to take us for a couple of days."

Nico. Genesis takes him into the back of the bar, and suddenly he's giving us a private tour of the most beautiful series of beaches in Colombia. Of course.

"Tayrona?" Ryan's brows rise. Our parents spent their honeymoon hiking at the foot of the Sierra Nevada mountain range, through the famous system of natural beaches connected by patches of unblemished jungle. The *parque* was my father's favorite place in the world.

Genesis knows we can't turn down a trip to Tayrona. And if we stay in Colombia with her, then this trip isn't just another impulsive rule-breaking binge orchestrated by a spoiled heiress. Suddenly, her reckless jaunt across international borders looks like the gift of closure to her grieving cousins, plus an overdue visit to her isolated *abuela*.

"I reserved a couple of cabanas, but it's a two-hour jungle hike from the entrance to the most isolated beach at Cabo San Juan. So dress accordingly and bring a swimsuit." Genesis eyes my pajama bottoms, as if they're indicative of what I'd wear for a hike.

"I haven't said I'm going," I snap, but she dismisses my protests in favor of a fresh *arepa*, which wouldn't be on her raw, whole foods diet at home.

"We're already here." Ryan pulls me close with one arm around my shoulder. "We may as well stay and see the sights."

"Go, *flaquita*," my grandmother urges. "Have fun on the beach for a couple of days. I'll deal with Hernán *y tu madre*, and we'll get caught up Monday night, when you get back."

I can practically feel myself falling onto the life-sized chessboard at my cousin's feet.

Checkmate.

92 HOURS EARLIER

GENESIS

Penelope Goh pulls me into a hug as she steps out of the back of the black car. "Sorry I'm late. We got stuck behind a blockade. My driver said the police found two bodies in a burned-out van last night."

"Of course they did." Holden shrugs. "Because why *wouldn't* my girlfriend's sense of adventure drag us into a war-torn third-world country?"

"You sound like my father." But Colombia is a different place than it was when my dad and his widowed, pregnant mother emigrated. Nana wouldn't have moved back if that weren't true. "We're perfectly safe here," I insist.

"Then why does it look like you're fleeing the country?" Penelope eyes the hiking packs lined up on my grandmother's front porch.

"Because once again, Genesis has confused danger with excitement." Holden wraps one arm around her as the driver opens the trunk to retrieve her luggage, and his stage

24

whisper is perfectly audible. "Maybe we should show her what real excitement looks like."

I roll my eyes at him. Holden likes to push boundaries, but we both know what lines not to cross. "We're going hiking in the jungle." I link my arm through my best friend's arm and pull her away from him. "A shopping spree was the only way to talk Neda out of her four-hour mud facial in favor of actual mud and sweat. I got you some gear."

"You're serious," she says as the driver carries her luggage past us into the foyer. "Does Neda understand that there's no Wi-Fi or filtered water in the jungle?"

"The cabanas have both, and I *might* have downplayed how little time we're actually going to spend in them."

Penelope laughs as her gaze wanders over the supplies I had packed for each of us.

"I probably *shouldn't* be surprised by the 180-degree pivot from spa day to jungle hike, but . . ."

"You really shouldn't. The car will be here in half an hour. Come say hi to Nana, then you can change clothes and stuff your swimsuit into your pack."

"So how was the event?" Holden says as Penelope's car pulls out of the driveway. "Actually, *what* was the event that made you willing to forgo the private jet in favor of flying commercial?"

"Judging for the Special Olympics, jackass." Penelope and her Olympic silver medal on the uneven bars are in high demand for appearances since she retired from competition two years ago. She reaches around me to give Holden a playful shove. "*You* should try giving back."

"We'll be there next time," I promise. Holden grumbles, but doesn't argue. He'll do the right thing, even if it makes him uncomfortable. I never have to worry about him when there's a live audience.

"Speaking of private jets, your dad offered to have his pilot drop me off in the Bahamas after my event. I had to tell him I'd already booked a flight to keep this trip on a need-to-know."

I squeeze her arm tighter. Only a true friend will lie to your father's face for you.

"So what'd I miss?" Pen asks as we head toward Nana's front door, her couture sandals clicking on the colorful stone walkway.

"A true sign of the end times." Holden holds the door open for us and we step into the foyer, where Pen's bags are waiting and the scent of *arepas con huevo* still lingers. "Neda and Maddie agree about something."

"About what?"

"That we shouldn't have let Genesis plan this trip."

I shrug. "Maddie's mad because I didn't ask her mommy if she could come."

Pen laughs again as she grabs her makeup case and the smaller of her two suitcases. "So your preachy cousin has fresh material for a new sermon, your hot cousin doesn't drink anymore, and Neda's just been denied the spa treatment you said would help her drop two pounds of water weight in a day. Remind me why I came?"

"Because you love me. Because you're my best friend. And because when we get back from Tayrona, the full-day spa package is on me."

My phone buzzes again with another message from my dad.

Genesis, WHY aren't you on the plane?

88 HOURS EARLIER

MADDIE

"Is anyone else being eaten alive by mosquitoes?" Neda slaps at a bug on her calf.

"No," I say, even though I have three bites on my left arm. During the four-hour drive from Cartagena to Parque Tayrona, her voice surpassed the shrieking of my alarm clock as my least favorite sound on the planet. "The rest of us found the risk of contracting malaria more compelling than the possibility of staining our clothes with bug spray." Which is especially ironic, considering that she's already splattered with mud.

"Why can't we just go back to the cabana?" Neda whines. "Hiking isn't a vacation. Hiking is *work*."

I'd rather sleep in the sand with a rock for a pillow than bunk in the cabana with my cousin and her spoiled, ignorant entourage.

Neda complains about every step, and Nico's jaw clenches tighter and tighter until I'm sure he's going to dislocate his own jaw. Finally he pulls a small radio from his bag and drowns her out with salsa music. When the first song ends, a newsbreak reports that police found two bodies in a burned-out van on the edge of Cartagena last night.

My insides twist into knots. My father's body was discovered the same way, nearly a year ago.

"What's wrong?" Neda demands, and Nico summarizes the Spanish-language newscast.

Her forehead furrows. "It's probably guerrilla warfare," she announces, turning to me with an "I told you so" expression.

Genesis scowls at Nico. "Why would you translate that for her?"

"It's not guerrilla warfare," he snaps at Neda, his accent thickened with irritation. "FARC has disbanded. It's just an isolated incident."

He's right. The conflict between activists and the Colombian government is all but over. This *has* to be a random act.

"Then it must be drug violence," she insists.

I speak through clenched teeth. "Believe it or not, Neda, sometimes people in Colombia commit crimes unrelated to drug trafficking. Just like in the rest of the world."

Still, I wish Ryan hadn't heard. The reminder of our father's death might not send him into a backslide, but it won't help him either.

"Was it in the jungle?" Neda asks, as if she didn't even hear us. "Guerrillas are always kidnapping and murdering people in the jungle."

"Kidnappings are passé," Genesis assures her, before Nico's head can explode. "Today's fashionable guerrilla makes his money in illegal gold mining and extortion. Besides, anyone who tried to kidnap you would give you back within the hour." She links her arm through Neda's. "You're an acquired taste."

Neda grins and flips her off. "Money is such a petty reason to ruin someone's life."

"Not for those who can't afford food and shelter," Nico insists. "But the gang riots and school shootings in the States truly *are* pointless."

"I don't condone *any* violence." She stands straighter and looks down her nose at him. "I don't even wear real fur."

"How very enlightened of you." I can hear my voice getting sharper, yet I can't seem to stop it. "But while American minks are running around with their precious skins intact, Colombian farmers are being driven out of business because of US interference."

Neda rolls her eyes at me. "The US does *not* put Colombian farmers out of business."

"Their economic policies do," Nico insists. "They also pour millions into the 'war on drugs,' yet nothing into helping feed and clothe the impoverished masses *they* helped to disenfranchise."

For one long moment, Neda is quiet. Then she frowns down at the mud on her feet. "If this is the only way to get to the beach why haven't they paved the path yet?" she whines.

I step over an exposed root and push aside a tall fern

reaching into the path. "Because pouring concrete wouldn't exactly preserve the natural beauty of the jungle."

She stops in the middle of the trail to wipe a smudge of dirt from a delicate leaf detail on the strap of her left sandal. "I'm more interested in preserving my shoes."

"Why didn't you change into your hiking boots?" Genesis asks, and the frustration in her voice makes me smile.

Neda stares down at her manicured toenails, tucking a loose strand of straight, dark hair behind her ear. "Ferragamo says T-strap flats are perfect for any occasion."

Genesis sighs. "For any occasion that doesn't involve thorns, snakes, rocks, and mud." For the first time in the history of their couture-based friendship, Neda has failed at shopping, and my cousin seems to find no humor in the situation.

I, on the other hand, think watching nature bitch slap a spoiled heiress is hilarious.

GENESIS

"How long is this hike?" Neda demands as we round another muddy curve in the path. "I can't walk another half hour in these sandals."

"That's too bad, because Cabo San Juan is two hours away." Maddie looks smug as she passes us on the narrow trail. "Maybe you should head back to the *parque* entrance and call for a car to take you home."

"Nobody's going home," I snap at my cousin. "Nico, how many beaches will we pass on the way to Cabo?"

"Two," he says as he holds back a protruding branch for Penelope.

"You'll be fine," I tell Neda.

Ryan hangs back to walk on her other side. "By the time your feet get sore, we'll be at Piscine beach, and you can jump into the water to cool off. And if your sandals can't hack it, there will be a piggyback ride in your future." His smile mollifies her, and she picks up her pace.

"I'm taking you everywhere I go from now on," I whisper to Ryan as I step over a muddy patch in the trail.

"Because I'm willing to give Neda a piggyback ride?"

"Yes." But mostly because Ryan is my most valuable

asset out here where I can't just send Maddie and Neda—or Holden and Nico—into separate corners.

"She's just feeling lost," he says. "I've been there, and I wouldn't have made it through without friends and family."

All I did was pick out the rehab facility. My dad paid for it, and Maddie convinced him to go, but ultimately, Ryan took control of his own future.

He *is* a Valencia.

By the last leg of our hike, Neda is squealing constantly, convinced that every vine is a snake and that within each shadow lurks a crouching jungle cat. Holden doesn't complain much, but every root he has to step over and vine he has to push aside deepens his scowl.

When the rest of us have to wade through a shallow stream, Penelope makes a show of crossing it on a narrow fallen log—walking on her hands.

If I didn't love her, I would totally hate her.

I am ready to feed them all to jungle predators by the time we finally arrive at Cabo San Juan, the best beach in the national park for swimming, surfing, and snorkeling.

As soon as we step onto the beach, I drop my bag and take off my boots so I can curl my toes in the sand. I breathe deeply, taking in the salt-scent of the air and the bright Caribbean sunshine. The waves here are gentle, and a couple dozen people are waist deep in them, throwing Frisbees and dunking each other.

With one glance at the water, Neda seems to have forgotten everything she hates about hiking. "It's beautiful," she says when she's caught her breath, and I nod.

"This is why we're here."

Suddenly, everyone's smiling. Clothes land on the sand as we strip to our swimsuits, showing off tan, firm bodies sculpted by Olympic coaches, world-class personal trainers, or years on the soccer field.

Naturally, people stare at us. Neda and Holden pretend not to notice, but I can see discomfort melt from their postures as they register the admiration of the small crowd.

Maddie hangs back, still fully dressed, obviously trying to establish a distinction between herself and the rest of us. As if she were actually in danger of being mistaken for a world-class athlete or a fashion-forward trendsetter.

I turn to thank Nico for bringing us to this exotic paradise, but he's already fifty feet down the beach, talking to three of the half dozen patrolling soldiers. Like those who searched us for drugs and alcohol when we entered the park, they obviously know him. But they don't seem happy with him.

Nico is gesturing angrily. I can't hear what he's saying, but when he sees me watching, he cuts the argument off. He's smiling as he rejoins our group, but his shoulders are tense.

As two of the soldiers strike off down the beach, I realize the third isn't a soldier at all. He's the guy Maddie made out with on the dance floor last night, in Cartagena. Sebastián.

What the hell is he doing at Cabo?

86 HOURS EARLIER

MADDIE

The waves are fierce and foaming as they crash over the rocks, as if the Caribbean is Mother Nature's heart and the waves are its beating. Regardless of the advantages I've missed, not being born to the wealthy Valencia brother, this is the only privilege that matters.

"Hey, Ryan, wanna hit the—" I turn, expecting to find my brother waiting for me, ready to dive into the water. Instead, I find him on a wide stretch of grass between the sand and the jungle, surrounded by tents. He's kneeling in the dirt, using a hand pump to inflate a pretty stranger's small air mattress while she expertly negotiates the arched poles and canvas of a bright yellow tent.

"Wanna hit the water?" I drop onto the sand next to my brother.

Ryan shades his eye from the sun as he looks at me. "You go ahead. I told Domenica I'd play soccer with her, if she can find a ball."

Domenica gives me an amused look. "I said I'd play

with him if *he* found some balls." She is tall and athletic, with a pouf of dark curls and beautiful brown eyes. I have no doubt she can hold her own against my brother, in any sport.

"Oh. Okay." Even I can hear how disappointed I sound, and suddenly I feel like an idiot.

"You're welcome to join us," Domenica adds as she slides a flexible pole into the slot forming the apex of her small tent. Her accent isn't Colombian like my father's or Cuban like my mother's. Maybe . . . Peruvian?

Her offer seems genuine, but Ryan gives me a small headshake. He clearly wants time alone with his new friend.

"That's okay. You guys have fun." I let my gaze wander the beach again, where several dozen people are surfing, swimming, wading, throwing Frisbees, and sunbathing.

Sand sticks to my feet as I head down the beach, to where Genesis is laying out designer Italian beach towels.

"I really admire the fashion risks you take, Maddie," Neda says in a tone so convincing I'm not entirely sure I'm being mocked until she continues. "I could never pull off 'discount chic.'"

I clench my jaw and let a retort die on my tongue. I swear, Genesis collects designer companions like some girls collect shoes or handbags. Though she collects those too.

She and the Versace vixens are the only other people I know here, but I'd rather puncture my own eardrum with a tent pole than listen to Neda's voice for one more second.

We're in one of the most beautiful places in the world, surrounded by travelers from every corner of the globe. If

Ryan can make new friends, so can I. I pluck my bag from the sand, but before I've taken three steps away from my cousin, something hard crashes into my hip. "Ow!" I look up to find two guys jogging toward me, backlit by the afternoon sun.

"*Pardon!*" The guys stop two feet away and one smiles as he bends to reclaim his Frisbee. "Benard has terrible aim."

The second guy runs one hand through dark, tousled waves. "*Casse-toi!* I hit what I was aiming for." He winks at me, and my breath catches in my throat. Benard is *gorgeous*. His gaze takes a tour of my body with a thrilling boldness, and despite two years on my school's debate team and a year in Youth and Government, I can't think of a single intelligent thing to say.

"You're French?" I finally ask, after several seconds of dumbfounded staring.

"Belgian. I'm Benard and this is Milo. Come play with us, *belle*."

I glance back to see Penelope elbow Genesis, and suddenly all three of the Burberry brats are watching, waiting for me to fall on my face or frighten off both of the beautiful globetrotters with some other act of social ineptitude.

"I'd love to." I smile up at Benard.

But Milo's attention has snagged on the device clipped at my waist. "You are ill?"

I swallow a familiar, bitter lump of irritation. "I'm diabetic. Don't worry. It doesn't slow me down." I snatch the Frisbee from Milo and take off down the beach to prove my point. Near the water's edge, I spin to throw the Frisbee to Benard, and before I know it, I'm laughing as I jog up and down the beach with the two hottest guys I've ever met.

"You're pretty good," Benard says as I jump to snatch the Frisbee from the air.

"My brother started putting my toys on high shelves when I was four. I wouldn't have survived childhood without a little vertical reach." I shrug and push hair back from my face as he crosses the sand toward me, sunlight highlighting every plane of his bare chest. He's shiny. I can't tell if that's sunscreen or sweat, but I'm struck by the sudden urge to touch him and find out.

"I'm thirsty." Sand flies from beneath Milo's feet as he skids to a stop. "Let's get a drink."

I follow his gaze to see that the open-air restaurant is serving dinner. There isn't much of a line yet, but that won't last long. "Sounds good."

Benard puts one hand on my lower back, escorting me toward the long pavilion thatched with palm leaves, and leans in to whisper conspiratorially. "You get a table, and we'll order. *D'accord?*"

I choose an empty white plastic table near the back.

A few minutes later, the Belgian boys come back from the bar carrying two bottles of beer and a bright red cocktail in a clear plastic cup, garnished with a slice of starfruit. "The selection is limited," Benard says as he sets the cup in front of me. "Just beer and a couple of fruity cocktails. This one is sparkling wine and corozo berry–infused gin.

They say it's a local specialty."

I take a sip. The cocktail is both sweet and tart, yet much stronger than the margaritas I had at the bar last night. "Delicious." My voice comes out hoarse. "Thank you." I'll have to adjust my insulin intake to make up for the sugar and alcohol, but a beautiful cocktail with a beautiful Belgian boy is totally worth it.

Benard and Milo don't know me as the lesser cousin of Genesis Valencia, heiress to a shipping empire. They aren't intimidated by my father's recent death. They're taking me at face value, and they seem to like what they see.

I like what they see.

Is this what life is like for Genesis all the time?

84 HOURS EARLIER

GENESIS

Holden sets his empty beer bottle in the sand, next to his towel. "Why isn't there anything to do here?" he demands, shooting an irritated look at Nico over me, Pen, and Neda. "I thought there'd be more . . . recreation."

"There's cornhole," Nico suggests. "Or Frisbee. Or swimming. Or soccer. Or cards. Or *conversation*." But I can tell from the sardonic upturn of one side of his mouth that he knows exactly what Holden means by "recreation."

My boyfriend knows Nico snuck something into the park, but his pride won't let him ask for a hit from the guy he caught kissing his girlfriend.

I haven't told him I have a joint tucked into my tampon case because I'd much rather watch this social experiment unfold.

"Why don't you guys go snorkeling?" Neda says.

I laugh. "Holden won't—"

"What, and mess up his hair?" Nico quips.

"That's a great idea." Penelope stands and holds one

hand out to Holden. "Come snorkel with me."

To my surprise, he lets her pull him to his feet, then digs my snorkeling gear from my bag. Halfway down the beach, she snatches his mask and he chases her all the way into the water.

"Look!" Neda sits up on her towel, and I follow her gaze to see that two men with drums and marimbas have pulled plastic chairs from the restaurant onto the sand. They begin improvising a lively rhythm, and a small crowd gathers. "What's that?" Neda asks when a woman joins them with a small wooden flute.

"It's called a *gaita*," Nico tells her as the first playful, airy notes mix with the marimba's melody.

The crowd grows, and people start dancing. The beat is infectious.

"Come on!" I pull Neda off her towel. She, Nico, and I head down to the spontaneous party, and I'm dancing before I even join the crowd. I can't help it. The sand is warm beneath my feet and the ocean breeze cools my skin. This place is the heart of Colombia. It's still a part of my father, even if he won't admit it. And now it's a part of me.

Neda, Nico, and I dance in a cluster, laughing and lost in the rhythm. The setting sun paints my shadow on the sand.

I don't see Holden and Penelope, but Maddie's laughing and drinking with two guys at one of the tables.

She's finally remembered how to have fun.

"Hey!" Penelope slides into the circle next to me. "The water's amazing! You should go in!"

"I will later. Where's Holden?" The crowd has doubled since we arrived this afternoon. So much for our exclusive retreat.

"He found some like-minded individuals." Penelope points across the beach, and in the dying light from the setting sun, I see my very high boyfriend clutching a fresh beer as he tosses beanbags with half a dozen guys who seem to be enjoying cornhole with more enthusiasm than it deserves.

"You want to get a drink?" I ask, and when Pen nods, we duck out of the crowd.

Penelope groans over the length of the line at the bar, but my gaze has snagged on a guy at the front, waiting for whatever he's ordered. Light beard scruff outlines his strong jaw. A narrow-brimmed straw hat blocks the setting sun from his hazel eyes.

The bartender sets an unopened beer and two bright red cocktails garnished with slices of starfruit on the bar. The guy in the hat slides the beer into a pocket of his cargo shorts, then takes both plastic cups. He stops in front of us, on his way to the beach.

"I over-ordered." The tilt of his smile mirrors the angle of his hat brim. "Could you two could help me out with these?" He holds up the cocktails.

Penelope's hesitation is no surprise. Until she retired from gymnastics, she didn't have time for a social life, and she's still behind the curve in experience. In fact, Holden is the only guy she seems truly comfortable with.

Which makes her the perfect wingman. She knows

when to bow out and is willing to keep my boyfriend company.

"Happy to help." I take the drinks and hand one to Pen.

"Thanks." She takes a sip.

"Wait, I did that wrong." The guy in the hat takes the drink from me and turns to Pen. "These are both for you."

Confused, she takes the plastic cup and before I can truly process the insult, hat boy steps back to study us.

"That's better." He smiles as if he isn't seconds away from sifting through the sand for the teeth I'm about to knock right out of his head. "Now that your hands are free . . ." He slides his left palm into my grip and tugs me toward the dancing crowd. I don't truly understand what he's done until we're both moving to the music.

"You could have just asked me to dance," I say, when the rhythm changes and he sways closer.

"Guys ask you to dance all the time, and you forget them before the music even fades. But you'll remember me."

I laugh as he twirls me, and the crowd backs away to give us space. "So, who exactly will I be remembering?"

He spins us in sync, with one hand at my back, and people are watching us now. "If I tell you my name, I lose my mysterious edge."

"Fine. Then where are you from?"

"South Bend." He pulls me closer when the music changes. His hand slides over my hair and down my back as we settle into a sexy Cuban salsa.

"You did *not* learn this in Indiana."

His laugh is low and hot. "I learned this in Santa Clara. But I was born in Indiana."

A Midwestern boy in a hat. Dancing sexy, street-style salsa on the beach.

I'm hooked.

We dance toward the edge of the crowd, and it closes in behind us. "So, Indiana, why were you in Santa Clara?" I ask, now that I can hear him better.

"Because that's where the bus dropped me, after Havana."

"Hey, Genesis, it's getting dark." Neda appears out of nowhere, staring nervously at the brilliant pink and orange sunset.

"Yes. That's a nightly event." I can't look away from Indiana.

"Maybe we should head back to the cabana."

"Relax. We won't let anything eat you." I turn her by both shoulders and point her back toward the crowd.

"You're staying at Cañaveral?" Indiana frowns. "That's a long hike in the dark."

"Change of plans." Who needs room service and real beds? "We'll rent hammocks and stay here."

"And you just decided that? For all your friends?"

"I always do."

The song ends and he steps back to look down at me. "Every now and then, you should let people make up their own minds." His gaze holds a strangely magnetic challenge. "That's how adventures begin."

Before I can figure out how much of that is innuendo and just how much adventure he might be up for, Holden materializes at my side.

"I won!" He less than subtly shows me the joint hidden in his palm—evidently the spoils from his cornhole battle.

"Congratulations." I glance at the soldiers gathered near the restaurant, but they aren't watching.

Holden's gaze hardens as he looks at Indiana. He lays a possessive hand on my arm. "Dance with me."

Before I can remind my boyfriend that he doesn't own me, Indiana tips his straw hat, then heads down the beach to join the cornhole game.

Holden and I dance with Pen and the rest of our friends. But my gaze keeps wandering back to the salsa-dancing cowboy.

83 HOURS EARLIER

MADDIE

"You do know that the Palmyra ruins in Syria are thousands of years old?" Benard says. "Destroying a community's history does just as much damage as destroying their homes and businesses. It's a blow straight to the heart of the people."

I sit back in my chair while I consider his point, then lean in to take a sip of my bright-red cocktail. I'm still not convinced, but Benard's eyes and the beach, both less than two feet away, are a perfect view. And a perfect setting for a debate.

"Of course," I concede. "But do you really think rebuilding some statues—"

"And temples!"

"Fine, rebuilding statues *and* temples will truly help people who have been displaced by years of war? Don't you think they're more concerned with necessities like food, shelter, and safety?"

He takes a drink from his beer, but his gaze never leaves my face. "I'm not saying those things aren't important, but think about the message rebuilding cultural symbols sends to the terrorists who destroyed them. 'Whatever you do, whatever pain you cause, you can't destroy our culture. You can't destroy who we are.'" He lifts one brow at me, punctuating his point. "That's pretty powerful, *n'est-ce pas?*"

"Yes, but what good will these symbols do, if the people you're building them for are dying of hunger and exposure?"

Milo chuckles. "You are not what we expected."

"Then you should reassess your expectations." I give them a half smile. Whatever is in this drink has definitely upped my sass factor. *"D'accord?"* My French accent is terrible—it sounds like I'm speaking Spanish—but I don't care.

Benard grins at my effort. "Okay, *d'accord.* But surely you agree that the media should dedicate more coverage to the problems people are faced with every day in a war zone?"

Hot and intellectually engaging? I'd swoon if it weren't cheesy.

Milo lifts his empty bottle. "I believe *la mademoiselle* needs another drink."

I glance down and am surprised to notice I've nearly finished my cocktail. And the sun is setting.

"À votre service!" Benard gives me a brief bow, and as they wind their way through the now-crowded restaurant for another round, I realize I'm buzzing.

Genesis and her entourage have been all over the world, yet I've never heard them debate anything of more significance than whether the shopping is better in Milan or Paris.

"Maddie? Is that you?"

I turn to find a boy in neon orange swimming trunks and a faded tee sitting at the table behind me. I recognize him, but at first I can't put a name to his face, because his face doesn't belong in Colombia. It belongs in Miami.

"It's me." He lays one hand over his chest, as if that will help. "Luke Hazelwood, from your calculus class."

"Oh, right." Seeing him here is disorienting. "What the *hell* are you doing here?"

He shrugs with a glance at the last half of a sandwich on the plate in front of him. "Eating dinner. It's this habit I have."

"No, what are you doing in Colombia?" Parque Tayrona isn't a typical American spring break destination—not that Luke is the party type.

Luke resettles his scruffy baseball cap over a headful of brown curls. "I'm on vacation." He shrugs. "My parents are snorkeling."

Of course he's traveling with his parents.

Though to be fair, if my uncle hadn't offered Ryan and me seats on his jet, we'd be at home with our mom right now. Swimming in our apartment complex's concrete pool.

"I saw you from behind, but I wasn't sure that was you until I noticed your arm."

Humiliation warms my cheeks. My hand slides over the jagged pink line of scar tissue on my left triceps.

Two seconds with Luke and I'm flashing back to the second worst night of my life.

Maybe he'd like to bring up my dad's death too?

"Not that the scar's your defining characteristic. You're definitely better known for your—"

I open my eyes to find him blushing furiously beneath the brim of his cap. His gaze drops from my face, and when he sees that I'm wearing a bikini, he looks away again, and his flush deepens.

Do I look this awkward to Genesis and her friends?

Luke's flush finally fades and he makes another valiant effort at communication. "You're not going to drink that, are you?"

My hand tightens around my nearly empty cup. "It's just one drink."

"I mean *that* one." He looks at something over my shoulder, and I turn to see Benard and Milo heading toward us with my second cocktail and two beer bottles. Luke glances at my insulin pump, and I bristle again.

"What do you know about it?" I already have a brother, mother, and grandmother looking over my shoulder. I don't need some boy from my math class telling me what to do.

Luke shrugs. "My dad has type one. He always eats when he drinks."

"*Voilà!*" Benard sets the fresh, bright-red cocktail on our table. I should apologize and tell him I can't have another one. But the heat in his eyes—and the sunlight gleaming on his broad chest—reminds me why I'm here in the first place.

"Thanks." I pick up the new drink and take a long sip through the straw.

Luke stands and sets his plate in front of me. "Ham and cheese."

I blink at the neatly cut sandwich half, then look up at him.

"I haven't touched that part." He steps off the wood plank floor and wanders off down the beach.

Benard sinks into the chair next to mine and places two bottles of water on the table. "Who was that?"

"Just a boy from my school." But I've already forgotten about Luke.

"You two have fun." Milo clinks his beer against Benard's and gives him a look I can't interpret. "The music calls . . ." He heads for a crowd gathered around an Afro-Colombian band playing outside the restaurant.

The sun continues to sink below the horizon while we talk. When I realize my cup is empty again, I look up to see that we're the only ones left in the restaurant. The owners are wiping tables.

Benard rises and pulls out my chair for me as I stand. Vertigo washes over me, and I clutch the table, waiting for it to pass.

"Are you okay?" he asks, and when I nod, he leaves the issue alone. He doesn't even glance at my insulin pump.

"Shall we find a spot on the sand?"

I grab my towel from where I left it hours before and follow Benard to a secluded spot on the dark beach. He spreads out the towel and sits, then laughs as I drop onto it next to him, still trying to find my balance. We're out of sight from the crowd, but we can still hear the music.

His arm around my waist steadies me. The rhythm of the waves lapping the beach lines up with the beat of the drums behind us. This moment is perfect.

"*Tu es très belle.*" Benard's lips brush my ear, and the warmth of his breath makes me catch mine. His fingers trail lightly up my neck and into my hair, and I shiver from the touch.

I close my eyes.

He kisses the back of my jaw, and a sigh slips from my throat. For a second, I feel embarrassed by my own inexperience, but Benard only groans and turns my face toward his.

His mouth finds mine, and suddenly I am kissing a beautiful Belgian boy on a moonlit night at the edge of the Caribbean Sea.

79 HOURS EARLIER

GENESIS

I take a hit and pass the joint to Neda, then I turn back to the window. A breeze blows through the two-story open-air hut, bringing with it the scent of the ocean. The hut sits at the top of a rock outcrop, jutting into the water, and the view is spectacular, even at night.

I feel like I'm floating high above the ocean, looking down at the rest of the world.

"Mind if I join you?"

I spin to find Indiana standing behind me. The crooked hat is gone, but the crooked smile is out in full force.

"I'm not going to forget you. You can stop stalking me now."

He laughs and takes the joint, then gestures with it to his hat, cradled in a blue-striped rental hammock. "I've been sleeping there for the past two nights."

Eleven other hammocks ring the center support column of the round hut like the spokes of a wheel, flickering in candlelight. My group has rented half of them. Ryan and

Domenica are already huddled up in one.

I lay one hand over my heart. "So you're saying *I'm* stalking *you*?"

He shrugs. "I think the evidence speaks for itself."

Neda giggles as Indiana passes the joint to her. "*This* is why you gave up the cabana," she whispers to me, loud enough for the whole world to hear. Then she takes a hit and leaves us alone at the window.

Indiana exhales, and the breeze steals his smoke. Laughter erupts behind us as the rest of my friends get high with the West Coast bros from the cornhole game.

"You're not really with them, are you?" I glance over his shoulder at the other West Coast bros, who are trying—and failing—to pass a joint completely around their circle before someone laughs or exhales.

"I met them at the park entrance a couple of days ago. They're entertaining and well supplied, so . . ." He shrugs, then looks right into my eyes. "I've met a lot of interesting people here."

"I've only met one." I can practically feel the air crackle between us. "Let's take a walk on the beach," I say as I take his arm.

He shakes his head slowly, holding my gaze. "I like the view from up here." Finally he turns back to the window. "The moon's reflecting in the water so clearly that it looks like there are two of them."

I follow his gaze. He's right about the moon.

"So, how long are you here?" I ask as I stare at the water.

Indiana's shoulder brushes mine as he shrugs. "Until I get bored or run out of money."

I turn to him, surprised. "You're not in school?"

"I'll probably go back for my senior year next fall. But for now, I'm taking a break from the drama."

Maybe it's the pot talking, but for the first time in my life, that sounds kind of peaceful, rather than boring.

Movement at the stairs catches my attention, and when I turn, I see my best friend and my boyfriend on the top step, their backs to us. Holden has his left hand in the air, and Penelope is practically climbing onto his shoulder, trying to get to the joint he's holding.

She laughs and grasps for his hand again, but every time she reaches, he pulls the joint farther out of her range. He's playing keep-away.

But she's not keeping away. She is all over him.

Alarm slices through me. It's a small pain. But like a paper cut, it stings.

"Where are you from?" Indiana asks, and there's a strange tone in his voice. It sounds like . . . sympathy.

"Miami." But I hardly hear myself speak, because Penelope has climbed onto Holden's lap to pull his arm back into reach. She smiles as she looks down at him. His hand is on her hip.

"Genesis," Indiana whispers, and I have to blink to keep my eyes in focus.

"They're just high." I can't look away. It's like staring at a train wreck.

Indiana exhales. "Things aren't always what they look like."

But it's exactly what it looks like—my boyfriend and my best friend are drunk and high, and moments away from hooking up right in front of me. Which is why Indiana pointed me toward the window, instead of down the stairs to the beach.

Penelope settles onto the top step, and Holden holds the joint for her while she sucks on it. There's something intimate and familiar about the way they touch each other. As if it's not happening for the first time. As if I'm watching something I was never meant to see.

They're together.

My face burns. I inhale, trying to put out the fire kindling deep in my chest.

My relationship with Holden may not conform to standard norms and boundaries—we're hardly your standard couple—but we *do have* boundaries. And he *will pay* for breaching them.

I square my shoulders.

"I've been where you are," Indiana whispers. "Acting on impulse cost me two friendships."

I squeeze his hand lightly as I remove it from my arm. "I *never* act on impulse."

I walk across the room as if nothing's wrong—as if my best friend and my boyfriend haven't crossed a line none of us can ever uncross. Holden and Pen are laughing. They don't know I'm there until I lean down between them and pluck the joint from Penelope's hand.

"Thanks." I take a long hit and hold it for a second. Then I blow it into their faces. "Since we're obviously sharing things now."

I leave them staring after me as I head down the stairs toward the beach.

75 HOURS EARLIER

MADDIE

Something pokes me in the side. My eyes open, and bright bolts of sunlight spear my head. "Wha . . . ?"

Someone groans near my ear, and the entire world seems to sway around me. And beneath me.

"Maddie!"

I freeze, then roll my eyes to see as much of my surroundings as possible without triggering another nauseating sway.

Ryan stares down at me through a fine sheet of mesh, which my groggy mind labels "mosquito netting." Because I'm in Parque Tayrona, in a hut on the beach. In a hammock.

That groan comes again, and an arm falls over my bare stomach.

Oh, shit. I'm in a hammock *with a guy*.

"Help me up," I whisper, humiliation burning in my cheeks. How did I wind up in a hammock with a guy half wrapped around me?

My brother pulls back the mosquito netting and helps me climb out of the hammock without waking . . . Um . . .

Benard.

The boy from Belgium who speaks French, Spanish, English, and German. Who knows about Greek philosophy, French wine, and Caribbean tides.

The boy I spent the night with.

No no no no . . . Panicked, I glance down and am relieved to see that I'm still wearing my bikini and board shorts. The rest of my memory falls into place as Ryan shoves my T-shirt at me.

Benard and I shared a couple of puffs of whatever Nico passed us, then came back to his hammock, where we made out for a while, then . . .

Did I fall asleep in the middle of a hookup?

My flush deepens. Two drinks and a couple of hits shouldn't have been enough to knock me out. Should they?

I check my insulin level as I follow my brother down the steps to the beach. It's a little low, but not terrible.

"Are you okay?" Ryan drops a granola bar at my feet as I plop down on the sand. "Do I need to go beat some manners into that predator?"

"Relax. Nothing happened."

My brother sighs as he sinks onto the sand next to me. "I'm not judging. I'm worrying."

"I can fend for myself." It's not Benard's fault I can't handle my liquor. "And he's not a predator. He's a classics major."

"The two are not mutually exclusive," Ryan insists.

I roll my eyes at him and grab the granola bar. "If I eat this, will you go away?"

Ryan scruffs my hair, like he used to when I was a kid. "Only long enough to get us some water." He heads toward the restaurant, and his shadow stretches across the sand behind him.

"*Bonjour, belle*," Benard says, and I turn as he steps onto the sand from the stairs. Something flutters deep in my stomach as he pulls me to my feet and slides his arms around me. "The night got cold, and I enjoyed your warmth." He leans in to press a kiss beneath my ear, and suddenly I am tingling all over.

"I enjoyed yours too." I slide my arms behind his neck and inhale the scent of his sunscreen.

The sun casts a halo around his dark hair. "Will you excuse me while I find my toothbrush?"

"Of course." I need to find mine too.

Benard kisses my forehead, then heads back up the stairs.

I head for the restaurant to find my brother, hoping he packed toothpaste, and on the way, I hear Holden and Genesis arguing behind the communal bathroom.

"You're completely overreacting." His tone drips with tedium. "I don't know what you think you saw, but—"

"You crossed a line. So here's how this is going to go." Genesis's voice is like a wall of ice. "You're going to be the *ideal* boyfriend for the remainder of spring break. If you even look at Penelope again, I'll slip the nearest soldier a fifty to give you a *thorough* search for contraband. Which he *will* find. And I *will* leave your ass to rot in a Colombian prison."

I squat to brush sand from my feet, trying to listen inconspicuously. I can't help myself.

"Don't you think that's a bit extreme?" Holden demands, but his question lacks conviction.

"Extreme would be calling in Colombia's finest right now. I'm being pretty damn generous. So go pack. We're done with Cabo."

No way. We *just* got here!

"Nico's taking us to see some ruins in the jungle."

Queen G has spoken, and her subjects will no doubt follow her into the wilderness. But that doesn't mean *I* have to go.

When I stand again, I find Benard heading down the beach from the hut, wearing a fresh set of swim trunks. Sunscreen glistens on his skin. I start to jog toward him, but someone grabs my arm.

"*Salut,*" Milo says as I pull my arm from his grip.

"*Salut,*" I return. But my gaze is glued to Benard as he heads for a group that's just emerged from the jungle path, carrying hiking gear.

Unease crawls over my skin. Something feels wrong.

Benard wraps his arms around a girl at the front of the group, lifting her off the ground with the enthusiasm of his embrace.

I stare, and in spite of the bright, warm sun, I feel suddenly cold.

"That's his girlfriend," Milo says, so close to my ear that I jump, startled. "So, maybe you won't mention sharing a hammock with him, *oui?*"

I'm too humiliated to speak. Of course he has a girlfriend. Of course she's tall and beautiful and graceful, even at a distance.

Of course yesterday was too good to be true.

"We are all adults, *non?*" Milo says in his stupid French accent.

I nod. That's the only response I can manage.

He leans down to kiss me on the cheek. "I knew someone as mature as you would understand."

67 HOURS EARLIER

GENESIS

"Hey." I fall into step with Indiana, before he can hit the water in his snorkel gear. "We're going sightseeing. Come with us."

"'We'?" He looks past me to where Neda is complaining about the upcoming hike, though Nico, Penelope, and Holden are too mired in an uncomfortable silence to pay attention. "*All* of you?"

"Yeah. Though I should warn you that no one's really in a good mood today, except for Ryan." Now that he's not a raging alcoholic depressive, he could have fun standing on the edge of an erupting volcano.

But Indiana is only looking at me. "What kind of mood are *you* in?"

"That depends. Are you coming with us?" I'm not flirting—not really. And I feel a little guilty for asking him to come on a trip pretty much guaranteed to end with one of my friends either punching or sleeping with another one of my friends.

But I could really use an ally.

"I'll get my stuff."

"We're waiting for the porters to bring our gear from the cabanas. Meet us in front of the restaurant in about fifteen."

"Porters? As in, plural?" He raises one eyebrow. "You have enough gear to require professional assistance?"

I laugh. "Admit it. You won't forget me either." I feel him watching me as I walk away.

Halfway across the beach, I find my cousin watching the Belgian boy and his girlfriend as they feed each other gooey bites of *pain au chocolate*. No wonder she was so willing to leave Cabo.

She actually liked him.

Maddie doesn't notice me until I'm standing right next to her, shading my eyes from the sun with my hand. "The only way to protect yourself is to assume everyone else is lying."

She crosses her arms over her bikini top. "That sounds like step one from the *Conspiracy Theorist's Guide to Mental Health*."

I nod at Benard. "You can get over it, or you can get even."

"Karma will take care of him." But her jaw is clenched and her cheeks are flushed. That Belgian bastard humiliated her.

Maddie may be naive and sanctimonious, but she's still a Valencia.

"Fine. Call me Karma." But she grabs my arm before I get two steps away.

"*What* are you doing, Genesis?"

"What you don't have the nerve to do." I pull my arm from her grip. "Teaching him a lesson." I let my hips swing as I march across the beach toward Benard. He's still holding his girlfriend's hand when I spin him around and kiss him like he's the only source of oxygen on the planet.

His girlfriend sputters in shock, and when I finally let him go, Benard is too stunned for words.

"Last night was great," I practically purr as I let my hand trail down his chest. Then I turn to the girlfriend. "Don't let this one get away. He's a keeper."

MADDIE

I will never be able to unsee Genesis kissing Benard.

Still, that was awesome.

As I head for the restaurant, I glance back to watch Benard's girlfriend yell at him, and my shoulder hits something firm but yielding.

"Ow!"

"I'm so sorry!" I turn to see who I've run into and find myself face-to-face with Luke Hazelwood.

"Hey, Maddie." He looks disappointed when he notices my backpack. "Where you goin'?"

"My cousin is dragging us back into the jungle." As if I'm not thrilled to be escaping Benard and his girlfriend.

"Cool. Can I come? It's just that . . ." He looks really young and needy. Even for fifteen.

"Yeah," I say, still mired in my own drama. "Wait, what?"

"I'll grab my stuff and meet you back here." Luke takes off down the beach at a jog before I've even figured out what I just agreed to.

"Wait, Luke! I—" *Damn it.*

The porter and his donkey have arrived with the rest of our luggage, so I grab my backpack and meet Genesis in front of the restaurant. Domenica, Ryan's new Peruvian friend, has packed up her tent to join us, and Holden has invited most of the bros and some old guy I can only assume is the source of their supply.

Our group has doubled in size.

"Who's your new man?" Genesis asks with a grin, and I turn to see that Luke is already awkwardly running toward us in the sand, as if he's afraid we'll leave without him. Suddenly I'm very aware of how pale and skinny he is. Of how his goofy grin is as big and awkward as the pack he wears.

I glare at her. "He's not—"

"He looks like he should be carrying a lunch box," Neda says.

Genesis laughs. "Or a cute little heart-shaped collar that reads, 'If lost, please return to Maddie Valencia.'"

"*Shut up!*" I snap as he jogs to a stop three feet away. "Genesis, this is Luke Hazelwood." I plead with my cousin silently to just smile and nod, for once. "I know him from school. I told him he could come with us."

"My parents are fine with it," he adds, then he immediately looks like he wants to stuff the words back into his mouth and swallow them. Like a poison pill.

"Well, as long as it's okay with Mommy and Daddy," Penelope sneers, but Genesis only rolls her eyes. Gen and Pen have been joined at the hip since they were eight, but obviously Genelope couldn't survive Hurricane Holden.

"Sure," Genesis says to Luke, but I can tell that's not the last I'll hear of this. "We're not very selective anyway, are we?" She glances from Pen to Holden, who is audibly grinding his teeth.

Luke flushes, and I already regret telling him he could come.

My cousin and her friends are going to eat the poor boy alive.

65 HOURS EARLIER

GENESIS

"So, where is this ancient ruin, exactly?" Neda asks as she pushes a branch out of her way.

"It's not on the tour circuit." Nico flips open his water bottle as he steps over an exposed root. "Not many people go, because the hike is kind of a pain."

I shoot him an angry glance; *why* would he tell her that?

"Hey," Ryan says, when Neda's groan begins to resemble a wildcat's growl. "Think of exploring this ruin as the sightseeing equivalent of an early glimpse at the new Manolo Blahnik scarf."

Neda laughs. "Manolo Blahnik doesn't make scarves."

"Or maybe he does, but no one knows yet. Anyone can go to the beach, but not just anyone can go see the Manolo Blahnik scarf of ancient ruins. After *you* go, *everyone* will want to go."

Neda laughs again. Ryan's logic is ridiculous, but she's smiling now. Better yet, she's not complaining.

"Hey, who's that old guy?" Domenica whispers as she hangs back to walk with us. "The one with a never-ending supply of pot." She nods at the cluster of stoners keeping Holden blissfully oblivious of anything but his own buzz.

"I'm calling him Rog," I tell her. "For Random Old Guy."

"He's, like, some kind of professional loser," Penelope adds, and I can tell from the way she keeps glancing at me that she's testing the waters of our friendship. Waiting to see if I'll try to drown her. "He looks like he's been wandering around the jungle for years."

"Maybe he lives out here, hiking from campsite to campsite, trading weed for food so he doesn't starve," Neda suggests with a giggle.

"Or maybe he betrayed his friends, so they left him out here to wander until he dies all alone," I counter, looking right at Penelope.

She flinches and looks away.

"Rog it is," Neda says. "Judging from the cloud of smoke he lives in, I doubt he even remembers his real name."

Rog turns and exhales a ring of smoke. "I've forgotten a lot of things—most of 'em on purpose—but my name isn't one of them. Never really liked it, though." He shrugs and taps ash from the end of his joint. "I could answer to Rog."

The old guy turns back around, and Neda gives me a wide-eyed, embarrassed look.

Indiana laughs out loud.

The minute the Ecohabs come into sight, Maddie stops

to look up at them with a dramatic sigh. "What a waste," she says, while the rest of us pass her. "We didn't even sleep there."

Penelope shrugs. "Once you pay for the rooms, they're yours to do whatever you want with."

Maddie stomps down the trail after us. "That is such a *typical* American philosophy of waste and entitlement. The money spent to rob some other poor tourists of their vacation plans means nothing to you because you have plenty of it. They lost their hotel room for *no reason*."

"You do know you're American too, right?" Neda says as she slaps at another mosquito on her leg.

"Fortunately, we don't all fit the stereotype," Maddie snaps.

"What you call a waste is actually a conservation of the local resources," I tell my cousin.

"How on *earth* do you figure that?" Maddie demands.

"Since no one was in our rooms, no water was wasted washing towels and beddings. Which means less detergent was emptied into the local water source, and less electricity was used."

"And the staff had less work to do, yet they still got paid," Indiana adds with a shrug.

I give him my brightest smile. "I'd call that one a win for everyone. Including the environment."

Maddie's mouth opens and closes for a second, as if her shock needs a way to escape her body. She's still staring at me when I settle into the hike, feasting on private satisfaction.

A minute later, Indiana falls into step beside me.

"Just how far off the grid are we?" Holden asks through a cloud of smoke, as our narrow path begins to climb,

"The grid isn't an actual thing, *mono*." Nico is breathing easily, in spite of the exercise and the increase in altitude. "So I can't judge our distance from it."

I savor Holden's scowl as I pull myself uphill with a good grip on the nearest thin branch.

Penelope props one foot on a fallen log and reaches back for the bottle of water strapped to the side of her pack. "So, if someone were to get hurt, how long would it take the rescue team to get here?"

Nico chuckles. "What makes you think they'd find us?"

64 HOURS EARLIER

MADDIE

"Please tell me that's a joke." Neda stares out at the jungle with mistrust. As if it hasn't been dangerous all along.

Genesis rolls her eyes. "Of course it's a joke." But she directs a questioning look to Nico for confirmation, and suddenly I'm uneasy about how deep into the jungle we might actually be.

We didn't tell anyone where we were going.

That's my cousin's standard operating procedure, not mine. I was so eager to get away from Benard and the drama on the beach that I let Genesis herd us into the jungle without even trying to get a message to Abuelita.

Nico shrugs at Genesis. "You said you wanted remote and private." And again, she's gotten exactly what she wanted. But unlike soldiers and park staff, snakes and caiman can't be bribed.

Still, Nico is a real tour guide. Right? He knew most of the soldiers on patrol at the park.

"We'll be fine," I insist as I pull my water bottle from

my pack and charge ahead.

When the trail flattens out a few minutes later, our hike develops its own rhythm. We actually make decent progress until we come to a stream rushing quickly downhill. Sunlight gleams on the surface from overhead.

"It's not very deep, but the rocks get slippery," Nico says. "So set your feet carefully."

The rocks are actually a series of small boulders sticking up from the water, forming a crooked, perilous path to dry—er, muddy—land on the other side.

"You *have* to be kidding," Neda groans.

"Come on, Neda, this is an adventure!" My brother slides his arm around her and winks at me over her head.

Nico re-centers his pack on his shoulders and ventures onto the first rock. He makes it across with a series of nimble steps.

"Come on!" Penelope shows him up with the skill of a retired Olympic gymnast, and once Rog and the bros have crossed, I suck in a deep breath and go for it.

Water splatters my calves as I step carefully from rock to rock, resisting the urge to slap at mosquitoes and upset my balance. My foot slides a little on the third boulder, but two steps later I'm across, grinning like an idiot from the adrenaline rush.

Neda and Ryan are the last ones left on the other side. "You got this," my brother says as Neda steps onto the first rock.

She takes the first four boulders slowly, listening as

Genesis and Pen encourage her. Basking in the attention. When she's down to the last step, arrogance shines in her eyes. Indiana reaches out to steady her, and she clings to him as she makes a bold hop from the last boulder into the mud.

Her couture sandal slides out from under her. Her foot folds at an awkward angle.

Neda's shrill scream sends birds fleeing from a treetop to our west.

I roll my eyes, sure she's exaggerating for attention. But before Ryan can make it across the stream, her ankle has swollen so badly that she's openly lamenting the tragic and premature end of her (nonexistent) career on the runway.

"I need ice!" she cries, while Nico kneels to palpate her injury.

"Lucky for us, this jungle is famously situated over the very last of the Caribbean glaciers," I tell her.

Indiana and Luke laugh, but Neda only moans louder.

Ryan kneels next to Nico and gently lifts her mud-coated foot. "I'm sure it's just a sprain, but we'll wrap it. I have an Ace bandage in my pack."

She looks at him with actual tears shining in her eyes as he wraps her muddy ankle. "I need to call my orthopedist."

"Neda," I snap. "We don't have ice or cell service. Those are the hallmark traits of 'off the grid.'"

"Come on, beautiful." Ryan winks at Domenica as he reaches down to pull Neda up. She flinches when her foot touches the ground. "I'll give you a ride, and when we make camp, you can put your foot up." He hands his bag to me. Then my brother actually kneels in the mud so the spoiled heiress can climb onto his back as if he were a beast of burden!

"Who are you trying to be?" I mumble as I trudge past him. "Prince Charming, or Cinderella's horse and carriage?"

61 HOURS EARLIER

GENESIS

The first real tears come during Holden's piggyback shift. "I can feel my ankle expanding by the second," Neda moans, practically choking him with her arms wrapped around his neck. "What if that's permanent? They won't let a girl with jiggly ankles anywhere *near* a runway."

"The swelling will go down," I assure her, before Holden can tell her that it won't be her ankle keeping her off the runway.

"Are you sure? How far is it to these ruins?" She clutches Holden tighter as he veers around a big rock, and a branch snags in her hair. "I can't take any more of this jostling. Did anyone pick up my sandal?"

"We have to get rid of her," I whisper to Nico, while I ignore Penelope's millionth attempt to catch my gaze. "Or at least shut her up." I would gag Neda with the strap from her Tom Ford calf-hair clutch, if that wouldn't be a waste of a damn fine bag.

"We should be about an hour from a bunkhouse used

as a campsite by various tour groups," Nico tells me as we round a sharp bend in the trail. "They get supply shipments by helicopter every other day for the soldiers who patrol the *parque* and the popular ruins. I can probably get the pilot to airlift Neda back to Cartagena."

"If we camp there, we won't get to see the ruins today."

"We wouldn't anyway." Nico gives the sinking sun a pointed glance. "Your friends move too slow."

"Okay. The car's coming for us at Cañaveral tomorrow night. If we get a decent start in the morning, can we see the ruins and make it back to the park entrance by nightfall?"

He nods. "If you can light a fire under your friends' feet."

"Done." I turn around to address the entire group as I walk backward. "We're camping at an army bunkhouse tonight." I let my gaze linger on Holden, driving home my threat to have him searched. "Let's go."

The bunkhouse turns out to be a short, squat building made of rough wood planks, in the middle of a large clearing. A patch of bare dirt to the west of the building has been designated for helicopter landings, and a dozen other tourists have pitched tents on the opposite side of the bunkhouse.

"How long am I going to be stuck here?" Neda demands as Ryan, Domenica, and Maddie start unpacking their gear. Holden, Rog, and the bros drop their packs and head straight for a large campfire, where people are already grilling hot dogs and passing around bottles of beer.

Penelope hangs back, glancing first at Holden, then at

me, as if she needs my permission to get within ten feet of him.

She does.

I leave her standing there while I help Neda hop toward the bunkhouse, where Nico is making arrangements to have her removed from our company. I totally owe him a beer.

We can already hear her ride coming, but in the end, I have to part with a fifty-dollar bill—US currency—to buy Neda a one-way ticket out of the jungle.

It's money well spent.

"You should still try to have fun without me," Neda shouts as the helicopter descends into the clearing, blowing back our hair and our words. "I totally don't blame you for dragging me into the jungle without telling me I'd need boots. So don't let that ruin your hike, okay?"

I laugh as I return her hug and shout into her ear, "I promise I won't let your lack of coordination and common sense plague my vacation." Now that she's leaving, I'm sure I'm going to miss her, for the entertainment factor alone.

"I'm not uncoordinated. The jungle was out to get me," she insists with a grin.

"Take it easy when you get back. In fact, have a spa day in Cartagena, on me. They have my card on file from the reservation we canceled."

"A spa day by myself?" Neda pouts, but she's clearly pleased. The spa is all she wanted in the first place.

Nico and one of the other guides help her into the helicopter, and we watch, our hair whipping around crazily, as it rises into the air. Neda waves from the open side of the helicopter, her heavily wrapped ankle propped up where we can all see it from the ground, in case we're tempted to forget about her hardship.

The moment she disappears over the treetops, our party begins.

59 HOURS EARLIER

MADDIE

With Neda gone, my day brightens by about 300 percent, even as the sun drops beneath the jungle canopy to the west. And seriously? Removed from the party by her own couture sandals? Those strappy death traps may have cost her a fortune, but the irony is truly priceless.

I take a seat at the campfire, as far from my cousin's asshole boyfriend as I can get, and Luke sits between me and a middle-aged tour guide wearing a stained white T-shirt and dark cargo shorts.

"I'm Nixon," he says with a thick but clear accent as he shoos a small, scruffy-looking mutt away from his hot dog.

"Maddie."

Luke sticks his hand out in front of me. "Luke Hazelwood."

"Are you going to Ciudad Perdida?"

"No. We have to be back in Cartagena tomorrow night," I tell him as the dog begs for a bite of meat.

"*Vamos*, Caca," Nixon says, and I can't help laughing

over the dog's name. "Fetch my pipe."

The dog yips, then runs off toward the small city of tents.

"Why did you name your dog after . . . poo?" I ask.

"What else would you call a smelly brown lump on the ground at your feet?"

Caca comes back with a hand-carved wooden pipe in her mouth. "Good girl." The tour guide takes it, then tosses a hunk of meat at her.

The other hikers are friendly and laid-back, but the soldiers watch us in small groups, wearing muddy boots and holding automatic rifles. They don't seem to care about the alcohol and pot being passed around the campfire, but a cold, hollow feeling swells in my chest when I notice them whispering to each other on the edge of the light cast by the fire. I try to listen, but all I can make out is something about increased foot traffic on some jungle path.

"What's with all the soldiers?" Penelope asks when she notices me watching them. "Is this a police state?"

"They're for security, on the beaches, and they patrol known drug trafficking routes in the jungle," Nico explains.

"See?" Holden turns on me. His eyes are glazed and his words are slurred. "There *is* drug trafficking here."

"There's drug trafficking everywhere," I tell him. "But no one ever tries to paint that as the defining characteristic of the US or Canada as nations. The truth is that the RDP—La Revolución del Pueblo, the People's Revolution—is in talks to end the guerrilla rebellion, and the Moreno cartel was nearly eradicated last year." According to my dad, the

CIA made some shady backdoor deal with another cartel to drive them out of business, and while I don't support the approach, Colombia is better off now that its citizens—and its tourists—have little to fear from armed militants.

Bored with my politics, Holden joins a drinking game with the bros. Luke takes a little of everything that is passed to him, and soon, I notice him staring into the fire, tracing bits of burning ash as they rise from the pit.

"You okay?" I ask.

He stares through the flames. "The fire makes your cousin look evil."

"Wings and a halo could make my cousin look evil," I mumble. When the joint comes our way again, I try to pass it to the bro on Luke's other side, but he intercepts my arm with a scowl.

"Hey. You can't just skip people."

I've seen Ryan wasted often enough to know that the fog Luke's mired in can't be penetrated with logic. Which will make him easy to bargain with. "Would you rather have a hit from this or from the bottle?"

Luke gives the decision more thought than it deserves. "I want the weed!" He sucks deeply on the joint, determined to get the better end of a choice he was under no obligation to make.

When he starts to tilt sideways, I guide him to his bright blue tent.

"Thanks for inviting me," Luke says as I help him into his sleeping bag. "This is the best vacation I've ever had."

I start to tell him how sad that sounds, but then I notice how long and thick his guy-lashes are, now that his hair isn't falling into his face.

With Luke tucked in, I head toward my own tent to crash, free from both the bite of mosquitoes and the sting of Miami's queen bee.

As I duck beneath the flap, I notice the silhouette of a man holding a rifle, backlit by the campfire in the distance. The soldier stares at me in the dark until I zip up my tent.

Even in my sleep, I can feel him watching me.

53 HOURS EARLIER

GENESIS

When the campfire has died down and Holden and the bros have passed out, I zip up my tent and collapse onto my sleeping bag, still buzzing from several shots of *aguardiente*. My phone screen is lit up for the first time since we arrived at Tayrona—I have one-bar reception at this outpost. There must be a tower somewhere nearby, which makes sense, considering that this bunkhouse is a point of communication for soldiers and tour guides.

I have twelve missed calls and three text messages. They're all from my dad.

Genesis, answer your phone!

Call me as soon as you get this message. I want you on that jet ASAP!

Go back to your grandmother's house as soon as you get this, Genesis. THIS IS NOT A GAME.

No, it's not a game. It's my *birthright*. Colombia is my history. It's in my *blood*, just like it's in my father's, and he has no right to try to take that from me just because he wants nothing to do with his homeland anymore.

My return message reads:

We'll come home tomorrow night, I promise.
Everything's fine. Te amo.

Seconds after my head hits the folded blanket I'm using for a pillow, my phone buzzes again. My message has failed to go through; evidently the incoming signal is stronger than the outgoing. I set an alarm and resign myself to the early hour, so I can try to resend the text before we leave the bunkhouse and its isolated, if weak signal.

If he doesn't hear from me soon, my father will *lose* it.

46 HOURS EARLIER

MADDIE

My tent is still dark when my brother shakes me awake. I grumble and roll over, but Ryan won't be ignored. "Wake up, Maddie! We have to go!"

"What?" I sit up, adrenaline driving my heart at a crazy speed, and my knee knocks over a half-empty bottle of water. "It's the middle of the night. What's wrong?"

"The sun will be up in a few minutes. Come on! They're going to leave without us."

"Who?"

"There's a cocaine manufacturing . . . facility—or whatever—about an hour from here. Some of the hikers are going to see a demonstration, and I thought we could—"

"This is about sightseeing? Wait, isn't that *incredibly* illegal?"

"Nico says it's just a gimmick for tourists." Ryan grabs my backpack and digs around inside it, no doubt making sure I have plenty of food and water. "Everyone'll probably be wrist deep in powdered sugar. It'll be hilarious!"

I snatch my bag from him. "It'll be exploiting a stereo-type."

"Come on." Ryan grins at me and stuffs another bottle of water into my pack. "You *owe* me a picture of you with powdered sugar caked beneath your nose, after you stole my funnel cake at the fair and *I* got blamed for *your* diabetic shock."

"I was seven! And I didn't steal it. You gave me half." Because I'd begged, and he never could say no to his little sister. Ryan has looked out for me ever since that day, even when that meant giving up sweets to keep from tempting me. Even though I've had several drinks right in front of him since we got to Colombia.

"Fine." I throw back the corner of my sleeping bag and crawl out of it. His grin is contagious, and I've hardly seen him since we got off the plane. "One picture. But you can't post it."

I pull my hair into a ponytail, then use a camping wipe to clean my face and armpits. When I emerge from my tent carrying my backpack, Ryan and two of the bros are wait-ing for me, along with the six other tourists who got up in time to see the gimmicky demonstration before breakfast. The campsite feels eerily quiet—almost dead—as we set off through the jungle on a narrow, well-worn trail, leaving everyone else asleep in their tents.

Not gonna lie. I wish I were still sleeping too.

Two protein bars into the excursion, I remember to check my insulin pump. I blame the lapse on the disorienting wakeup call.

"How's it look?" Ryan asks.

"My blood sugar's fine. But . . ." Guilt washes over me. I should have checked before I even left my tent. "Um . . . my insulin vial is gone. It must have fallen out of my bag."

Ryan groans. "What's left in the pump?"

"About an eighth of the reserve."

He exhales heavily. "What is that, a few hours' worth?"

"A little more, maybe. I'm sorry! I was going to change the infusion set this morning, but I got distracted by the field trip."

Everyone has stopped hiking to listen, and I *hate* being stared at.

"You go ahead," I tell Ryan. "I'll find my insulin, and I'll see you after the demonstration." I start to head for the bunkhouse, but he grabs my arm.

"Maddie, if you can't find that vial, we have to go back to Cartagena now and call in a refill."

He's right. I have *maybe* half a day's supply left in the pump. But I really want to see the ruins, and I really *don't* want to be the reason the rest of our group has to miss it.

Ryan turns back to the tour guide. "You guys have fun. But not *too* much fun." He swipes one finger across his nose suggestively, and several people laugh.

"That's just more for us, man!" one of the West Coast bros calls out as we head back toward the bunkhouse.

"I'm sorry about your demo."

"It was just a stupid gimmick." But his smile is stiff. This isn't the first time he's missed out because of me.

We're still several minutes from the camp when a scream tears through the jungle, silencing the ambient birdsong.

I freeze. Chills race down my spine and pool in my stomach. "Was that Penelope?"

45 HOURS EARLIER

GENESIS

A scream slices through my sleep, leaving the edges of my dream frayed and dangling. I bolt upright, my heart pounding, and pull on my shorts. I glance at the time on my phone—it's not quite seven in the morning—then shove it into my pocket and unzip my tent flap.

Before I can peek into the aisle between the rows of tents, more shouting startles me.

"Come out!" a man yells. "¡Venga!"

I scramble back and pull on my hiking boots, but then I freeze when heavy footsteps clomp past my tent, accompanied by deep voices speaking rapid-fire Spanish. Most of the words are too muffled for me to understand over the whooshing of my own pulse, but my name comes through loud and clear.

I recognize the heavy click and the scrape of metal as the footsteps fade. Someone has just chambered a round in a large gun. Something bigger than anything I've ever fired on the range with my dad.

Strange men are carrying rifles through our camp, ordering people from their tents.

They're looking for me.

The metallic whisper of a zipper comes from the tent next to mine and I go still as I listen.

"*¡Salga!*"

"What?" Penelope's voice is high-pitched and terrified. "I don't understand—"

"Come out of the tent!" the voice orders in a heavy Spanish accent.

Penelope's air mattress squeaks. "Can I please get dressed?" Her words are shaky.

There's no reply, but a shuffling sound comes from her tent as she digs through her bag.

My pulse races so fast I can hardly think.

Clear your head and get out of your own way. The voice of reason sounds like my trainer guiding me through a Krav Maga workout. *Let your senses do their job. Let the information in.*

I close my eyes and take a deep breath.

Heavy footsteps. Heavy weaponry. Commands issued in Spanish, from several different voices. They probably don't outnumber the hikers, but they're armed. Resisting or fighting back would be suicide.

Watch for your opportunity, my instructor's voice says.

The barrel of a rifle slides inside my tent. I gasp and scramble backward, but can't tear my gaze from the muzzle aimed at my chest.

The gun is military issue. Semiautomatic. The same general type carried by the soldiers at Tayrona. There's no move in my self-defense repertoire that can be executed faster than a bullet leaves the barrel of a gun.

A face appears in the opening. Dark eyes glance around my one-person tent, taking in my air mattress and supplies. Below the face is a torso wearing jungle camo.

"¡Salga! Bring your passport and your cell phone."

My hands shake as I grab my passport and my cell phone on the way out. Pen is standing in front of her tent a few feet away. She holds her hands up at head height, one clutching her own passport, the other her cell phone. Down the row of tents to my right, more hikers stand in the same position. They all look terrified.

The man with the rifle turns to unzip the tent across from mine, and through the opening, I see Holden still asleep facedown on his sleeping bag. After a binge, Holden could sleep through the Apocalypse.

"¡Levántate!" the soldier orders. When he gets no response, he kicks Holden's foot.

Holden mumbles an obscenity as he rolls onto his side, his eyes still tightly closed. "People are trying to sleep."

The soldier aims his rifle at my boyfriend's head, and my airway tries to close. "Get up!" he shouts, and Penelope flinches.

Holden's eyes open. He blinks, his forehead furrowed in anger, and I can tell the instant reality comes into focus for him, because his eyes widen and his jaw snaps shut. He's never been on the wrong end of a rifle.

"Come out with your phone and your passport."

Holden stumbles out of his tent on bare feet, clutching his phone and a well-worn passport. His stunned gaze finds me, and his eyes narrow. *"What the hell did you do?"*

I frown at him. What did *I* . . . ?

"Am I under arrest?" he demands. "I have the right to a lawyer!"

Holden thinks I've hired these soldiers to pay him back for sleeping with Penelope.

"Shut up!" I tilt my head toward the campers lined up on my right. His mouth snaps shut. Blood drains from his face when he realizes we're *all* being held at gunpoint. But something else has caught my attention.

None of the soldiers' camo matches. They aren't carrying standard issue canteens or sleep rolls, and they're armed with three different rifles.

Terror blazes a path up my spine.

These are not soldiers. We are not under arrest.

We've been taken hostage.

MADDIE

Penelope's scream echoes through the jungle, raising chill bumps on my arms.

Ryan's eyes narrow and his jaw clenches. "Wait here." He starts to take off toward the camp, then spins to face me again. "I changed my mind. Stick close and be quiet."

"She probably just saw a spider," I whisper as we tiptoe over roots and fallen branches. But neither of us believes me.

"*¡No se mueva!*" another voice shouts from the direction of the bunkhouse, and I realize I'm breathing too fast.

"Ryan," I whisper, but the word hardly carries any sound. He reaches back for my hand, and I slide my palm into his grip. We stand frozen, listening to the rush of our own pulses in a jungle that has gone strangely quiet.

"*¡No se mueva!*" the voice repeats, and I jump when a burst of gunfire punctuates the order.

Ryan squeezes my hand. I suck in a breath and hold it as a wave of panic washes over me.

"*¡Pónganse en fila!*" that voice shouts again, ordering people to form a line.

"Ryan!" I whisper, my voice shaky with fear. "What's happening?"

"Stay here," he says, but I can barely hear him. "Hunch down behind that bush and don't come out unless I call for you. Okay? And watch out for snakes."

"What are you doing?" I demand as quietly as I can.

"Recon." His eyes hold a reckless determination. "I need to see what's happening."

"No!" I clutch his hand, but he pulls it from my grip and points to the clump of brush again. "Don't leave!" Then he quietly pushes toward camp.

My focus flicks from tree to tree, shadow to shadow as fear fuels my racing heartbeat. Careful not to step on anything loud, I drop into a squat behind the brush, then nearly scream when a lizard scurries over my hand.

Alone, I can only listen and wait, terrified.

"¡Vete de la carpa!" another voice barks, ordering someone to come out of a tent. Another burst of gunfire makes me flinch. More people scream.

Was my brother one of them? Was my cousin?

I stand, terrified of going closer to the gunfire, but even more terrified of not knowing. A twig snaps behind me. I gasp and whirl around.

A man in green fatigues aims a rifle at my face.

GENESIS

Are they going to kill us? Penelope mouths to me from a few feet away, where she's still standing in front of her tent.

I shake my head. If these men wanted us dead, they could have shot us in our sleep.

My thoughts race as I evaluate our situation, running through the threat assessment steps from the survival class my father made me take two years ago.

Assets: my fellow campers.

Liabilities: my fellow campers.

As far as I know, none of my friends have had a single self-defense course, and Holden's the only other one who's ever fired a gun—a hunting rifle.

Thanks to my paranoid father, I know how to handle myself one-on-one—or even one-on-three—but there are nearly a dozen armed gunmen.

Nico and the other guides can get us back to civilization, if we can escape, but Maddie—

Maddie and Ryan aren't standing in front of their tents. Neither are Luke and at least two of the bros. Maddie probably chased a rabbit into the jungle to make sure it wasn't being exploited as a native resident, but the guys could be anywhere.

"*¡Pónganse en fila!*" one of the armed men shouts, waving his rifle at an open area between the outdoor showers and the tent village. Scared campers begin to form a rough line, and Holden, Pen, and I file in with them.

Holden reaches for my hand as we walk, but one of the men in camo uses the barrel of a rifle to shove him away from me. He stumbles and curses, then scowls as he slides his hand into his pocket.

In the clearing, Indiana and Domenica line up next to us, in front of the bunkhouse. She looks scared, but Indiana watches quietly, drawing no attention to himself.

"Be chill," Rog whispers to the bros. I'm surprised by how focused he sounds now that he isn't high.

"Should I call my dad?" Holden asks me, when the nearest gunman's gaze travels away from us down the line of hostages.

"Do *not* reach for your phone," I whisper. "Those are not soldiers."

"They're carrying military issue M16s, M4s, and AK-47s." Rog lets out a long, soft breath. "That is *not* chill."

I watch the campers still falling into line, searching for Maddie and Ryan, yet I hope I don't find them. If they've avoided being captured, they'll be able to report the kidnapping.

Nico is among the last out of the tent city. "Everything

will be fine," he whispers as he steps into place next to me.

Holden's eyes narrow. "Either your English isn't very good or something got lost in translation," he whispers. "Because this is pretty damn far from fine." A toxic blend of fear and rage burns in his eyes.

We're being taken captive by armed gunmen, yet it's Holden who makes me nervous.

"I thought you said this shit doesn't happen anymore," he hisses at me. "You said this place was *safe*."

"It is," Nico insists before I can answer. "They're probably RDP. Their problem is with the Colombian government, not with us," he insists as his gaze travels over our captors.

"Oh, well, then I guess it's okay that we were dragged out of bed at gunpoint by a bunch of psychos. Whose side are you on?"

Nico scowls at Holden. "I'm just saying that it could be worse."

His last word is swallowed by a burst of gunfire. Several of the women in line scream. Holden takes my hand, and I let him hold it because while I get focus and calm from meditation, he gets them from anger. His grip is rock-steady.

"Everyone shut up and listen."

The female voice surprises me, and at first I think one of the other hostages has spoken. But then I see a female kidnapper, her rifle still aimed at the air. Instead of fatigues, she wears a green tank top with her camo pants and black boots and her makeup is as dramatic as her fierce brown eyes. When her gaze settles on me, I see nothing soft or yielding in her expression.

Like her voice, this woman is all hard planes and sharp edges.

"Three of my men are going to walk down the line," she says. "You will give the first man your cell phone, the second your passport, and the third any electronics, watches, or valuable jewelry."

Her accent is thick, but her English is flawless. She doesn't ask if we understand, even though the hostages represent at least six countries, and I'm not sure they all speak English. A woman like this cannot be negotiated with. She will not bend to either sympathy or logic.

She will not let us go until she has whatever she wants.

"If you try to escape or call for help, you will be shot," she says as her men make their way down the line, confiscating our property. "If you refuse an order, you will be shot."

Holden hesitates, clutching his phone, and I grab his hand again because I see rebellion in his eyes. In his entire life, the worst-case scenario has never once applied to him. He's been the exception to every rule.

He doesn't truly believe the kidnappers will shoot him, even if they're willing to kill the rest of us.

"Do you know who I am?" he demands, holding his phone over the open bag, and I flinch. If our captors didn't already hate him personally, they will now.

"Just give them the phone," I whisper, but it's too late.

"*¿Qué pasa?*" The woman in charge stomps toward us, and the casual way she aims her rifle at Holden's gut makes my stomach churn. "Passport." She holds out her free hand, and Holden slaps his passport onto her palm. Her eyes narrow and she opens it one-handed. "Holden Wainwright." She looks up at him again, one brow raised. "Is that supposed to mean something to me?"

Holden scowls. "Wainwright. As in Wainwright Pharmaceuticals."

My friends and I have always found it amusingly ironic that his parents' wealth comes from one of the largest prescription drug manufacturers in the world, considering his fondness for recreational chemicals.

"You're worth something?" The woman looks him up and down, as if she finds that hard to believe.

"Only a couple billion," Holden snaps, evidently as angry about the lack of recognition as he is about being taken hostage.

"Go stand over there, Wainwright Pharmaceuticals." The woman points to an unlit torch post near the front of the bunkhouse.

The strange satisfaction in Holden's eyes makes no sense—until I realize he thinks he's been invited to the VIP lounge of this hostage situation.

"Óscar!" the woman shouts at one of her gunmen.

"Sí, Silvana." A gunman about my age jogs toward her with his rifle aimed at the ground.

Silvana pulls a pistol from the back of her pants and hands it to the gunman. "If Wainwright Pharmaceuticals moves, shoot him in the leg."

Holden's step falters. His shoulders stiffen. Now he understands.

But when Óscar takes aim at his left thigh, Holden doesn't even flinch. He's eyeing the pistol. He thinks he will have revenge.

I am *terrified* that his revenge will get us killed.

Silvana turns to me. "Genesis Valencia. Of Genesis Shipping." She's not asking. She doesn't need to look at my passport. She knows who I am, and she knows what I'm worth.

I've been the target all along.

MADDIE

"*¿Hablas español?*" the man with the gun says as his dark eyes burn into me.

All I can see is the rifle pointed at my face. "*Sí.*" My voice sounds strangely hollow. My heart is beating too hard.

This can't be happening.

"*Marcha.*"

Numb with fear, I slowly turn around, praying that I'm not about to be shot in the back. When I hesitate, he shoves me with the barrel of the gun, and I gasp. I've never touched a weapon in my life. I've never been threatened with anything worse than the confiscation of my phone.

I walk forward, and I hear nothing but the roar of my pulse, even as my boots crunch through twigs and leaves.

My breath freezes in my throat, and my legs stop working. Is this what happened to my father?

"*¡Ándale!*" the gunman shouts, and I flinch. "Back to the bunkhouse."

"Okay." Slowly, I lift my arms to show him I'm not resisting. "Who are you?"

He shoves me in the back with the rifle again, and I stumble forward. My heart races and my vision begins to swim. The jungle starts to spin around me.

Calm down, Maddie. You're still alive for a reason. Think it through.

I take a deep breath and take another step. Then another. Finally my legs are working on their own, and so are my thoughts. "Is this about cocaine?" Have we gotten caught up in some kind of drug trafficking . . . incident?

"*¡Cállate!*" The gunman shoves me again, and my jaw snaps shut. "No talking."

It's going to be fine, Maddie. But I've never been a very good liar. Not even to myself.

44 HOURS EARLIER

GENESIS

"Who else is with Genesis Shipping and Wainwright Phar-maceuticals?" Silvana demands.

To my surprise, Indiana steps forward.

After a second, Domenica joins him. I hear her whisper as she passes Silvana, "*No soy americana. Por favor, no me mates.*"

"I don't care if you're not American." Silvana motions her toward us with the butt of her pistol.

Penelope finally takes one shaky step forward, staring at the ground.

"I'm their tour guide," Nico says as he joins us.

Silvana shoves him back into line. "You four, over there." She waves us toward the post where Holden stands. Then she studies the remaining hostages one at a time. After a couple of minutes, she shoves Rog toward us, then orders everyone else to lie facedown on the ground with their hands behind their backs.

Armed gunmen don't tell people to lie facedown on the ground because they're about to hand out candy and send everyone home. Chill bumps rise on my arms and legs. The tour guide's stray dog lies by his side and tucks her nose beneath her paws.

Penelope watches with wide, teary eyes, and Indiana looks sick when one of the gunmen comes forward with a bundle of zip ties. He begins binding the prone hostages' hands at their backs.

Two of the women are crying, their wet cheeks pressed into the dirt, and I want to look away. My own terror is more than enough to deal with. But I know what's going to happen to them, and I won't turn away from their pain.

Not this time.

"Don't look, Genesis." She's choking on tears, face-down on the floor, but I can still understand her. "Close your eyes, baby."

"Listen to your mother." The man's face is in shadows, but light glints off his knife.

"Just keep your eyes closed, baby, no matter what you hear." She's sobbing, and I don't know what to do. "It'll all be over in a minute."

So I close my eyes.

I refuse to look away.

But when the gunman has bound them all, he only

stands behind them, rifle at the ready. He's going to drag it out. He's going to torture them with the inevitability of their own deaths.

Bastard.

"Silvana! *¡Vamos!*"

I follow the voice to find another man in fatigues coming out of the bunkhouse carrying an automatic rifle.

"Oh, *shit.* Sebastián." Nico's friend, who danced with Maddie in Cartagena. He didn't just follow us to the beach. He *led* us to Tayrona, through Nico. Then he led us into the jungle.

I clench my hands together to keep them from shaking.

We've been targets since the moment we stepped off the plane.

MADDIE

The shouts from camp get louder as the man with the gun marches me closer.

"¡*Silencio!*"

"¡*Formen una línea!*"

"¡*Pongan sus teléfonos en la bolsa!*"

The hikers are being kidnapped. *I'm* being kidnapped.

Twigs snap beneath my feet. A branch slaps my arm. I have to *do* something, but I don't know what to do, other than to keep putting one foot in front of the other.

I step into the clearing with the rifle pressed into my spine. Terror shoots through me. There are at least eight gunmen, and two of them are soldiers stationed at the bunkhouse. The men who watched me get into my tent last night. Who are supposed to protect tourists from things like this.

Most of the hikers lie facedown on the ground, bound with plastic zip ties. I recognize two of the bros and Nico, but Ryan, Genesis, and Luke aren't with them.

Near panic, I search the rest of the clearing. Genesis and her friends are in front of the bunkhouse, with two gunmen. My brother isn't with them.

Genesis looks relieved to see me, but then she mouths

Ryan's name, her brows arched in question.

I can only shrug, but a small buoy of hope bobs to the surface of my fear. They haven't caught Ryan. He can go for help.

"Silvana," the gunman at my back calls.

A woman in camo pants with a headful of poufy curls turns. Her brows rise. "What have you brought me, Moisés?"

"I found her in the jungle."

Silvana comes closer, an automatic rifle slung over her back. Her gaze takes in my cheap boots and faded tee, then settles on the lump at my waistband. She reaches for the hem of my shirt and I flinch away from her. Moisés holds me in place while she lifts my shirt and eyes my insulin pump.

I can see her weighing some decision, as if my worth can be established by a column of pluses and minuses. Genesis and her friends are going to be moved, but the people on the ground have guns aimed at their backs.

My head spins so fast the campsite blurs around me. "I'm stronger than I look. I can hike."

I don't want to die.

She points toward the bound hostages. "Lie on your stomach and put your hands behind your back." My strength and determination have not moved her. My life means nothing to her. She looks at Moisés. "If she tries to get up, shoot her."

"No! Please!" I shout as he drags me across the ground. My tears blur the clearing. "*Please!*"

"Wait!" Genesis shouts. "She's my—" But another gunman aims a pistol at her head, and her mouth snaps shut.

The captives on the ground strain to look up at me. Several of the women are crying.

Moisés throws his rifle over his shoulder and hauls me past the picnic tables. I stumble, struggling for each panicked breath. My feet drag the ground.

I grab a branch as Moisés pulls me by a thick clump of brush, and it skins my palm as it slides through my grip.

The brush rustles. A blur in dark pants and a familiar blue T-shirt lunges into the clearing.

My brother slams into Moisés's shoulder. The gunman falls, pulling me down with him. The impact drives the air from my lungs.

Ryan reaches for me. Fear lines his forehead. Over his shoulder, I see another gunman take aim.

"No!" I shout.

The rifle thunders. Ryan stumbles forward.

Blood blooms on the front of his shirt like a rose opening in time lapse. He collapses onto his side, just out of my reach.

"Ryan!" My brother's name scrapes my throat raw, but he doesn't answer. He doesn't even move. "Ryan, look at me!"

He's still breathing, yet the pool of red beneath him keeps expanding.

One of the guerrillas races across the clearing, shouting, *"Dame tu chaqueta."* He drops onto his knees next to Ryan, and when he looks up to take the jacket one of the other gunmen offers, I realize I know him.

Sebastián. From the bar in Cartagena. I don't understand. I kissed him. Now he wears camo and holds an automatic rifle while he presses the jacket to my brother's wound.

Sebastián's focus settles on the pendant hanging from a chain around Ryan's neck. His forehead furrows and his hands clench around the jacket. His eyes close, as if he's praying.

Finally Sebastián stands and orders one of the other men to take over for him. "Maddie." He meets my gaze. "*Lo siento.*"

My tears run over. "You're *sorry*? Do something!" I shout. Putting pressure on the wound isn't enough. "Call someone who can help!"

Sebastián gestures to two men, who lift my brother, then carry him into an orange tent. I can't see him.

"No! No, Ryan!" Desperate, I turn to Sebastián. "Bring him back!"

Sebastián shakes his head and gives me a somber look.

Moisés drags me away, and I scratch and flail and kick, but I may as well be fighting a concrete wall. I scream as the world collapses beneath me.

I scream as people stare at me, and point guns at me, and shout orders I can no longer hear.

And once I start screaming, I don't know how to stop.

43.5 HOURS EARLIER

GENESIS

The gunshot echoes in my head and Ryan hits the ground. Shock hits me like a punch to the chest. "No!" I lurch toward my cousin. Rifles swing in my direction.

Indiana pulls me back and pins me against his chest. I feel his breath against my ear, but I can't hear what he's whispering.

Maddie shouts as she kicks and claws at the man trying to drag her away from her brother, but I can't hear her either. I can't hear anything over the ringing in my ears.

Indiana won't let me go.

My hearing comes roaring back. Gunmen are shouting. People are crying. The tour guide's little dog is barking so forcefully that her whole body shakes.

But Maddie . . .

Maddie starts screaming, and everyone else falls silent. Her voice is an earsplitting tide of grief and anguish as she fights to get to her brother.

The rest of the world slides out of focus as I stare at Ryan, willing his lungs to expand. Willing him to breathe.

Come on, Ryan.

The wound is too big. There's too much blood.

This can't be real.

Please, God, let this not be real.

Finally Ryan's back rises, so slightly I'm not even sure of what I'm seeing.

"Julian!" Silvana grabs the shooter's rifle and slams the butt into his nose. Blood bursts from Julian's ruined face, and he howls until he starts choking on it.

"Ryan!" Maddie screams, but his name is half swallowed by sobs, and I can hardly see her through my own tears. "Call someone to help him!" she demands again, but Silvana only shrugs.

"There's no point."

"No!" Maddie's legs fold, and Moisés has to hold her up. Two men carry Ryan into a tent.

Indiana lets me go, and I lurch toward my cousin. But then I stop, frozen. I know eight ways to take down an unarmed opponent, and three methods for disarming one. But I can't take on this many armed men at once.

Maddie finally fights free. Moisés aims his rifle at her, but looks to Silvana for an order; after Julian's nose, the guerrillas are afraid to act on their own.

Maddie keeps screaming and backing away from the gunman. Her voice is hoarse. Her eyes are wide and her hands are shaking.

Silvana nods to one of the gunmen. "Shoot her."

"No!" Sebastián lunges for her, but I'm faster.

I push Maddie behind me and stare, breathless, at the rifle now aimed at my chest. "I've got her!" I shout, my pulse thundering in my ears. They can hear me because Maddie's voice is almost gone. "She's my cousin." I reach back and grab her arm to keep her behind me. Out of the line of fire.

Silvana frowns, and I can see the order hanging from the tip of her tongue. She wants Maddie facedown on the ground, and nothing less than absolute obedience will satisfy her.

Sebastián steps between me and the gunman. "*¡Deténganlas! ¡Las necesitamos!*" he shouts at Silvana. Sweat breaks out on my forehead while I wait to see if his insistence that they need us will outweigh Silvana's ego.

She scowls and aims a dismissive wave our way. The gunmen lower their rifles. Breath I didn't realize I was holding explodes from my lungs.

Sebastián marches past Silvana and tugs Maddie out from behind me.

"*Lo siento.*" He points toward the tent where they took Ryan, and my grief swells. "An accident." Then he turns back to Silvana. "Madalena *vendrá con nosotros.*"

"Fine," Silvana snaps. "Madalena comes." Then she addresses the rest of our group. "You have five minutes to gather food and supplies, but nothing that can be used as a weapon. Anyone who runs will be shot." Her focus finds me, then slides to Maddie, who's staring at the ground with an unfocused gaze. "Anyone."

I hate Silvana with the fire of a thousand hells, and that is *exactly* what I will bring down on her before this is over.

I lead my cousin toward the tents with the others, escorted on both sides by armed men. As we pass the tent they put Ryan in, she reaches for the flap, still sobbing.

"Maddie!" I hiss as I pull on her arm. Silvana is already marching toward us, pistol drawn.

Indiana steps up on her other side, and we help her into her own tent.

Alone in mine, I dump my backpack, then quickly repack only the essentials. A change of clothes and my waterproof blanket. My remaining protein bars and packets of tuna. Bug repellent. My flashlight. Every bottle of water I can find. I roll up my sleeping bag and strap it to my bag, then step out of my tent.

Óscar rummages through my things and tosses out the flashlight, because it's big enough to be used as a weapon. Which is exactly why I packed it.

"What are they going to do with us?" Penelope whispers from my left as she settles her backpack onto her shoulders.

"Don't worry," Rog says as the only other female kidnapper searches his bag. "When they get what they want, they'll let us go."

Penelope shudders and wraps her arms around herself. "What if what they want is us, dead?"

"They're not going to kill us," I say as I watch Domenica's and Indiana's bags being searched. "They're going to march us deeper into the jungle."

"How do you know?" Pen asks.

"They need us alive." For now.

43 HOURS EARLIER

MADDIE

A shadow falls into my tent. "Maddie." Genesis puts one hand on my shoulder and I flinch.

"They shot Ryan." It's not what I meant to say. But all I can hear is the echo of gunfire. All I can see is my brother, covered in blood.

"I know." Genesis dumps my backpack and starts sorting through my things. "We have to pack."

"I'm not going." I've already lost my dad. I can't lose Ryan too.

She rolls up one of my clean shirts and shoves it into my bag. "If you don't, they'll shoot you."

"If I go, they'll let Ryan die."

"There's nothing we can do for him." Her voice cracks, and for just a second, I can see her pain.

Rage crackles like fire inside me. I rip my bag from her hands. She has *no right* to that kind of pain. She wasn't there when we got the call about my dad. She didn't visit Ryan in rehab. Letting him party with her friends made him worse, not better, and she doesn't have any right to—

Genesis holds my gaze, as if she can read my thoughts. "I love him too, Maddie."

I can't think.

My cousin tugs the bag from my grip and starts shoving things into it.

"We can't leave him," I whisper.

She sets the bag aside and starts rolling up my sleeping bag. "Staying here won't help Ryan, but it will get us killed."

She's right. I need a better plan. "Did you bring a satellite phone?"

"No. The whole point was to be out of reach for a while." She buckles my sleeping bag to the bottom of my pack, then picks up a small glass vial that was hidden beneath it. My missing vial of insulin. "Do you need this?"

My eyes fill with tears again as I stare at the vial. "I lost it."

Genesis slides the vial into a pocket on the side of her hiking shorts and zips the pocket closed. "We can't let that happen again."

"He wouldn't have been shot if I hadn't lost it." I can't stop my nose from running.

Genesis sets my repacked bag in front of me. "Julian pulled the trigger. Not you."

"So we're just supposed to *leave* Ryan here?" My words sound half choked. Fresh tears blur the inside of my tent.

She lowers her voice until I'm practically reading her lips. "They'll pay for this, Maddie. I *swear*. But until then, you need to keep your mouth closed and your head down."

My tears won't stop coming. "But he'll *die* if we leave him."

"*We'll* die if we don't." She exhales slowly. "And what good would we do him then?" I can practically see her shoving pain and fear back from the surface of her thoughts. Turning it all off like she did when her mom died.

That scares me more than an entire crew of armed kidnappers.

GENESIS

"Sebastián!" Nico strains his neck to look up from the ground, where he's bound with fifteen other hostages. "Don't do this!" His focus flicks from me to our captors. "Take me, please. Let me help!"

"Leave him!" I shout as I swing my backpack onto my shoulder. The thought of having that backstabbing bastard around makes my skin crawl. "He's done more than enough!"

"Genesis, I didn't . . ." Nico struggles to lift his head high enough to see me. "This wasn't—"

"¡Cállate!" Silvana shouts, looking up from the map Sebastián holds. "Or I'll put a bullet in you myself."

Nico's jaw snaps shut, but he keeps watching us.

"¿Estás listo?" Silvana asks Sebastián.

"Sí. Vámonos." Sebastián folds the map and shoves it into his back pocket while Silvana gives an overhead "round-'em-up" signal to her other men.

No one speaks as we're marched out of the clearing flanked by seven of the nine gunmen. The eighth is in the tent with Ryan, and the remaining gunman stands over the captives bound facedown on the ground.

Indiana walks at Maddie's side as she plods in front of me. Penelope and Domenica stare at the ground as if they're afraid that seeing or hearing too much will get them killed. I take in every detail. As my father says, forewarned is forearmed.

My father also says Colombia isn't safe. But how was I supposed to know he was serious about that, when his everyday level of paranoia sentenced me to years of Krav Maga, self-defense, and survival classes?

If he'd told me there was a specific threat in Colombia, I never would have paid the pilot to bring us here. My friends and I wouldn't be heading into the jungle at gunpoint.

Ryan wouldn't have been shot.

Maddie sobs as we pass Ryan's tent. Then she lurches away from Indiana, headed for her brother.

I grab for her arm, but I'm too late. Sebastián catches her around the waist and hauls her back to me.

"*Anda*, Maddie," he whispers in her ear.

To me, he says, "*Ayúdala, o ella va a salir lastimada*," and the warning sends chills all over me.

"What did he say?" Indiana asks as Sebastián jogs toward the front of our group, pulling his map from his pocket.

"He said that if I don't help her, she won't leave the jungle alive."

I take one of Maddie's arms and Indiana takes the other. For the first few steps, we have to drag her along. She's determined to stay with Ryan, even if that means being buried with him.

I can't let that happen.

Maddie may feel responsible for what happened to Ryan, but all of this is my fault. I dragged us into the jungle. I *have* to get us out.

42.5 HOURS EARLIER

MADDIE

He's not dead. He's not dead. He's not dead.

I walk without seeing the path. Without truly hearing the birds, and frogs, and monkeys. I can't process anything through the funnel of grief narrowing my focus to that one moment. To the sight of my brother falling to the jungle floor.

"Maddie," Genesis whispers as we crunch into twigs and push dense clumps of brush aside. "I need you to keep your head in the game. Don't make me avenge Ryan all on my own."

Avenge?

I force the world back into focus. She looks just like her dad.

Fine. Let her avenge Ryan. Genesis is *great* at revenge.

I have to get back to my brother. But if I run, I'll just get shot. I need a distraction. Or an opportunity.

I pull free from my cousin's grip, and when I don't bolt this time, she leaves me alone.

Genesis thinks I've given up. But she's about to find out just how much we have in common.

42 HOURS EARLIER

GENESIS

"*Yo no quería esto.*" Julian's nose has finally stopped bleeding, but his whispered insistence that this isn't what he signed up for sounds like a nasal whine. "*No me gusta esa puta.*"

Moisés nods.

Obviously there's dissension in the ranks, and if that's about more than the broken nose, I should be able to exploit their anger and drive a wedge between our captors.

But it would help if I knew why we were being kidnapped. Unfortunately, I know nothing about the Colombian political situation, except that Maddie says both the drug wars and the guerrilla revolution—the main sources of the violence my father remembers—are practically over. Either she's wrong, or this is about something else.

Silvana knew who I was. The gunmen called my name as they searched the tents. My father will let me go anywhere in the world, except Colombia. This has to be about more than local politics.

This is about me. But why?

My dad and his mother moved to Miami when he was twelve. My uncle David was born six months later, and he was obsessed with his Colombian heritage, but my dad never talks about his childhood in Cartagena. As far as I know, he hasn't been back since the day he left.

I squat on the trail to retie my boot lace, letting Rog and my friends pass me until I'm within eavesdropping distance of Óscar and Natalia, the other female kidnapper, who're bringing up the rear. But the only thing I learn from their smutty whispering is that she's definitely *not* his sister.

As I stand, a gunshot echoes through the jungle.

Maddie turns to me, her eyes wide and swimming in tears.

"No," I whisper as I take her arm. "No, Maddie, it wasn't Ryan."

"How do you know?" she asks through halting sobs.

I know because they don't need another bullet to kill Ryan. All they have to do is leave him alone.

"*¡Vamos!*" Silvana shouts, and Maddie jumps. Indiana takes her backpack and wraps one arm around her shoulders, urging her forward.

A second shot rings out from behind us, and Penelope starts crying. Then she stops walking.

"Get her moving, or she's next," Silvana orders, marching backward so she can look at me.

I swallow a groan and wrap my arm around Penelope. I can't let her die, even if she did totally stab me in the back.

"Hey," I whisper close to her ear. "You have to keep walking."

"I can't." She grabs my arm, and her grip is so tight my fingers start to tingle. "They're going to kill us. We're next."

"They're not going to—" We both flinch as the third shot rings out.

Rog closes his eyes and bows his head for a second.

"March!" Silvana shouts.

I tug Penelope forward as the fourth shot echoes toward us. We march, her hand tight around mine, as bullet after bullet is fired, each separated by a short pause.

Pen flinches with each one, but I count them.

Seventeen shots. But we only left behind sixteen hostages tied up on the ground.

41 HOURS EARLIER

MADDIE

The forest goes gray and silent around me. I hear nothing but the echo of gunfire.

Seventeen shots, sixteen bound captives. Including Nico. It only makes sense if I count Ryan.

Unless they found Luke.

Guilt brings fresh tears to my eyes.

My legs stop moving, but Indiana tugs me forward. "We don't know what this means," he insists. "They could have fired into the ground, to make us think they're willing to kill. To keep us in line."

I cling to his logic, because it's what I need to hear. If they're willing to kill us, why would they try to save Ryan? Why not shoot the other hostages in front of us?

Nothing has changed. My brother could still be alive.

I cling to that thought as our path steepens, and I have to grab on to bamboo and handfuls of vines to pull myself over obstacles in the trail. I am sweating too much and drinking too little water. But then the narrow path turns downhill, and hiking gets easier. I watch for a chance to run.

"Five-minute break!" Silvana shouts when we reach a clearing, and I exhale slowly.

Holden, Penelope, Indiana, and Domenica gather around Genesis on fallen logs while they snack on food from their packs.

Queen Genesis could hold court in hell, with nothing more refreshing than boiling water to offer. Nothing has changed, socially. Yet she doesn't even seem to be listening to them.

"How's your glucose level?" she asks as she abandons her entourage.

I shrug. My eyes water as I dig a protein bar from my bag. Ryan always made sure I had plenty of low-carb snacks.

"Maddie." Genesis puts one hand over my food, so that I have to look at her. "What does your pump say?"

I check the display. My blood sugar is around eighty. Too high. "I just need a snack." Soon I'll have to change my insulin pump site and install a fresh cartridge, but that will take time and energy I don't want to expend right now.

"*¡Vamos!*" Silvana yells, and we are on the move again.

"Where do you think they're taking us?" I ask Genesis as I wipe sweat from my forehead.

She shrugs. "Getting a ransom will take time. They haven't even sent out any demands yet. So they must have a camp somewhere."

"Ryan doesn't *have* time," I murmur.

Holden steps up on my cousin's other side. "Wake up,

Maddie. Your brother's *dead*," he whispers fiercely, and I suck in a deep breath, trying to hold back fresh tears. "The only way to stop that from happening to the rest of us is to take action. We need to—"

"*Shut up!*" Genesis shoves him with both hands, and Holden stumbles into a tree. Rifles swing toward us. The hike comes to a sudden halt.

Holden pushes himself upright. His face is bright red and furious. "What the hell?" he demands through clenched teeth.

"Be useful, or be elsewhere." Genesis grabs my arm and tugs me away from him.

Silvana laughs. "*¡Vamos!*" she shouts. And the hike resumes.

GENESIS

"Do you hear that?" I frown into the jungle, concentrating on the new sound. "Hiking downhill usually leads to—"

"Water," Indiana says. The sound of the current gets louder with each step, then the narrow trail opens into a broad clearing. Yet there's no river. After a second of staring into empty space, I understand why.

The clearing ends in a cliff overlooking a roaring rapid so far below that I can't see the water from where I stand.

I drop my pack on the ground and ease toward the edge to peer down at the river. Indiana follows me, one arm extended. Ready to grab me if I fall.

"Damn it." Frustration weighs down my arms and legs. We're tired, hungry, and filthy, and I can't justify drinking any more of my water until I know I can refill the bottles.

"Did you think you were going swimming, *princesa?*" Silvana sneers, standing well back from the cliff. "Let's go."

"Madalena . . ." Sebastián's voice holds an eerie tension, and I turn to see my cousin walking slowly toward me. Toward the edge. Her hands are shaking.

"Maddie." Chill bumps pop up on my arms, in spite of the heat. I reach for her, but she lurches even closer.

"Grab her," Silvana orders from the tense silence behind us. But no one else is close enough, because you'd have to be crazy to get this close to that kind of drop.

Or desperate.

"Maddie," I say, but she's not listening. Her gaze trails downriver. The river runs to the east. In the direction of the bunkhouse.

"Don't do it," I tell her, while the tense silence behind us stretches on. "It won't work." I look down, and my head spins.

The toes of her boots hang over open air and I inch forward to meet her. My boots scrape loose tiny clods of dirt, which tumble into the water far below. I take her hand. "Come on."

Maddie lets me pull her back one step. Then another. On the third step, I exhale slowly. On the fifth, I let her go.

Indiana lays his hand low on my back, and the touch is reassuring.

"¡Vamos!" Silvana shouts, gesturing to us with her pistol. "¡Vamos!" Her men follow her lead, trying to corral with rifles and fierce looks.

Maddie glances at me, while everyone else is distracted. Desperation shines in her eyes. She races toward the edge of the cliff.

I grasp for her, but I already know I'm too late.

Maddie launches herself over the cliff.

GENESIS

I drop to my knees and stare over the edge, but Maddie is already gone.

I close my eyes and suck in a deep breath, then let it out slowly. I push everything away.

Then I stand.

Shoulders square, I open my eyes and turn around.

Domenica stares at me, her hands clasped over her mouth.

"Oh shit," Penelope breathes. "Ohshitohshitohshit. Gen—"

"Stop it." I grab her arm and look right into her eyes. "Get your shit together *right now.*" Panicking won't help. Crying won't help. When you lose someone, you pick yourself up and you *move on*, because that's the only thing that makes sense.

Penelope flinches away from me. I let her go.

"*Mierda.*" Silvana finally edges toward the cliff and peers over.

"They're gonna kill us," Penelope whispers. "Maddie just screwed us all."

"*Idiota,*" Silvana declares, and several of the gunmen

laugh. She turns to me. "Your cousin just saved me a bullet." But there's something off in her voice. She's trying much too hard to convince us that she's happy about that.

"¡Vamos!" Silvana calls. "Genesis Shipping! Let's go!"

I stare back at her without moving, five feet from the cliff. All the guns in the world can't truly put her in control of me.

"Get her," Silvana orders.

Moisés grabs my shoulder, but I break his grip with the back of my forearm. Seizing the inside of his bicep, I swing his arm forward, and slide behind him. I've done this maneuver so many times I don't even have to think about it.

But the next part . . . If I try for a choke hold and use Moisés's weight against him, I'll drag us both over the cliff. Instead, I dig in my heels and shove him forward.

He falls to his hands and knees. His rifle swings on its strap, scraping the ground.

Shocked silence descends on the cliffside clearing. That's when I realize I've messed up. I let muscle memory do the work my head should have done, and now I've tipped my own hand.

While Moisés stands, I glance over my shoulder just as something bobs to the surface of the river.

Maddie's backpack.

Moisés grabs me again, fury burning in his gaze, and I jerk my arm from his grip.

"If you ever touch me again, you'll pee sitting down for the rest of your life."

Silvana aims her pistol at my rib cage. Her gaze is cold. "On your knees, *princesa*." She points to the cliff. "There."

"Do what you've got to do," I say, counting on the fact that she can't kill me. They took me hostage for a reason. "I'm not going to kneel."

Silvana's eyes narrow. She swings the pistol in Penelope's direction. "Kneel, or I put a bullet in your friend's head."

Pen gasps. Tears fill her eyes. She stares at me as if I might actually let her die because she slept with my boyfriend.

She *will* pay. But not like this.

I walk backward toward the cliff, so I don't have to turn my back on Silvana. Fear fuels my rapid heartbeat, but I clench my jaw and steady my steps. I glance over my shoulder again and again as the edge draws closer.

Pen and Domenica are pale with terror. Holden and Indiana both look torn, as if they can't decide whether an intervention would make things better or worse for me.

"Kneel," Silvana orders.

Less than a foot from the edge, I drop carefully onto my knees; then sit on my heels. My certainty that she won't shoot me wavers as I stare at the barrel of her pistol.

"You!" Silvana shouts at Penelope. Then she turns to the rest of the group. "All of you. Join her." When no one moves, she flips her pistol around and aims the butt at my face.

I flinch and close my eyes, bracing for the blow.

"Wait!" Indiana calls, and I look up to see him heading toward me. Rog escorts Penelope with one arm around her shoulders and Domenica follows right behind them, clutching the straps of her backpack so tightly that her fingers are white. Her expression is grim.

Holden comes last.

In spite of his bravado about taking action, he doesn't know what to do when there's a gun aimed at my head. When there's a problem that neither his money nor his name can solve.

We're lined up, kneeling on the brink of the cliff, execution style. Silvana waves her men forward, and they aim rifles at our heads.

I fight to steady my breathing. On the edge of my vision, Penelope's chest hitches with panicked hiccuping and a high-pitched, terrified whine I don't think she even knows she's making.

We are going to die here, on our knees. Humiliated and defeated.

And *I* am the one who brought us all here.

Silvana holds up one hand, fingers spread. My heart slams against my chest as her fingers fold one at a time, counting down the seconds until my death. "Five. Four."

One of the gunmen smiles. Natalia shifts uncomfortably, and I notice that she's not looking at any of us.

Not all of Silvana's people are happy with this demonstration.

"Three."

Behind the line of executioners, Sebastián and Óscar stand with their rifles aimed at the ground. Sebastián's jaw is tight. Óscar stares at his feet.

"Two." Silvana has only her pinkie finger left.

Penelope sobs.

"I'm so sorry for getting us into this," I whisper to her. My rebellion has made it easier for our captors to kill us than to put up with us long enough to claim a ransom.

Silvana drops her hand without saying the last number. "That's how long it will take to kill you if you try to escape."

Penelope trembles so hard on my left that I'm afraid she's having a seizure. I let my head fall forward, waiting for my pulse to slow.

"Álvaro." Silvana nods to the soldier in front of me. I look up as he unsnaps a machete from a loop on his belt. He brings the blade to my throat.

I gasp, then freeze. The warm metal presses into my flesh. If I take too deep a breath, I'll spill my own blood.

"And this is what will happen if anyone tries to rescue you," Silvana says. "Are we clear?" My fellow hostages nod on the edge of my vision, but I'm too scared to move.

Silvana makes another gesture, and the gunmen lower their weapons.

The man with the machete at my throat winks at me, and chills slide down my spine. When he finally steps back,

I fall forward, bent over my knees, wiping tears from my face as fast as they form.

I am not dead.

As I pick up my backpack and fall into line again, I pass Silvana and Moisés. *"Busca el cuerpo,"* she whispers to him.

My jaw clenches until my teeth creak. She just told him to find Maddie's body.

40.75 HOURS EARLIER

MADDIE

I scream as I plunge into the river. Water fills my mouth.

The river slings me downstream, and I flail against the current. My elbow smashes into a rock. My lungs burn.

I fight toward the surface and suck in as much water as air. The current is too strong. My backpack is too bulky. The river rips it from me as I ricochet off rocks and floating branches.

I'm *flying* down the river.

Totally out of control.

GENESIS

Rain begins to fall mid-morning—just enough moisture to keep us damp and irritable.

No one talks. We are each stuck in our own heads, islands of fear and exhaustion isolated by the sound of the rain and the difficulty of the hike. As I lower myself down muddy hills with handfuls of bamboo and dangling vines, skinning my palms and bruising my knees, I think about Maddie and Ryan.

My cousins. Gone. Just like my mother.

Every breath is hard to take. Each step requires staggering effort.

Could I be wrong? Are they still alive? Can they be for much longer?

The only thing I'm sure of is that this is all my fault.

40·5 HOURS EARLIER

MADDIE

I slam into something jutting out from the bank. A thick root. Water rushes around me. Pulling at me. Roaring in my ears. But I hang on.

I take a deep breath.

Then I pull myself hand over hand toward the bank.

39 HOURS EARLIER

GENESIS

"Fifteen minutes for lunch!" Silvana shouts.

I'm no stranger to exercise, yet I ache all over from the grueling pace of the hike. My clothes are wet from the intermittent rain, and my boots are caked in mud.

Indiana and Domenica drag a fallen log through the mud toward me, and my friends all gather around, pulling food and half-empty bottles of water from their bags.

I'm starving, yet already sick of tuna and protein bars, so I trade Indiana one packet of lemon-pepper flavored tuna and twelve soggy crackers for (approximately) two tablespoons of peanut butter and an oatmeal cream pie.

What I wouldn't give for a ramekin full of crème brûlée. Or even just a turkey sandwich.

"So?" Rain drips on Penelope's unopened gourmet PowerBar. Her focus follows mine to where our captors have split in two cliques—one surrounding Sebastián, the other seated around Silvana. "What's the plan?" Her lip quivers. "Are we just going to wait to be ransomed?"

"No." Holden takes the spot next to her on the log. "I saw Sebastián with a satellite phone, but they haven't called in any demands yet." He rests his hand awkwardly on his own leg. As if he wants to pull Pen into a hug, but knows that if he touches her, he'll have more to fear than our kidnappers. "We're not going to be ransomed any time soon."

"That can't be good," Domenica whispers.

No, it can't. It means this is about more than ransom money. It means they're prepared to hold us for a long time. It means they don't have to keep all of us alive to get whatever it is that they want.

I give her a steady, confident look as I shield my face from the last patters of rain with one hand. "It just means they're waiting until they get to their base of operations to figure out who to call and what to ask for."

Holden rips open a bag of peanuts with more force than necessary. "What it means is that this isn't going to end any time soon unless *we end it*."

38.75 HOURS EARLIER

MADDIE

I collapse on the wet ground, panting. A leaf sticks to my cheek. Grass clings to my soaked clothes.

My elbow throbs. My shin is scraped raw. My limbs weigh a hundred pounds each. But I am alive, and only slightly woozy from insulin deficiency.

Insulin . . .

Groaning, I push myself up and lift my shirt to check my pump. My shoulders sag with relief. Still working. Nothing else matters.

Nothing but getting back to my brother.

I scrub my hands over my face. *Think!*

We couldn't have hiked more than an hour west of the bunkhouse, and the river carried me southeast. Ryan can't be more than an hour's hike north.

North-*ish*, at least.

I stumble in what I hope is the right direction, grabbing branches and roots to haul myself up muddy inclines. Pushing farther and farther to the northeast.

Closer and closer to my brother.

"Please be alive."

Tears blur the jungle. My boot catches on something and I slam into the ground. I push myself up again, and now I am running.

Branches slap my face. Thorns catch my clothes.

I keep running.

GENESIS

"With Moisés gone, there are six of us, and six of them." Holden tears open a package of salted almonds as he walks, and several of them fall onto the trail. "The odds are even."

"Guns tip the scale in their favor," Indiana points out as he steps over a mud puddle.

Holden shrugs. "So we take a couple of them."

"Brilliant." I have to fight not to roll my eyes. "I mean, surely they'll just hand over their weapons if we ask nicely."

Holden's gaze hardens. "I've seen you talk your way past club security with nothing more than a low-cut blouse. Hell, you got us a private tour of the park by making out with Nico." He shoots a glance at Indiana, clearly hoping for a reaction, but Indiana is immune to drama, and that only makes Holden angrier. "Surely you could use your super-powers for good this time. Distract a couple of the guards long enough for us to get their guns."

My face flushes, then my embarrassment flares into white-hot anger over his hypocrisy. I glance pointedly from Holden to Penelope, then back, and Pen flinches. But I don't call them out on their betrayal, because unlike my hot-tempered boyfriend, I don't need to throw a fit to make a point.

Instead, I call his bullshit.

"Let me get this straight. You want me to take not one, but *two* of those gunmen into the brush and get naked with them so you can try to take their guns?"

Holden's gaze takes on a cruel glint. "You'd do it eventually, so why not now?" He's trying to make me lash out at him, to prove that my temper's as volatile as his. That I have no more self-control than he has. "You kind of owe it to me."

"Hey, man." Indiana tries to step between us on the trail. "That's not—"

"I *owe* it to you?" I cut Indiana off, because I don't want him drawn into the muck that is me and Holden.

"To all of us." Words fall out of Holden's mouth so fast I can hardly follow them. "You're the reason we're here. Genesis says jump, and we all launch ourselves at the sky. Genesis says hike into the jungle, and we all stock up on bug spray." He jumps down a small incline, where water has washed earth from beneath a large tree root, then turns to glare at me. "If it were up to me, we'd be partying on the beach in Cartagena right now." His whispered tirade takes on a fiercer, colder tone, and spittle flies from his mouth with each syllable. "This is *your* fault, so you're going to take off whatever you have to take off to keep those jungle savages occupied!"

Domenica flinches.

Penelope lays one hand on his arm. As if just touching him could calm him down.

"Okay, that's *more* than enough out of you." Indiana swings himself over the exposed root and lands in the mud in front of Holden, fists clenched.

Silvana notices the conflict, and pulls a huge knife from a sheath at her waist. "Shut up and get moving," she says, pointing the knife at each of them in turn. "Or one of you will lose a finger."

Indiana turns and offers me a hand over the root, but the tension still feels thicker than the oppressive jungle air.

"Okay, offensive slut-shaming and pimping aside, this isn't a cartoon, Holden," I snap softly, determined to bring his reckless plan to a screeching halt. "I'm not wearing my Kevlar lingerie."

Holden only rolls his eyes. "It's not like I'm asking everyone to do something I'm not willing to do. I'll take Natalia. But there are only three of you girls and five men with guns, so . . ." He shrugs. "You do the math."

"Yeah, my calculation looks a little different." I step into Holden's personal space and look up at him as if I were towering over him—a skill I learned from my father. "Penelope was strike one. This is strike two. One more, and *you're out*."

MADDIE

No matter how hard I push, I can't get there fast enough.

Ryan is dying.

Vines slap my face. Mud sucks at my boots. Perspiration drips into my eyes. I wipe my forehead, but my sweaty arm and damp sleeve are no help.

My leg itches, and when I scratch it, blood streaks across my skin. The red smear seems to float in front of me, and when I squint, I see tiny bits of mosquito scattered through it.

My stomach heaves, but there's nothing to vomit. I can't remember the last time I ate.

I pull up my wet shirt and squint at the display on my pump. My glucose level is at sixty-four. Not good. I drop my shirt, and the world spins again. I catch myself against a tree and breathe deeply until the vertigo passes.

If I don't eat soon, I will pass out. Then I will die on the jungle floor, and there will be no one to help Ryan.

I push forward again, but every few steps, I have to stop and rest against a tree.

Score one for the jungle.

GENESIS

Domenica glares at Holden as Sebastián give us a "get going" gesture. "I'm not taking anything off," she says

"Nobody's taking anything off, and we're *not* going for their guns," I whisper. We veer west along the muddy trail again, facing into the sun. "Our plan needs to be one hundred percent less smutty and suicidal."

"Agreed." Indiana ducks under a low-hanging vine. "What do you have in mind?"

But then Óscar and Natalia pull even with us on the path, and we have to march in silence until they move ahead, fifteen minutes later.

"Soft targets and psychological manipulation," I say when they're out of earshot.

"Well, you are uniquely qualified for that one." Holden means it as an insult, but I value every weapon in my arsenal.

"Silvana may as well be carved out of stone," I whisper, just loud enough for the three of them to hear. "But Sebastián tried to help Ryan. I don't think he wants anyone to get hurt. We can use that."

Holden looks at me as if I've lost my mind. "So you want to what? Get him on our side?"

I shrug. "Or at least off Silvana's side. He's different from the others. He doesn't seem to like violence, and he's Nico's friend."

Holden rolls his eyes. "Nico's had his tongue in your mouth, so naturally you trust his friend with your life. *That's* a solid decision-making strategy."

My gaze narrows on him. "And pimping out your girlfriend to an armed kidnapper in exchange for a gun is a much better plan?"

"*Yes.* Nico's *in on this*, Genesis," he insists. "We can't trust anything he's said or done."

I thought so too, at first. But the kidnappers left Nico behind. They probably shot him. I think they've been using him from the time we landed in Cartagena.

From the moment I walked into my grandmother's house and saw him fixing a cabinet, they were using him to get to *me*.

MADDIE

Bananas. Bunches of them. But they're all too green and hard to eat.

I stumble on, shoving blurry vines and branches out of my way until a familiar greenish-brown fruit catches my eye.

It's some kind of jungle mirage—my brain showing me what I need to see, rather than what's really there.

But then I pluck one of the avocados hanging a foot above my head. It's real.

Its skin is soft enough to pierce with my thumbnail, so I kneel in the mud and pull back a section of the green peel. I eat the meat like a mushy apple until I get to the pit.

Then I pick three more and eat them as I walk.

Food brings the world back into focus, and I realize I have no idea where I am.

I look from tree to tree, from vine to vine, searching for a familiar landmark.

Ryan doesn't have time for this.

Calm down, Maddie. Think.

I close my eyes and take a deep breath. *Use the sun.*

I look up. Since I'm in the Southern Hemisphere, facing the sun means I'm facing north. So I turn to my right and head as close to east by northeast as I can.

Within minutes, I come to a narrow path. In the middle of it is a moss-covered log I tripped over shortly after the kidnappers started to march us out of camp.

Relieved, I take off down the path at a jog. Fifty yards later, I find a cigarette butt with Silvana's lipstick staining the tip. I start running, stumbling with every other step, and when I see the top of a bright yellow tent, I stop in the middle of the path, sobbing.

I've made it. All on my own.

Score one for the girl with diabetes.

Fighting the urge to race through the camp in search of my brother, I creep along the back side of the line of tents instead. I listen for the footsteps and voices of anyone who might have stayed behind, but I hear nothing louder than the roar of my own pulse.

Ryan was shot at the end of this row of tents. I'm just yards away. A single orange tent blocks my view.

My heart pounds so hard it threatens to throw me off balance. I push back the flap of the orange tent.

Ryan is gone.

The camp is empty.

But there is a pile of loose earth beneath a tree on the edge of the clearing.

A single grave.

37 HOURS EARLIER

GENESIS

The gunmen prod us with their rifles, forcing us to move faster and faster in the slick mud, until we're virtually sliding downhill. Penelope's eyes are unfocused, and every time we need to climb over or under something, I have to practically shake her back to reality.

The temptation to slap her awake is almost irresistible, but she's in too much shock to understand that my motivation is at least as much retribution as friendship.

If I hit her, I want her to understand why.

Indiana tries to help me keep her going, but Holden is lost in his own thoughts, and I can tell from how often he glances at the gunmen's rifles that his thoughts are going to get us killed.

Finally Silvana calls for a bathroom break. "Five minutes," she shouts. "*Nada más.*"

Pen, Domenica, and I head into the woods to relieve ourselves, escorted by Natalia and her rifle. On my way back to the clearing, I hear Sebastián and Silvana arguing in hushed voices. I stop behind a tree, trying to listen, but I can only pick up bits and pieces.

"*No se suponía que iba a morir . . .*" Sebastián hisses. *He wasn't supposed to die.*

They're talking about Ryan. My hand clenches around my backpack strap, and the buckle bites into my skin. Do they *know* he's dead or are they just assuming?

"*. . . mi jefe se pondrá furioso . . .*" *My boss will be pissed.*

"*My* boss won't give a shit, as long as he gets what he wants," Silvana replies.

My head spins. She doesn't work with Sebastián. And she obviously doesn't care if some of the hostages die. She could be part of some splinter political group or maybe a member of a drug cartel. Maddie said the conflict in Colombia was over, but it's not like people have stopped using drugs.

A stick breaks beneath my foot, and I suck in a startled breath, waiting to see if they've heard me. But they're still arguing.

Silvana lets her rifle hang from its strap and props both hands on her hips. "You deal with the hostages and let me do my job."

Does that mean *he's* in charge of us?

"*Llámale,*" he replies, pulling the satellite phone from his bag. "*En seguida.*" *Call him. Right now.*

Silvana glares at him. But then she takes the phone and presses a button.

I hear a series of soft tones as the phone autodials. She holds it to her ear, and a second later she speaks. "*Buenas tardes,* Hernán. *Tenemos Genesis, Ryan, y Madalena.* You know what we want for them."

The realization washes over me like the shock of a cold rain. "Dad!" I run at her, grasping for the phone, but Sebastián catches me around the waist. "Dad!"

"Genesis!" my father's voice is soft, stretched over the distance and the wireless connection, but I can hear the power in it. He's shouting. In his office at home, the glass case behind his desk is probably rattling.

"Let go!" I slam the heel of my boot into Sebastián's shin. He only tightens his grip. I shove my elbow into his ribs. He grunts, and his hold weakens. "We're in the jungle!" I shout. "Somewhere near the—"

Silvana pulls her pistol left-handed and aims it at me.

"Stop," Sebastián whispers into my ear with a thick accent.

"She's lying!" I yell. "They don't have—"

Sebastián's hand covers my mouth.

"Give us what we want, and you'll get all three of them back," Silvana says into the phone.

"Don't touch her!" my father shouts. "Silvana, if you hurt her, I'll—"

"You have until three p.m. tomorrow. Twenty-four hours, Hernán."

Silvana gives me a smug smile and ends the call.

MADDIE

I sink to my knees in the dirt. Tears fill my eyes, blurring the clearing around me.

It's not Ryan. It can't *be.* We heard seventeen shots. Anyone could be buried under that tree.

But seventeen anyones could not. It's a single grave.

I crawl toward the fresh earth. Rocks bruise my palms and cut into my knees. The rest of the camp blurs into nothing on the edges of my vision.

I have one mission, and it has only two parts.

Dig up the grave.

See *any face in the world* other than my brother's.

I pick up the first clod of dirt, then I'm digging, frantically tossing handful after handful over my shoulder. Soil cakes beneath my nails. Bugs land on my neck, but I hardly feel the bites. My breath hitches with each inhalation. I'm choking on my own fear.

Eighteen inches down, I scrape a muddy swath of cotton. I fall back on my heels and wipe my eyes with both grimy hands, breathing through the fierce ache wrapped tightly around my chest.

I *claw* at the dirt now, sniffling, and each bit I remove

exposes more of a blood-and-dirt-stained shirt.

My finger scrapes metal, and I freeze.

No.

I brush the dirt away. My hand trembles as I clutch the medallion.

My father wore one just like it. They used it to identify his remains, in the burned-out van where he was found, on the outskirts of Cartagena.

Like my father, Ryan never took his medallion off.

"No, no, no." I pull Ryan up by his shoulders, devastated by the pliant resistance of his weight as I hug him to my chest.

"Ryan . . . Ryan!" This can't be real. He can't be gone.

A twig snaps to my left, and I look up, still clutching my brother's body.

Moisés stands fifteen feet away, his rifle aimed at my head. "Well, isn't that sweet?"

GENESIS

"Why did they only call in *her* ransom?" Domenica asks as we wade into the narrow river.

Penelope picks her way across several small rocks sticking up from the surface. "Her dad owns the world's largest independent shipping company."

"Like, UPS?" Domenica frowns. "How big could it be, if I never heard of it before this morning?"

"Genesis Shipping is freight transportation," Pen explains. "Gen's dad has a huge fleet of trucks, planes, trains, and cargo ships moving merchandise and materials for companies all over the world. He even has contracts with several governments. Ransoming her is a *massive* payday."

They think I'm too upset to listen.

They don't know me at all.

"I'm worth more than she is," Holden insists. But our kidnappers clearly think they can get three ransoms from my dad, as long as he doesn't know about Maddie and Ryan.

But he *should* know. My aunt and grandmother should know.

I can't be the only one who knows what happened. Not again.

*"Genesis. Mija. Where is your mother?" My father
kneels next to me on the living room carpet. He looks
scared.*

I've never seen my father scared.

"Genesis."

*I see him. I hear him. But I can't answer. Maybe if
I close my eyes, I won't even be here anymore.*

*He takes my hands, then drops them and stares
in horror at the blood on his palms. At the blood on
mine. Then he looks past me. Into the kitchen.*

"Genesis." Indiana takes my hand, and I let him tug
me into the shallow water. It's easy to pretend I'm mired in
shock, rather than in thought, and the more the kidnappers
underestimate me, the better off I'll be.

My father was *right there.* I wanted to tell him that I'm
sorry for bringing us here. For lying to him. For putting us
all in danger.

I mentally replay the phone call as I step out of the
river onto the opposite bank, but it still makes no sense. My
dad knew Silvana's name. She didn't bother to set a price
because she thinks he already knows what she wants.

Understanding hits me like a knife to the gut. Whatever is happening here is the reason I've never been allowed
in Colombia. It may even be the reason Uncle David was
killed.

My kidnapping and his murder within a year in the
same country *can't* be a coincidence.

36.75 HOURS EARLIER

MADDIE

Moisés's lips turn up in an ugly sneer, his brows bunched toward the middle of his forehead. "Get out of the hole."

"No." I am covered in dirt from my brother's grave, holding his still-warm body, yet suddenly a seething storm of anger churns deep in my belly.

"*Salga del agujero* unless you want me to bury you in it."

Slowly, I lower my brother back onto the ground. My tears leave wet trails on his cheeks, as if he cried them himself. "You're not going to shoot me," I say as I run one hand through the hair at Ryan's temple, arranging it the way he wore it. "You weren't supposed to shoot my brother either." My uncle may not be the man my father was, but he will pay to get me back.

He would have paid for Ryan too.

I stand slowly, wiping my palms on my shorts, but that does no good. I'm covered from head to toe in grime.

"Silvana needs me, doesn't she?" I make myself look away from his trigger finger and meet his gaze.

"She thinks you're dead. She'll be happy to see you breathing, no matter how banged up you get on the way."

I swipe one hand across my nose, smearing snot and tears through the dirt on my face, punctuating my determination not to cry anymore. "I'm diabetic, and I'm on the verge of an insulin reaction from too little food and too much exercise." I show him my insulin pump. "If you make me hike, my body will shut down and I'll die. How pissed will Silvana be if you lose her *another* hostage?" I can hardly believe my nerve. But he's not going to kill me, and I have nothing left to lose.

"I'll worry about Silvana." Moisés shifts his rifle into a one-handed grip and pulls a length of nylon cord from his belt loop. I recognize the cord—he cut it from one of the tents on his way to the clearing. "You turn around and put your hands behind your back."

I can't outrun him. Not without rest, food, and insulin. But I can't give in either.

Heart pounding, I take a step back and trip over a lump of dirt, then fall into my brother's grave. The impact slams my teeth together. Blood pours into my mouth from my bitten cheek.

Moisés swings his rifle onto his back, then hauls me up by one arm. "You spoiled Americans are all the same." He throws me to the ground. My hands and knees hit the dirt, and I grunt from the impact.

"You think the rules don't apply to you. You think there's nothing that can't be bought, but you're about to learn—"

Moisés's rant ends in an *oof* of pain, and his hands fall away. He lands on the ground next to me, his eyes closed. A fist-sized rock lies a foot from his head.

I scramble back on my hands and knees, eyes wide.

Luke stands ten feet away with his right arm pulled back, staring at the unconscious gunman. Ready to throw another rock.

GENESIS

"*¿Tenemos tiempo para descansar?*" Julian asks as he and Óscar haul a fallen tree out of the path.

"No!" Silvana shouts. "We keep moving!"

Domenica groans as she steps over a log. I shift my backpack from my left shoulder onto my right, and the relief is immediate. Being driven through the jungle at breakneck speed is more grueling than any workout I've ever had.

Despite her Olympic pedigree, even Pen looks wiped out.

At the front of our ragged procession, Sebastián and Silvana are arguing again. I move closer so I can hear.

"What are they saying?" Indiana asks as he falls into step with me, holding a packet of peanuts.

"Sebastián wants to know why she's pushing us all so hard," I whisper.

"*Porque el envío se realizará en esta noche,*" Silvana answers.

"Because the shipment will be in tonight," I translate.

Indiana takes my hand and pours several nuts into my cupped palm. "What shipment?"

"I don't know. They're being very careful with the

details, because they know some of us speak Spanish." What Holden speaks is more the pig latin version. "Thanks," I say, holding up the peanuts. Then I toss them into my mouth.

Sebastián breaks away from Silvana with a huff of disgust and takes up a position at the rear of the group.

This could be my chance. My friends are all here because of me, and when Silvana decides they're too much trouble, she'll kill them. Even if a couple of them are worth a fortune.

Unless I can convince Sebastián to let us go.

"I'll be right back," I whisper to Indiana. Then I drop back to walk next to Sebastián.

"What do you want?" His accent is thick, but his words are clear.

"I want an end to this before anyone else dies, but I'm not going to deal with Silvana." I've seen my dad work people over in business a million times. Running an international shipping company is all about forming relationships. Part flattery, part truth, and all Valencia spine. "*You*, I'll negotiate with."

"Negotiate?" Sebastián rests his hands on his rifle as we walk, settling in for what he clearly thinks is a game. "What are you bringing to the table?"

"Cash. Name your price." I wait a heartbeat, while he decides whether or not to take me seriously. Then I move in for the kill. "For *all* of us."

Offer them something they want, but on your terms, Genesis.

My father taught me that strategy when I was eleven. It's been useful at school, and even more useful with Holden. But out here, it might save lives.

Sebastián's dark brows rise. "You think you can get your *papá* to pay for six hostages?"

"I can get him to pay for eight. He doesn't know Maddie and Ryan are . . . gone." I shove back my grief and rage and push through with my initial offer. "If you knew my dad, you'd know he'll give me whatever I ask for, and he can have a plane here in a couple of hours. You'll get credit for bringing in the ransoms. What do you want? A hundred grand each?"

Sebastián laughs, and I have to work to unclench my jaw.

When in doubt, add another zero, my father's voice says in my head.

"One million each. That's *eight million dollars*." My dad keeps more than that in his emergency safe at home.

But now Sebastián looks insulted, and alarm bells go off in my head. I have no idea how much they were going to demand for our release.

"Name your price. Just let me call my father," I insist. But he's already shaking his head. Frowning. I'm missing something. "Unless . . . this isn't about money?"

My backpack suddenly feels heavier than it did a second

ago. Have I read this whole thing wrong?

"Why is everything about money with you Americans?" Sebastián demands, and those alarm bells swell into a siren. "We need your *papá's* resources." He pulls me to a halt and leans in until I can't see anything but his gaze burning into me. "We need Hernán Valencia to remember where his loyalties ought to lie."

MADDIE

"Holy shit." Luke blinks, stunned, and the unused rock falls from his hand. "I can't—" He blinks again, then scrubs his face with both hands. "Do you think he's okay?"

"I hope not." Moisés is breathing, but the gash on the back of his head is oozing blood and already swelling into a huge lump. "How did you do that?" I push myself to my feet. "Do you play baseball?"

"Only on my Xbox. I didn't even have my eyes open, Maddie. Total lucky shot." He puts one hand on top of his baseball cap, still stunned, and the reality finally hits me.

Somehow, he's still alive. And un-captured. And he just saved my life.

"Luke—" I pull him into a hug, and he feels a lot more solid than I expected. "I thought you were dead."

He returns my embrace with an awkward one of his own. "I left camp to pee right before the soldiers came, and when I heard them rounding everyone up, I hid in the brush. Are you okay?"

"No." I let him go and swipe at my face with shaking, dirt-caked hands.

"We should probably . . ." He slides the automatic rifle

out of the gunman's reach with his foot.

The gash on the back of Moisés's head is still steadily leaking blood. "I wish you'd killed him," I whisper.

"I don't."

I glance at Luke in surprise. "He and his friends—" The word gets stuck in my throat. "They *murdered* my brother!" They *all* deserve to die for that.

"They're killers. I'm not. We need to tie him up." Luke plucks the nylon cord from Moisés's relaxed fist, then squats over his thick thighs, but I can only stare as I struggle to keep the world in focus.

None of this feels real.

"Hey, Maddie? A little help?"

I squat in the dirt and lift Moisés's arms into position behind his back. Luke winds the cord around the gunman's wrists, then ties some kind of complicated knot.

I home in on his fingers. "Where'd you learn that?"

"Scouts."

Of *course* he's a Boy Scout. Because what else would get a fifteen-year-old math genius/gamer out of the house on weekends?

"I'll get more rope." I slide a large knife from the sheath strapped to Moisés's belt and march to the nearest tent, where I cut a long section from one of the cords holding it in place. When I get back, Luke has emptied everything from the gunman's pockets. He's found a small fishing kit, a bottle of water, a folding multi-tool, and a large, clunky two-way radio.

"Here." I hand him more cord to tie Moisés's ankles together. "Does that radio work?"

"Yeah, but we're not within range of any others. All I heard when I tried it is static."

"If we *were* in range, we'd hear . . . what? The other kidnappers?"

Luke shrugs as he finishes his knot. "Assuming we're tuned to the right frequency."

My gaze is drawn back to my brother.

Ryan's eyes are closed. He looks like he's sleeping, but he's *gone*, and I'm never going to get him back.

My brother is never going to wake up. But Moisés will.

Rage pours in to fill the hole left in my heart as I stare at the unconscious gunman. I pull my foot back and kick his thigh as hard as I can. But there's no reaction, and that only stokes the fury crackling inside me.

So I kick him in the ribs. Again and again.

Something cracks, and he wakes up screaming.

GENESIS

"Silvana," I call in a loud, clear voice as I make my way to the front of the line. Holden gives me a small shake of his head, and Penelope looks terrified. Indiana's gaze skips from captor to captor, assessing their reactions with his usual quiet intensity.

Rog watches me somberly, and I have no idea what he's thinking.

"What's wrong, *princesa?*" Silvana sneers. "Need a break to repair your nail polish?"

"Let's end this." I still don't want to deal with her, but if that's what it takes to drive a wedge between our captors . . . "I'm prepared to give you whatever you want."

Sebastián shakes his head at me in warning.

"You're prepared . . . ?" Silvana laughs, and most of her men chuckle. "*You're* just a spoiled little girl."

"You're right. My dad will give me whatever I ask for. Let me talk to him."

"So you can tell him your cousins are dead?" She shakes her head, and her earrings jangle. "Get back in line."

"I swear I won't tell him."

"And I should believe you because you look so sweet

and innocent? Hernán Valencia's daughter would take food from orphans, if that's what it took to get her way. Just like her father. Let's go."

Anger burns beneath my skin like hot coals. "I *am* just like my father." In the sense that she has *no idea* what either of us is really capable of. "I'm not going to tell him about Maddie and Ryan, because pissing you off wouldn't be in my best interest. So just tell me why you need his resources and I'll make it happen."

Silvana stomps toward me, mud splattering around her boots with every step. She grabs my jaw in a bruising grip, and I fight the urge to pull free, because I know what this is. Like Holden, she needs to believe she's in control—right up until the moment I show her that she's not.

"Resources?" Her furious gaze slides from me to Sebastián, confirming that I've just driven the wedge between them deeper. He wasn't supposed to tell me that.

"What do you want? Trucks? Boats? What are you trying to sneak across the border? Or, *who* are you trying to sneak across?"

Silvana snorts, and her men grumble angrily.

"Why do Americans always assume everyone else wants what they have?" Álvaro demands.

"Because they're spoiled and egotistical," Julian answers.

"We're not smuggling people into the States. We're going to use your dad's 'resources' to teach you and the rest of your privileged, arrogant countrymen a lesson in humility."

Chills wash over me as Silvana's gleefully cruel smile

drives her point home. My dad's resources can deliver anything to anywhere in the world, in a matter of hours, but I doubt she plans to teach us a lesson with reams of paper and pallets of lip gloss.

She'll use Genesis Shipping to smuggle weapons. Or explosives.

Bombs.

Silvana and her men aren't just kidnappers. They're *terrorists.*

Fear freezes my tongue to the roof of my mouth, but I hold her gaze to disguise my horror.

If my dad cooperates to save my life, he'll be helping them kill who knows how many hundreds of innocent people.

MADDIE

I kick Moisés again. Then again. And again. With each blow, he cries out, cursing me in Spanish.

My next kick splits his lip, and blood pours from his mouth.

"Maddie!" Luke shouts, but I hardly hear him over Moisés's grunts and the roar of my own raging pulse.

My boot splits open Moisés's cheek. I pull my foot back for another blow, but Luke wraps his arms around me and drags me away from my target.

"Let me go!" I thrash and kick, trying to break his grip, but he's stronger than he looks.

"Maddie. Killing him won't bring Ryan back." He has to say it right into my ear to be heard over Moisés's shouting. I really *did* hurt the bastard.

"I know." I stop struggling and he lets me go. "Let's shut him up before he brings every gunman in the jungle running."

"I got it." Luke heads for the line of tents, then comes back with a scrap of white cloth and a roll of duct tape so quickly that he could only have gotten them from his own stuff.

He shoves the material into Moisés's mouth, then tapes over it with a strip of duct tape. A striped bit of elastic sticks out above the tape. "Is that . . . underwear?"

Luke shrugs. "It's clean. It's the only thing I had that was small enough to fit into his mouth. Not that my underwear is small." His face turns bright red. "Not that it's big either. I mean . . ." Finally he gives up with a sigh. "Stop talking while you're ahead, Luke," he mumbles.

"I'm not sure you were actually ahead."

I kneel at my brother's side and carefully unclasp his medallion. It's all I have left of him and of my father, so I fasten it around my own neck and tuck it inside my shirt.

Luke clears his throat as he backs toward the bunkhouse, obviously reluctant to intrude on my private moment. "Um . . . I'll go get the shovel. I put it in the utility shed."

"You . . . ?" I blink at him in sudden understanding. "*You* buried him?"

Luke shrugs. "I couldn't just leave him there."

"Thank you." I stand and pull him into another hug, and my tears fall on his shoulder. "You . . . Thank you."

When I let him go, he gives me a self-conscious nod, then scruffs his hat over his curls and heads toward the bunkhouse.

While Luke is gone, I position Ryan's arms over his chest, then I start pushing the dirt over him again. Moisés has stopped yelling behind his gag, and the ambient wildlife sounds have faded into the background—for a moment, it feels like the entire jungle is honoring my brother with a moment of quiet.

Fresh tears blur my vision as I work, and I am sniffling again when Luke's hand lands on my shoulder.

"Let me do it."

I stand, and he gently shovels dirt over my brother's face while I fight fresh tears. "Ryan nearly died once before," I whisper. "Last year. After our dad died. He started drinking, and I used to find him passed out. Barely breathing." My finger traces the pink line on the back of my arm. "So one night I showed him what he was doing to himself."

"That's how you got your scar?" Luke asks as he wipes sweat from his forehead.

I nod. "At my cousin's Halloween party. I matched him drink for drink, until I passed out and my arm went through a glass bottle. He checked into rehab the day I got out of the hospital, and he hasn't had a drink since. He—" My voice breaks. I clear my throat and start over. "He decided to live."

GENESIS

"Teach us a lesson?" Penelope hisses as she pushes her way between me and Indiana on the narrow trail. "They're going to punish us just for being American? What did our country ever do to them?"

"Poison their crops, livestock, and people with herbicides," Domenica says over her shoulder, from a few feet ahead. "And not just in Colombia. It happened to my uncle's farm in Peru."

"That is not true!" Penelope insists.

Domenica actually laughs. "Your country's 'war on drugs' involves crop duster planes bombing Colombian coca and poppy farms with toxic chemicals that make people sick. They cause miscarriages. And they're devastating to poor farmers, who don't profit from the drug trade like cartels do."

Penelope rolls her eyes and steps over a mud puddle. "There is *no way—*"

"And your CIA sponsors backdoor deals with one drug cartel to assassinate members of a rival cartel, to cripple the drug trade."

"She's right," I say. My dad followed that story pretty

closely when it broke, then he signed me up for another self-defense class. At the time, I thought he was being paranoid.

"Are you with us or them?" Holden demands through clenched teeth.

"There *is* no us or them," I snap, annoyed when he takes up a position on Pen's other side. "These terrorists don't represent all of Colombia any more than we represent all of the US."

"Well, the part they represent wants to blow up the part we represent," Penelope insists, with a glance at Holden. "It should be pretty simple to decide which side you're on."

"None of it is simple." Indiana steps up on my other side. "These guys don't have the right to bomb the US just like the US doesn't have the right to kill their crops and poison their people."

"What they don't have the right to do is make us pawns in their homicidal political statement," Holden says, so softly I have to listen hard to hear him over the twigs crunching beneath my boots. "If Gen's dad refuses to ship their bombs, they'll start picking us off one by one to show him they're serious. We have to get out of here before that happens."

"And go where?" I whisper. "People who wander into the jungle unprepared usually don't make it out."

"We'll take everything we can carry and head back to the base camp." Holden's pack gets caught as he climbs over a log on the trail, and Penelope reaches up to unhook him. "There'll be another helicopter tomorrow, and we can report these psychos as soon as we're out of here."

"That's the only way we're going to get out alive, Gen," my former best friend says.

Maybe so. But . . . I glance around to make sure none of our captors are close enough to hear. "Silvana gave my dad a twenty-four-hour deadline. If he gives in, she'll get her plane, or ship, or whatever she's asking for by tomorrow. A cargo plane is the worst-case scenario. Assuming we even make it to the base camp in time to catch the helicopter, if she asked for a plane, she could *already* have gotten her bombs into the US—or flown them into a building. It's only a two-hour flight to Miami."

"What are you saying?" my boyfriend demands.

"No one else knows about this, Holden." I give them a moment to let that sink in. "There's no one else to stop this terrorist attack. There's only us."

36.25 HOURS EARLIER

MADDIE

"Let's round up everything we can carry." I jog toward the abandoned tent city, fired up in spite of my exhaustion by the driving need to *be on the move*. "They have a six-hour head start."

"Who?"

"Do you still have your cell phone?"

"Yeah." Luke pulls it from his pocket. "The signal isn't strong enough for a call, so I texted my mom but I can't tell if it went through."

My gaze falls on the small bunkhouse. "Surely there's a radio."

"They smashed it. This is all we have." He pats the two-way radio now clipped to his belt.

"Tayrona's a day's hike to the east, right?"

"I don't know." Luke shrugs. "I lost track of our direction during the detour to the bunkhouse. If we start on the wrong heading, we could be lost in the jungle for days."

"Okay." I can't afford to get lost. My insulin is almost

gone. "And that helicopter that brings supplies for the soldiers comes every other day, right? So it won't be back for at least twenty-three hours."

"I think so."

I brush dirt from my hands onto my pants, struggling to think now that the adrenaline boost is starting to wear off. "No one knows they're missing, and there's no one left to help them."

"Who?" Luke shakes his head when my intention sinks in. "Maddie, we can't go after them."

I watch Moisés thrash on the ground like an angry caterpillar. Silvana and Sebastián and their men killed my brother and kidnapped my cousin. Sebastián *used* me in Cartagena. They *have* to pay for that. But I can't drag Luke into any more danger. He wouldn't even be out here, if not for me.

"You're right. You should find somewhere to camp nearby until the next supply shipment comes. You can't wait here. This is the first place they'll look when Moisés doesn't come back." I duck into my brother's tent in search of supplies. "Keep trying to get ahold of your parents. With any luck, I'll be back before the helicopter gets here."

"Maddie—"

I grab my brother's spare clean shirt, and when Luke realizes I'm changing, his face flushes and he turns around.

Dressed, I say a silent apology to my brother, then I dump his pack on the floor of the tent to take inventory. My hand closes around a familiar shape in one of his backpack pockets, and I hold my breath as I pull out an insulin reservoir and clutch it like the life raft it is. Ryan saved the leftover insulin I usually throw out when I change my pump injection site. Just in case.

The cartridge is one-third full, and I still have a little left in my pump. That's around thirty hours' worth of insulin, at the rate my body typically uses it.

But my body doesn't typically hike through the jungle three days in a row.

"You can't take off into the jungle by yourself!" Luke plants himself in the tent opening, blocking my path. "And you can't go up against armed kidnappers!"

So I slide the vial into my pocket before he can see it and borrow the partial-truth move from my cousin's playbook. "Genesis has the rest of my insulin."

Luke's mouth snaps shut, and I can practically see the gears turning behind his eyes "Fine. I'm coming with you."

I don't have time to argue with him. Silvana is getting farther away with every second we waste. "Then grab what you can carry and let's go."

We only find two other backpacks left in the camp: Luke's and Moisés's. And there's no blood where the campers were lined up on the ground. "Does this mean the other hostages were marched out alive?" I ask. Were the gunshots just for show, or were they shot somewhere else?

"I don't know." Luke stuffs several PowerBars and a flashlight taken from the bunkhouse into his bag. "I hid too far away to hear much more than gunfire, and when I came back, I only found your brother."

The reminder of Ryan's death makes my chest feel tight.

Luke kneels to pick up Moisés's rifle. "Ready?"

I swing Ryan's bag over my shoulder. "Do you even know how to use that?"

"In theory." The gun makes a metallic clicking sound. "I have a rifle badge, but I've never shot an automatic."

A Boy Scout with a gun. I'm not sure whether to be impressed or worried.

As Luke and I leave the bunkhouse with our backpacks loaded, I stop at my brother's grave and kneel in the dirt. "Ryan, I swear that when this is over, I *will* take you home."

36 HOURS EARLIER

GENESIS

Holden sits next to me on the damp log. Before he even opens his mouth, I know I'll hear his "reasonable" voice—the one he saves for authority figures and people he wants to impress.

The one he never uses with me because he knows I see through it. But Domenica and Rog are sharing a sleeve of cookies a few feet away, and they can hear everything he says.

"Hey, Gen. You and I have always made a good team." He glances at the terrorists gathered around a radio blaring static across the clearing. "We should really try to get on the same page."

I scoop tuna from a foil packet with one of my last crackers. "What page would that be?"

"We need to face the reality of the situation." He lowers his voice and makes very direct eye contact, as if he's speaking in some code I should understand. I almost expect him to wink, or signal for me to steal third base. "They've already killed everyone we left at the base camp. Unless there's another gang of murderers roaming northern Colombia—and I admit that's a possibility—these are probably the same guys who burned that couple in their car the other day. We have no reason to believe they're going to let us go, even if your dad gives them what they want."

He won't. My dad *can't* just let Silvana and her psychotic band of brothers kill hundreds—thousands?—of people.

But if he doesn't . . .

Holden's right. They'll probably kill us.

I take a deep breath and let it out slowly. I'm seventeen years old. I'm supposed to have the next eighty-five years or so to extend my youth with every designer cream and elective procedure money can buy. I'm supposed to change the world and look great doing it, then die in my sleep when I'm one hundred and four, surrounded by humanitarian plaques, design awards, and people who can't bear to think of the world without me in it.

The world will hate me if I let terrorists bomb the United States. *I'll* hate me.

But I'm not ready to die.

"We *have* to escape," Holden whispers. "And we all have to work together to do it, or someone will be left behind."

I crunch into my cracker and chew slowly. Letting him stew.

"I need you with me on this, Genesis. People listen to you."

He's right again. "That's why we have to stay." I lean

closer to whisper, well aware of how intimate our conversation must look. "I can talk Sebastián out of whatever they're planning." I *have* to. "He needs to make a statement, but I don't think he really wants to hurt anyone. He'll listen to me, once he knows he can trust me."

Holden's eyes narrow. "He's a *terrorist*. We are everything he and his friends hate about the world, and they will kill every one of us just to make a point."

"So you're going to run away and let them kill hundreds of innocent people?" I whisper fiercely, careful to keep my expression as neutral as I can, in case our captors are watching.

"Those people are *not our responsibility*. There's nothing you can do for them without putting *our* lives at risk. *We're* the people you should care about. We've had your back from the very beginning!"

"You've . . . ?" I fight to stay calm as anger explodes deep inside me. "You and Penelope have my back? You're the people I should care about?"

Holden rolls his eyes. "Fine. You're right about me and Pen. But we were just messing around."

"You were just messing around. With my *best friend*." It's like he doesn't even hear himself.

"It meant nothing. It never does. You know that."

"Does *she*?" I glance pointedly at Penelope, who's sitting cross-legged in a patch of moss, watching us with her hands clenched so tightly in her lap that she's at risk of breaking her own fingers.

"I don't know what she knows," Holden snaps. "Are you really willing to let us die out here in the mud because of a few stupid drunken hookups?"

"A *few*?"

"Gen, you're missing the point."

"No, *you're* missing the point." I lean in until I'm practically spitting in his ear, to disguise our argument. "Your life is worth no more than anyone else's." Saying that feels *so* good. "Neither is Pen's. Neither is mine. This isn't like court-ordered community service. This is *real*, Holden. Real life. Real death. Real responsibility. We have a chance to prevent something *terrible*.

"I am *not* going to let Silvana use my dad's company to slaughter innocent people. You need to man up and get on board with *that* reality, because if your escape attempt gets someone killed, that blood is on *your* hands. Not mine."

34.5 HOURS EARLIER

MADDIE

". . . but this would probably be a sandbox game, considering we can go wherever we want to out here. Or maybe not. We *do* kind of have to stick to the trail, to find your cousin. But it sure would be nice if we could lower the difficulty level, so we wouldn't have to eat to regain strength or energy. Or so we could gain XP faster—that's experience points—and learn how to, like, catch and skin rabbits for food. Like in *Red Dead Redemption.* Or—"

"Luke!" I spin to face him on the trail. "Do you have to fill *every* moment with the sound of your own voice?"

He stares at the ground, and I want to kick myself for hurting his feelings. I've put up with an hour and a half of endless chatter about which snakes are poisonous, which frogs are safe to eat, and which plant leaves should not be used as toilet paper, but I draw the line at debating the difficulty rating an "adventure" like this would have on some video game I've never heard of.

"Sorry. I just . . ." Luke adjusts his cap over his sweaty

curls. "At my grandmother's wake, everyone was really quiet, and that made it impossible to think about anything else." He shrugs. "So I thought talking might distract you from . . . Ryan."

I am the world's biggest asshole.

I push stringy strands of hair back from my face and exhale slowly. "I'm sorry. That's very thoughtful."

We continue down the trail. For several minutes, I hear nothing from him but the shuffle of his boots on the path. Luke is right. Silence is a lot less peaceful and a lot more awkward than I thought it'd be, so I clear my throat and press the reset button.

"Hey, Luke. What were you saying earlier about some kind of limbless amphibian?"

"Oh! A few years ago, they discovered a new species in Brazil that grows up to thirty-two inches long, and resembles—"

Luke's voice cuts off so suddenly that I turn to make sure he hasn't been eaten by something. His face is flushed the color of a cayenne pepper, and suddenly I truly am curious.

"Resembles what? Don't leave me hanging."

"It resembles . . . um . . . a certain male reproductive organ."

"Oh." I face forward and hike as if my feet are on fire, and I don't slow until I hear rushing water. A minute later, we reach the cliff, and I catch my breath, just like I did the first time. The setting sun paints ripples of fire across the surface.

"Holy shit!" Luke breathes as he peeks carefully over the edge.

"*That* is where I lost my supplies."

His eyes seem to take up half of his face. "You jumped?"

"From about two feet to your left." I could have died. I *should* have died.

Luke scoots back from the edge, sweat beading on his forehead. "How did you avoid the boulders?"

"Ryan says God keeps a close eye on those without the mental capacity to take care of themselves. My survival seems to prove his point." Thinking about my brother sends a fresh bolt of pain through my chest and I close my eyes, determined not to cry again.

This is the time for revenge.

"Let's go. It's getting dark." I take two steps, but Luke doesn't move.

"You're fearless," he whispers.

"I'm scared right now." What if Genesis is already dead? What if we never make it out of the jungle?

What if my brother's killers get away?

"Okay, but you use fear like a superpower. You harness it for good, or whatever." His focus drops to the ground, and I can see that he wants to take the whole thing back. Not because he doesn't mean it, but because he thinks it sounds stupid.

"You really think so?"

"You jumped off a cliff to help your brother. Stupid? Yes. But very brave." Luke's gaze holds mine with a bold confidence I've rarely seen from him, and something flutters deep in my belly.

"You're giving me way too much credit. Come on."

As we continue down the path, I stare at the ground, hyperaware that every decision I make from this point on could take us in the wrong direction.

I'm no longer retracing my steps. This is where the jungle gets real.

GENESIS

"*¡Vamos!*" Silvana calls from up ahead, and I assume she's talking to one of the hostages until I see that we've come to a small clearing centered around a semipermanent fire pit, where Julian has taken a seat.

"*Queremos café y tenemos que hacer pis*," he insists, and I have to stifle a laugh.

"What did he say?" Indiana asks.

"He told her that they want coffee and they need to pee."

"I'm with him on both counts," Indiana says.

I haven't had enough water in the two hours since our last rest to need a bathroom break.

Silvana curses in Spanish, but when Álvaro sits with Julian, she relents. "Don't get comfortable, *princesa*," she says when I set my bag on the ground. "We leave in twenty minutes."

Penelope groans. "The sun is setting. I thought she was finally going to show us a little mercy."

I sit on a patch of grass, and Pen takes my silence as an invitation to join me. "Holden and I didn't mean to hurt you, Genesis." She steels her spine and takes a deep breath. "It just happened."

"Nothing 'just happens' with Holden." I shrug and dig in my bag, as if this conversation means nothing to me. As if I'm not losing my best friend, when I've already lost everything else in the *world* today. "If it hadn't been you, it would have been someone else."

"But it *was* me."

I look up and hold her gaze. "And you think that makes you special? That you're different from his other hookups?"

The raw vulnerability in her eyes answers for her.

"I know you're socially stunted, from spending most of your adolescence on the uneven bars, so let me give you the SparkNotes version of *Hookups for Dummies*: if you start out as someone's dirty little secret, that's *all you will ever be*." I look right into her eyes and am pleased to see them watering. "You clearly have no respect for me, but you should at least try to respect yourself."

"Genesis, you hook up with guys all the time!"

"But I don't sleep with them!" I hiss, too low for anyone else to hear. "And I would *never* have hooked up with my best friend's boyfriend." I pause for a second, then drive the blade home. "I hope it was worth what it cost you."

Penelope flinches.

I swallow my guilt, pick up my bag, and leave her staring after me, so she can't see the moisture I blink from my eyes.

Most of our captors have gathered around a pot sitting over a fire someone has built in the pit. They hold camp mugs, and Óscar is distributing scoops of instant coffee from a canister.

Sebastián sits a few feet away, holding an empty cup and watching the flames. This feels like a good opportunity to make a personal connection. To convince him that the kidnappers can make their point without taking any more lives.

Suddenly I'm horrifyingly aware of how awful I must look, wearing almost as much sweat and mud as clothing. I haven't even brushed my teeth yet today. But I'm not going to get a better shot, so I dig a breath mint from my pack and sit next to Sebastián.

He looks up, surprised, and I point at Óscar's instant coffee. "If Colombia produces the best beans in the world, why is everyone drinking instant?"

Sebastián laughs, and heads turn our way. I can practically feel everyone watching us. "We export the best beans," he says in his thick but comprehensible accent.

"All of them?" It doesn't seem fair that those who produce the best coffee don't get to drink it.

Rog chuckles as he passes behind us. "Colombian farmers are too smart to drink their own cash crop, when they can sell it to Americans foolish enough to pay more in a month for coffee than on their cell phone bills."

Metal clinks, and I turn to see Óscar pouring hot water into cups held out by his fellow captors. He heads our way when Sebastián holds his mug up.

I've never needed coffee worse in my life.

When Óscar moves on, I make a show of sniffing the air and enjoying the aroma. "Smells good."

Sebastián looks amused as he holds out his metal cup

so I can see several small green leaves steeping in yellowish water. The scent of coffee is not coming from his mug. *"Té de coca,"* he says. "Want some?"

Do I want cocaine tea?

"There's no actual cocaine in it," Rog says, and I turn to see him sitting with his back to a tree, pulling his longish, frizzy hair into a low man bun. "A sip won't hurt."

So I accept the cup from Sebastián. He watches while I take a sip. I make a face. The tea is bitter and herbal-tasting.

He laughs again.

"Gracias." I give the cup back and watch him sip from it while I consider an approach that will drive the wedge between Silvana and Sebastián deeper, while letting him know he can trust me. "I'm sorry if I got you in trouble with Silvana." I look straight into his eyes to convey honesty. "Over my dad's 'resources.'"

Sebastián scowls. "I don't answer to Silvana."

"Oh." I fake surprise. "That's good. She's kind of . . . horrible."

"They don't pay her to be sweet."

"Well, if 'they' intended to hire a homicidal maniac, I'd say they got their money's worth. Who else would want to smuggle bombs into the US on a cargo plane?" It doesn't matter whether my guess is right or wrong. What matters is his reaction to it.

Sebastián leans closer and lowers his voice. "We don't want a plane."

I'm not sure I believe him. A plane would be the fastest,

most direct way to get a bomb into the country, and he didn't deny that they'd be smuggling bombs.

"You know everything that comes through customs is inspected, right?" I whisper as I study his reaction. "It's not as simple as just unloading a bomb at the airport and driving off with—"

Horror sends a wave of chills over me. Maybe they won't be driving off with the bomb. What if they're planning to blow up an airport?

When he says nothing else, I glance at Silvana, then give him a sympathetic look. "I know, you're not supposed to tell me what this is really about. She's such a control freak."

Sebastián chuckles. "If you were half as smart as you think you are, you'd be a very dangerous girl."

"If you had half the balls you pretend to have, you'd be calling the shots here," I return without missing a beat.

Sebastián looks insulted. Then he laughs out loud. "I'm calling plenty of shots. And that's all you need to know."

34 HOURS EARLIER

MADDIE

"There! Do you hear that?" I grab Luke's hand, and his fingers go stiff. "That's definitely water."

He smiles. "Good ear."

We veer to the north, and soon we find the bank of the very river I jumped into seven hours ago.

While Luke gathers dry twigs, I unpack the small wood-burning camp stove we scavenged from the technological treasure trove of Holden's abandoned tent, and together we manage to get a compact but bright fire going.

"Wait." He frowns at the stove, then at the plastic water bottles, which will melt at the first lick of flames. "We need something to boil the water in before we drink it."

"We have something." I sit on a fallen log and pop the top on two cans of soup, then hand one to him. "Eat fast."

We have to pour bites into our mouths straight from the cans because we don't have any spoons, and I smile when Luke lowers his to reveal a half circle of tomato soup rising from the corners of his mouth, like a grotesque clown smile.

"Yeah, well, you have a clam chowder mustache," he fires back with a grin while he wipes his face on his sleeve. For the first time in hours, I don't want to dig my own grave and lie down in it.

But then the radio at Luke's waist crackles, and my smile dies. We hear only static, but the fact that we're picking up anything at all means we're getting closer to Genesis and the other hostages.

Closer to my brother's killers.

I'm only going to get one shot at them. I will damn well be ready.

GENESIS

Everyone stares at me as I rejoin the hostages across the clearing. Indiana's subtle smile says he knows what I'm up to with Sebastián, but I'm not even sure I do, anymore. He's harder to read than I thought he'd be, and I still have no idea how they expect my dad to get a bomb past customs, or what they want to blow up. Or why.

"What the *hell* was that?" Holden demands in a whisper. In spite of his plan to distract a couple of the gunmen with my nudity, he's wearing jealousy like a wool sweater— as if it chafes.

"What was what?"

He leans in to whisper what probably looks like something sweet and soft, his breath brushing my hair. "You can't work Sebastián over in front of the whole world. You have to take him into the jungle and give him something better to hold on to than that rifle."

I shove him back until I can see his eyes. "Believe it or not, your sledgehammer approach isn't appropriate for every problem," I snap softly. "I can't stop whatever they're planning until I understand what that is. Which won't happen until Sebastián trusts me. I'm trying to make a connection."

Holden snorts. "We both know you don't need to talk to connect with a guy. Stick to what you're good at."

"You have *no* idea what I'm good at," I say, my cheeks flaming. Even Holden only sees what I show him, and I'm done showing him how to hurt me.

"You crossed a line with Penelope," I hiss, my hands curled into fists. "And you *damn well* know it. You should be on your knees right now, begging for forgiveness, but you're trying to pimp me out to armed terrorists instead. What the *hell* kind of apology is that?"

Holden glances around to see if anyone is close enough to overhear our quiet implosion. "You're totally overreacting," he whispers. "And we have bigger problems right now than—"

"Stay away from me." I let my voice carry, and everyone who wasn't already watching turns to stare. Pen is on the edge of her seat, waiting to see how this will play out. "We're done."

Sebastián and most of the other gunmen chuckle. Silvana makes a snide comment about Holden's inadequacies in Spanish, using his name so he knows he's being ridiculed.

Holden's jaw clenches so hard I can hear his teeth grind. I've never seen him this mad, but my anger matches his so fiercely that for the moment, I don't care how reckless it is to make new enemies, when I'm already being held at gunpoint.

He sits on the log next to Penelope and pulls her close for a kiss. I laugh out loud. Poor Penelope is the only one who can't see that his pathetic display is actually for my benefit.

Indiana watches me as he stores a nearly empty water bottle. His brow rises, asking a silent question.

Did that go as planned?

Are you okay?

Do you want to rethink this approach?

I'm not sure which of those he's asking, but the answer to all three is no.

33.5 HOURS EARLIER

MADDIE

"We can't hike all night," Luke says as he refills our last plastic bottle with the cooled water we boiled in our soup cans.

Yet that's exactly what I want to do. We're close enough to my brother's killers to pick up radio static, but they'll slip farther and farther away while we "rest." As if I'll be able to sleep while the kidnappers are out there getting away with murder. And hunting for me, if they've realized Moisés won't be bringing me back.

"Come on." Luke slides my backpack from my shoulders. "They won't be hiking all night either."

I should insist that we press on. That this is our chance to gain some ground. But the harder I push my body, the less predictably it will use the insulin I have left.

So as the last rays of daylight sink behind the jungle canopy, I reluctantly pitch our one-person tent on the bank of the river. While Luke gathers more wood for the camp stove, he lists his favorite movies in which people get lost in the wild. "And then there's *Alive*," he says as he shoves two more sticks into the stove. "That one about the plane crash in the Andes where the survivors resorted to cannibalism."

I frown at him as I look up from the last tent pole. "Do you think you could leave out all the movies that don't have happy endings?"

Luke's sudden silence does little to reassure me of our chances. Suddenly the jungle seems built of shadows, rather than trees.

"We're going to be fine," I insist as I crawl into the tent. "We're in the Sierra Nevada de Santa Marta. Not the Andes."

He climbs in after me, then zips up the transparent roof/door section. "True. Although we're not far from the northern tip of the Andes."

Of course he would know that.

33 HOURS EARLIER

GENESIS

Ahead, several flashlight beams pierce the darkness, illuminating slices of the jungle path as if they were thrown from a disjointed disco ball. Branches and vines seem to loom over us, jumping each time the light shifts.

I'm starting to think they're going to march us all night.

Holden and Penelope are near the head of the line, walking so close together that their shoulders keep brushing each other. Álvaro takes up a position on my right, and the way he watches me makes me feel like I'm still kneeling on that cliff. As if he still holds his machete to my throat, and he's waiting for me to flinch.

Fortunately, he loses interest in me when Óscar clips a small portable radio to the shoulder strap of his bag and begins dialing through the FM band.

The other gunmen argue in Spanish about whether or not we're close enough to their base camp to pick up a signal. When Óscar finds not one, but three different stations, the gunmen cheer, and I'm tempted to join them. If they can pick up a radio signal, they might also pick up a cell phone signal.

Not that either of those will help, unless I can get ahold of a radio or a cell phone.

Óscar turns up the volume and sound crackles over the airwaves. I trip over my own feet when I hear my name come from the radio.

". . . Genesis Valencia is seventeen. Her cousins Ryan and Madalena Valencia are eighteen and sixteen. Penelope Goh, an Olympic silver medalist on the uneven bars and a local celebrity, is seventeen. Holden Wainwright, only son of . . ."

At first, I am so shocked that the familiarity of the voice doesn't register.

"Neda . . ." Penelope turns to look at me, having evidently forgotten that the only reason she and I are still on the same continent is that we're being held at gunpoint. "How did she get on the radio?"

"Shhh!" Suddenly my feet don't hurt. My mosquito bites don't itch. The rest of the world fades away as the gunmen cheer over the realization that their efforts have made it onto an English-language radio show—surely the first part of whatever message they're trying to send.

I listen, desperate for information from outside the jungle. I've been without my cell phone for all of eleven hours, and I already feel like the world has moved on without me.

"Neda, what can you tell us about the others who were kidnapped in the north Colombian jungle along with your friends?" another voice asks over the static, and I recognize the practiced cadence of Bill "The Thunder" Lewis, one of our local Miami DJs.

Neda is being interviewed. Either Óscar's radio is picking up a signal from Florida—is that possible?—or the show has been syndicated.

Either way, our disappearance has obviously become *big* news.

"I don't have the names of all the others who went missing," she says. "But I'm working closely with the US authorities to answer their questions to the best of my ability. And I appreciate this opportunity to tell my story to the world. It was *such* a close call, Bill. If I hadn't been airlifted out of the jungle last night, I'd be out there right now, fighting for my survival. Only with my injury, I'd have a distinct disadvantage."

Yeah. Because Maddie's diabetes made things so easy for her.

"I can only imagine." Bill clucks his tongue in sympathy with the girl who *wasn't* kidnapped at gunpoint. "We need to take a quick break, then we'll be back with Neda Rahbar, to hear more about the six Miami teens who went missing in the Colombian jungle this very morning."

"They know we're missing!" Penelope clutches Holden's arm as the radio goes to a commercial break, and my teeth grind so hard I can hear my jaw creak.

Indiana gives me a sympathetic smile and aims his small flashlight at the ground in front of our feet, lighting the way.

"It sounds like they only know about the people your friend felt like talking about on the radio," Natalia says, and the pointed smile she shoots at Indiana, Rog, and Domenica looks extra smug in the indirect glow from Óscar's flashlight.

"Well, then they mostly know about Neda." I try to summon a smile, as if I think my absent friend's narcissism is in any way amusing while the rest of us are being held at gunpoint.

"At least they know something," Domenica points out as we trudge through a puddle of mud that Indiana's flashlight failed to illuminate.

Silvana's soft laughter is cruel. "Yes, they know you're out here *somewhere,* and they only have *seventeen thousand* square acres of dense jungle to search on foot in order to find you. You'll be rescued in no time!"

MADDIE

"So . . . what's the plan, Maddie?" Luke asks as he lies back on the floor of the tent with his hands folded beneath his head. "For real." His tone is carefully neutral, as if he's afraid of upsetting me with the question. "Why are we really out here, instead of waiting for the helicopter near the bunk-house?"

"I told you." I pick at a string hanging from the side of the sleeping bag and avoid eye contact because I don't want to lie to his face, even if that lie is partly true. "I have to find Genesis and get my insulin."

"You've hardly glanced at your pump all day. You don't seem very worried about running low."

I'll be more worried about my insulin if we don't find Genesis before tomorrow afternoon. But that's not what he's asking about.

"I'm . . ." Luke deserves the truth. But he's not going to talk me out of it. "Look, you didn't have to come. I told you to stay near the bunkhouse. You—"

"I wanted to come with you, and I'm not going to leave you out here," he insists. "But I need to know the plan. The *real* plan."

"They have to *pay* for what they did to my brother," I say as I finally look at him.

"Okay, but even if that were a plausible goal—and most critical thinkers would agree that it's not—what are you going to do?" He sits up, and now we're eye to eye. "There are two of us against who knows how many gunmen. Not to mention the jungle itself. Do you have any idea how many things could kill us out here, even if we never find the kidnappers? Jaguars. Piranha. Poison dart frogs. Caimans. Snakes. Spiders. We'll be lucky if we don't catch malaria from the mosquito that just bit me. Or we could drown in the river or fall off a cliff."

"I've already survived a cliff, a river, and more than one gunman. And this mosquito . . ." I reach up and smash it into the top of the tent, leaving a small smear of blood against the overhead view. "As for the rest, we'll just have to keep our eyes open."

"Maddie, Ryan's gone, but your cousin's still alive, and she needs help," Luke says. "We owe it to her and her friends to report them missing."

"Report to whom?" I demand. "Even if we find police or more soldiers, we can't be sure they aren't in on this like the soldiers at the bunkhouse."

Luke looks shocked, and I realize he didn't know that, since he missed the actual kidnapping.

"What did you overhear while you were hiding?" I ask.

He shrugs. "I'm in second year Latin, not Spanish."

My brows rise. How can anyone live in Miami and speak no Spanish?

Fear lines his forehead, and I try not to let him see how scared I am too. "Look. There's no one to report this to. There's no one else to help Genesis." And like her or not, I'm *not* losing another family member.

"Do you have any idea where they're taking the hostages?"

I shake my head. "All I know is that they were heading northwest. If you're not up for it, I understand. But I have to—"

"I'm with you, Maddie." He says it softly, but the words hold no doubt.

I exhale in the dark, grateful to know that I won't be out here in the jungle alone.

32·5 HOURS EARLIER

GENESIS

Everyone stops talking when Bill Lewis comes back on the air.

"Thanks for tuning in to Power 85 FM for this exclusive interview with local high school junior Neda Rahbar, whose friends disappeared in the Colombian jungle this morning. For those of you just tuning in, the US embassy received a report around ten hours ago from the mother of Luke Hazelwood, one of the missing Miami teens, after she got a text from her son, saying that armed gunmen had taken over a supply base in Parque Tayrona, on the northernmost coast of Colombia."

"Luke?" Holden turns to walk backward, and even in the dark, I can tell he's scowling at me. "Your dad didn't report us missing?"

"Hernán knows better," Silvana says with a laugh.

And Maddie's lovesick puppy dog has proved more resourceful than I gave him credit for. Yet he's evidently still missing.

"We have a special caller on the line," Bill "The Thunder" Lewis says over the radio, and everyone goes quiet again. "Hello, Mrs. Wainwright?"

"Yes, this is Elizabeth Wainwright."

Holden makes a strange choking sound from the front of the line.

"Thank you for taking our call. Please, tell us something about your son."

"Holden is my only child. He's a sweet boy," Elizabeth says, and she genuinely seems to believe that. "He's allergic to mold and he's never really been fishing or even camping without prepackaged meals, so the rain forest is truly a less-than-ideal environment for his health."

Silvana shines her light at him, and Holden's jaw is so tight I'm afraid he'll dislocate it. He loves to talk about going on safari with his dad, as if that makes him a badass, but he never mentions the private guide who cooks, packs the Jeep, and makes all the travel arrangements.

Holden camps like a rich boy.

"So, if whoever has him is listening, please tell us what you want. We'll do anything. Just *please* send our boy home."

The back of Holden's neck is flaming now. If he were a cartoon, fire would be shooting out of his ears.

"Mrs. Wainwright, we hope your son's captors have heard your plea. That's it for tonight, folks. Please tune in tomorrow when we come to you live with Neda Rahbar at the sit-in vigil at Elmore Everglades Academy. And don't forget you can pick up your 'keep hope alive' bracelets here at the studio!"

Silvana steps in front of Holden as Óscar turns off the radio. "'Oh, please send him back! He's good for nothing, but we'll pay anything!'"

The gunmen laugh, and she turns to play to her audience.

"If Wainwright's *mami* will pay a fortune for her *entire* son, what would she pay if we send back just a piece of him at a time?" Silvana pulls Holden to a stop by one arm and lays the blade of her huge knife flat against his left nostril. "How much for his pretty little nose?"

We've all stopped walking now. Most of the flashlights are trained on them, so we can all see the show.

Holden is frozen. Pen looks terrified, and I want to throw up.

This is all my fault.

Silvana's men laugh harder, and she lets him go, muttering in Spanish about how useless he is.

Holden fumes, humiliated. Penelope watches him, obviously unsure how to help.

I should stay away from him because when he's angry, he acts without thinking. But someone has to talk him down before he does something stupid.

"You okay?" I ask softly, while everyone else starts walking.

Holden turns on me. "First chance I get, I'm taking that bitch down." Spittle flies from his lips and he speaks through clenched teeth. "Are you with me, Genesis? Because if you get in my way, I'll take you down too."

As he marches past me down the dark jungle trail, I see the fury raging in every step he takes. I am terrified that even if the rest of us are ransomed, Holden is never going to get out of this jungle alive.

32 HOURS EARLIER

MADDIE

"It's Monday night." I sit on the foot end of our mummy-shaped sleeping bag and stare up at the trees through the transparent top of our tent, listening to the chorus of croaks and chirrups all around us. Everything feels oddly peaceful. "We've missed the car that was supposed to pick us up at the *parque* entrance. But Genesis's plans change on an hourly basis, and there's no cell reception in the park. Abuelita won't consider us truly missing until we're at least twenty-four hours late."

At the head end of the sleeping bag, Luke takes off his outer shirt and rolls it into the shape of a pillow. "Even if they didn't get my text, when I'm not back tonight, my parents will call in the National Guard. Or whatever the Colombian equivalent is."

"Do they know who you're with? Or where you went?"

"I told them, but there's no telling how much they processed."

"They don't care where you're going or who's with you?"

"It's not that, really. My friends whose parents are divorced think it's great that mine are still so into each other. But the thing about happily married parents is that sometimes they'd be just as happily married even if they weren't parents." He shrugs and unties his boots. "But once they realize I'm gone, they will definitely sound the alarm."

"Good."

"So . . . how do you want to do this?" Luke stares down at the sleeping bag so deliberately I realize he's avoiding looking at me. But there's nothing he can do about the flush creeping up his neck. "I'll sleep on the ground. You can have the bag."

"It's only fair if we share."

"Yeah. Okay."

I unzip the bag, but spreading it out in the cramped space is like playing Twister in a cardboard box. Luke's face gets redder every time I bump into him or have to duck beneath his arm, but he stays inside the tent, as if he needs to prove he's comfortable sharing it with me.

"We should get some sleep," I say at last. "We need to be up at first light."

My legs ache and my head is throbbing, and now that we've stopped hiking, I can't imagine taking another step before the sun comes up. Though it can't be any later than eight p.m., I've never felt more exhausted in my life.

After a couple of awkward attempts to get comfortable without touching each other, we finally give up and lay spine to spine, with Luke nestled between me and Moisés's rifle.

His warmth against my back feels surprisingly intimate in the chilly night. I am suddenly conscious of every breath I take, because he can feel the movement. I can't remember how to breathe at a natural pace.

If I breathe too fast, he'll think I'm nervous. If I breathe too slowly, he'll think I'm asleep, and I'll have to pretend I am.

"Hey, Maddie," Luke whispers.

"Yeah?"

"Are you scared?"

"Terrified," I tell him. "You?"

"Yeah. Me too."

I can feel his heart race through the back of his shirt, which makes me wonder whether he's more scared of armed kidnappers . . . or sharing a tent all night with me.

31.5 HOURS EARLIER

GENESIS

It feels like midnight as we finally trudge into the terrorists' base camp, but the sun's only been down for a couple of hours. It can't be any later than eight or nine p.m.

The camp is lit by fire pits, torches strapped to poles, and gas camping lanterns—the kind trembling men carry into dark caves in scary movies. There are at least a dozen men standing around, drinking coffee from dented metal mugs, but most of them don't wear military uniforms or carry rifles. Several are chatting in English with no obvious accent.

I can tell from the way Holden's focus skips over the men that he's counting. Trying to calculate our chance of an escape, now that we no longer outnumber our captors.

"Get back to work," Sebastián shouts and most of the men dump their coffee on the ground and head into the jungle on a well-worn footpath opposite the direction we've come from.

Indiana studies what we can see of the path, even once

the men are out of sight, and I realize he's listening to their footsteps. Waiting to see how long it takes for them to fade.

Penelope groans as she looks around the camp. There are no showers. There is no electricity. No running water. No beds.

At the center of the clearing is a small hut with a thatched roof and no windows—the kind indigenous tribes have been building for centuries. An acoustic guitar hangs outside the hut from one of its posts. Several fire pits are spaced around the site, each surrounded by a carpet of large leaves and straw mats.

Two long, improvised, open-sided tents hold rows of hammocks stretched between the support posts, but the third tent is an anomaly. It's a sturdy green military-style pavilion, enclosed on all four sides, so that we can't see who or what is inside. That tent is obviously the headquarters of the terrorist organization.

"This is *so* third world," Penelope whispers.

But what she sees as gritty, makeshift accommodations is actually a well-established and surprisingly functional base of operations. The terrorists have everything they need to live here indefinitely, and they've obviously been here for a while.

"*¡Vamos!*" Silvana shouts, and as we trudge behind her on a tour of the camp, Indiana nudges my shoulder with his.

"All the comforts of a prison camp," he whispers.

"None of the hope of a rescue," I shoot back, and Indiana laughs softly.

"*Los baños.*" Silvana pulls back the curtain hung in front of a hand-built bamboo stall on the far end of the clearing and shines her flashlight inside to reveal a plastic toilet seat nailed to a wooden platform. "After you go, sprinkle lime." She points to an unlabeled bucket. "But don't touch or inhale."

"How very civilized," Holden mumbles.

"You will bathe every other day," she orders, pointing at a stream that defines one side of the clearing.

Penelope groans softly. "How long are we going to *be* here?"

Silvana gestures to clothing hung from vines used as clotheslines over our heads. "Wash your clothes and hang them up to dry. If you don't stay clean, you will get sick, and if you get sick out here, you will die."

"She's right," Indiana whispers. "Fungi will grow in any dark, damp environment, including socks and underwear. That's the whole reason commandos were known for 'going commando' during all those jungle wars."

Penelope makes a disgusted face.

"You must boil water for drinking, and you may not leave camp without permission and an escort. If you fail to follow orders, I will start cutting off bits of you to send to your loved ones." Silvana wiggles her left pinkie finger in an absurd threat. "Now go to sleep." She points at the closest of the fire pits, assigning it to the hostages.

We stake out spots on the leaves and grass mats around our pit, and while everyone else rolls out sleeping bags, I begin picking up all the twigs and broken branches I can find in the clearing. Gathering firewood is just an excuse to eavesdrop, but the only thing I learn from what I overhear is that several of the men working for Silvana and Sebastián are, in fact, American.

I lay the scraps of wood on the ground, and start arranging them in the stone-lined pit.

"Wait. Start with this." Indiana kneels next to me and drops a handful of crunchy greenish-brown material in the bottom of the pit.

"Dried moss?"

He nods. "The *aggressively* malodorous gentleman guarding the supplies was kind enough to give us some tinder." His hand brushes mine as he takes several twigs from me. "Most people go with a lean-to or teepee construction, but a pyramid design makes the longest-lasting campfire."

I lift one brow at him. "Then why are you making a log cabin fire?"

He frowns. "I'm not—"

"Give me those." I take the twigs and arrange them in a large square around the tinder, then begin stacking that square with progressively smaller ones.

"You're pretty good at this," Indiana whispers as he watches. "Tell me the truth—have you been taken hostage before?"

I laugh. "Only by a father determined to escape everything but nature, at least twice a year."

When the pyramid is ready, Indiana lights an extra twig

at one of the other pits and uses it to start our campfire. I settle onto a mat with my back to the jungle and watch light flicker on his face while he stokes the blaze.

Somehow, two days' stubble has made Holden look tired and ragged, yet Indiana looks rugged and strong.

He sits back on his mat and even when he catches me staring, I can't look away. So we watch each other next to the fire, and though we're surrounded by both our captors and our fellow hostages, this moment feels somehow private.

Somehow . . . ours.

"What's your real name?" I whisper, staring into eyes that look more brown than green in the firelight.

"I'll tell you when we get out of here," he says so softly I can hardly hear him. "I promise."

"What if we don't get out of here?"

"Oh, I think you're pretty motivated." His smile is crooked. And totally hot.

Suddenly I'm aware that there's mud on my cheek and moss beneath my nails. "I'm wearing half the jungle," I say as I scrub my face.

He takes my hand, then holds it. "It works. You look *fierce*."

I can't resist a smile.

Indiana spreads out his sleeping bag next to mine, and as our captors settle in for the night—except a couple of armed men on patrol—I realize that beneath the normal jungle noises, I hear a steady pulsing sound I've known all my life.

I grab Indiana's arm. "Do you hear that?"

He closes his eyes, listening. "The ocean."

"Yeah," I whisper. "I think the beach is just down that footpath."

Indiana opens his eyes, and he looks as hopeful as I feel.

Where there's coastline, there will be boats, and where there are boats, there's a way to escape.

MADDIE

I wake up screaming in the middle of the night.

"Maddie!"

I open my eyes and find a man's silhouette hunched over me, two shades darker than the night itself, and my screaming intensifies.

"Maddie!" He shakes me by both shoulders. "Shhh! *Please* wake up and be quiet. You're going to draw every predator in the jungle!"

I recognize Luke's voice and realize the shadowy silhouette makes him look much bigger and more threatening than he actually is.

"You're okay," he says as I sit up. "It's just a dream."

"Yeah. I . . ." I don't realize I've been crying until I wipe my face with both hands and find it wet. "I dreamed my brother got shot, and I dug a grave for him, but my dad was already buried there."

"That's messed up," Luke whispers, and in reply, I fall back onto the shirt-pillow. He lies next to me with his hands folded beneath his head and stares up at the sky through the top of the tent. "It's still early. We can get more sleep."

But I'm not sure I want any more sleep, after dreaming about my brother's murder. "Sorry I woke you up," I whisper.

"You didn't. I had my own nightmare."

I roll onto my side, facing him, and Luke tenses beside me. "What happened in yours?"

"It's stupid. You don't want to hear it."

"I told you mine."

"Yeah, but your subconscious fears have merit. Mine are just . . . dumb," he insists, and though I can't see much more than his outline in the dark, I'm pretty sure he's blushing again.

"No fear is dumb. What happened in your nightmare, Luke?"

He takes a deep breath, still staring up at the trees. "I dreamed I woke up and you were gone. But you weren't missing. You just left me here and took all the supplies."

My hand goes to my heart. I feel like someone just kicked me in the chest.

I think for a minute, trying to figure out how to respond. I've never been the subject of someone else's abandonment issues. "Luke, I can't even carry all the supplies on my own. I need you as a pack animal, if for no other reason."

Finally he rolls over to face me, and my eyes have adjusted to the dark well enough to see his scowl. "I'm starting to think you and your cousin are cut from the same—"

I laugh, and his eyes widen.

"Oh. You're kidding."

"Of course I'm kidding. I'm not going to leave you alone in the jungle. Though you may actually be better off without me."

Luke smiles as he rolls onto his back again. "Neither of us is better off alone."

22 HOURS EARLIER

GENESIS

It's hardly even light yet when a boot digs into my side hard enough that I wake up gasping. The pain is disorienting, and at first I can't remember where I am. Then Silvana's outline comes into focus.

"Get up, *princesa*." Her sneer turns my father's nickname for me into an insult, yet makes me ache with homesickness. "It's time to boil water."

"*¡Arriba! ¡Es hora de levantarse!*" She wakes the other hostages with a shouted order to rise and shine. No one else gets a boot to the ribs.

I sit up and groan at the soreness in my arms and legs. No amount of jogging down suburban streets or working with my personal trainer could have prepared me for a twelve-hour hike through the foothills of the Sierra Nevada. In the rain.

"Morning," Indiana says, and I turn to see him looking up at me from his sleeping bag with both hands folded beneath his head. As if he were stretched out on a towel at the beach.

How the hell does he make being taken hostage look sexy?

Indiana unzips his sleeping bag and pulls a small plastic pouch from his backpack.

"Where are you going?" I ask as he stands.

"To brush my teeth. I might decide to kiss you later."

I don't realize I'm smiling until I see Domenica grinning at me. She heard every word.

I dig my toiletry kit from my pack, and when my compact falls out, I remember that I haven't looked in a mirror in more than two days. Nor have I brushed my teeth or truly washed my face.

I pluck a camping wipe from my packet and wipe down my face, neck, and arms, but before I can find my toothbrush, Silvana shouts at me from across the clearing.

"*¡Princesa! ¡Agua!*"

Which is just as well. I can't brush my teeth without clean water.

While I collect every kettle and empty tin can that will hold water, Julian gives each of the other hostages an MRE—military-style meals ready to eat in thick brown envelopes—and a piece of fruit picked straight from the jungle.

Penelope giggles and I turn to find her feeding bites of her oatmeal to Holden. They pretend they don't see me, but

I know exactly what Holden looks like when he's playing to his audience.

I hope the water she used in that oatmeal gives them some kind of parasite.

On my way to the stream, I notice that all the rifle-carrying, camo-wearing terrorists—including Julian and Álvaro—are gathered around one fire pit with Silvana. At the other pit, all the unarmed men in dirty tees and cargo pants—including several Americans—sit with Sebastián. Óscar and Natalia stand on the fringes of Sebastián's circle, and the three of them are the only ones in the group who are armed.

Now that we're at their base camp, our kidnappers have aligned themselves into two distinct groups, and they look too comfortable in their circles for this to be a new arrangement.

Suddenly I understand. We've been kidnapped by two groups working together. And if the tension between Silvana and Sebastián is any indication, neither organization is thrilled with the collaboration.

"¡Vamos, princesa!" Silvana's shout startles me, and I knock the full kettle into the stream. She and her men laugh while I wade in to fish it out.

When I have water boiling on grills propped over all three fire pits, I sanitize my toothbrush in one of the kettles. While I'm brushing my teeth, the green walled tent opens, then falls closed behind a man carrying a cardboard box. Sweat rolls down his forehead and drips into his eye. He blinks the sweat away, but never takes his focus off the box, even when he stumbles over a rock on his way to the narrow footpath leading to the beach.

He's *terrified* of that box.

Unease crawls up my spine as I watch him. Silvana's bombs are being made *here*. Twenty feet from the spot where I slept.

I won't be sleeping again until this is over.

By the time my teeth are brushed and I've used what passes for a bathroom, the other hostages are almost done with breakfast. Except for Indiana.

"Here." He sets a bulky brown meal packet on my lap when I sink onto the grass mat next to him. "I tried to snag you a piece of fruit, but Domenica's a beast before she's had some caffeine."

"I know how she feels." I hold up the brown envelope. "If there's no instant coffee in this thing, my descent into madness will be swift and terrible."

Indiana laughs. "I'll alert the men in white coats. So what will the hostages be feasting on this morning?"

"'Menu twenty-two: Asian Beef Strips,'" I read from the front of my packet.

"The breakfast of champions. I got 'Menu twelve: Fancy Penne Pasta. Vegetarian.'" He rips into his packet. "*Bon appétit!*"

I start to tear open my envelope, but when I look up, I find Sebastián watching me from across the clearing.

It's six thirty in the morning, according to Indiana's

waterproof camping watch. Eight and a half hours until the deadline Silvana gave my father. Time is running out.

"Thanks," I say as I reluctantly hand the MRE back to him. "But I think I hear opportunity knocking. Wish me luck."

"I've seen you handle yourself. You don't need luck," he whispers as I stand. But I can hear concern in his voice, and that makes me feel oddly warm as I cross the clearing.

Sebastián sees me coming, and his smile actually looks welcoming. "¿Qué pasa, Genesis?"

"I didn't get any fruit."

The men around him laugh, clearly amused by my willingness to make demands from a man holding an automatic rifle.

"We ran out," Sebastián says.

"Rumor has it, fruit grows in the jungle."

His brows rise. "You'll have to pick it yourself."

"Then I'll need an escort." I gesture toward the narrow footpath, as if I don't know it goes to the beach. "Lead the way."

He stands, then gestures in the other direction. Away from the ocean. As we head across the clearing, a crescendo of laughter and crude jokes from his men follows us.

I ignore them all and focus on Indiana instead. He's right. I don't need anyone to wish me luck.

Valencias make their own luck.

21.5 HOURS EARLIER

MADDIE

When the first rays of dappled sunlight wake me, I find Luke curled up to my back with his arm draped over my stomach, as if he'd tried to stop me from leaving in his sleep.

For a moment, I savor his warmth. But then reality kicks in.

Luke shouldn't depend on me. Following me into the jungle nearly got him killed. And it may still.

I shouldn't have let him come, but I can't leave him now, even for his own good.

I don't *want* to leave him.

I carefully lift his arm and sneak out of the tent. By the time I get back from relieving myself in the jungle, Luke is packing up our camp.

"Did you know that Parque Tayrona contains more than seventeen thousand square acres of jungle?" he says as he folds up the camp stove.

"So what?" I ask as I strap our sleeping bag to the bottom

of my pack. "You think we're still in Tayrona?"

"Probably. The vast majority of the *parque* is unexplored, unmapped wilderness."

I shrug into my backpack. "If this is a needle-in-a-haystack analogy, you know exactly where you can shove your odds and statistics. I *will* find them."

"I know. And I'm still with you. But I have an idea. Silvana was marching you guys northwest, right?"

"Yes. We were headed away from the rising sun."

He shoves the folded camp stove into his bag and zips it up. "Then I propose we head due north, instead."

"Why?"

Luke looks at me as if I should already have caught onto his point, and I hate how clueless that makes me feel. "Because the Caribbean is due north, and heading toward the shore means we'll be going downhill. Which will make hiking easier. We can turn west once we hit the water, and that'll be *much* easier going."

"You're leaving something out." I can see it in his eyes.

If we hike along the beach, we might see a boat, or run into other tourists, or pick up a stronger cell signal. "You're not trying to help me find Ryan's murderers." The betrayal feels like a bruise deep in my chest. "You're trying to get us rescued."

"I'm trying to do both," he insists. "We'll still be heading north and west, but at a much faster pace. And if we find help before we find the kidnappers, we can alert the authorities and let them take over. We *owe* that to your cousin and her friends."

"I know, but . . ." I don't want Ryan's killer apprehended. I want him dead.

"Maddie, you don't even have a plan." Luke throws his hands up in frustration. "Even if you're willing to kill someone—and I really hope you're not—we have a rifle you don't know how to use, and a grand total of five shells."

But five shells is plenty, because I *do* have a plan.

Find the kidnappers' base camp. Shoot from a hidden location. Flee with Genesis and her friends in the subsequent chaos.

The hard part will be deciding whether to aim for Silvana or Julian, in case I only manage one shot.

"You're low on insulin, we're both low on food," Luke continues. "And if we hike much farther, we won't make it back to the bunkhouse in time to meet the helicopter tonight. So if we're going to press on, we *have* to head for the shore."

I open my mouth to argue again, but he cuts me off.

"And if that doesn't convince you, think about this: Silvana and Sebastián are almost *certainly* heading for the shore too. There's no more convenient way for the kidnappers to get the supplies they need to keep themselves and their captives alive than by boat."

I frown, resettling my bag on my shoulders. "Then why didn't they march us straight to the beach in the first place?"

"Because they *don't* want to be found. And they probably wanted to keep you guys disoriented." He watches me for a second, letting me think it over. "This is our best bet, Maddie."

He's right.

"Fine." I smile and toss my pack over my shoulder. "Lead the way north, Boy Scout."

21 HOURS EARLIER

GENESIS

"*¿Qué prefieres?*" Sebastián asks as we pick our way through the jungle. His voice is low-pitched and smooth. It's the voice of an announcer or a politician. A voice people will listen to.

A voice like my uncle's. Like my father's.

"Bananas, if we can find them."

"You're in luck." He strikes off to the east, clearly leading me some place he knows well.

Every step I take through this untouched patch of jungle feels like the ticking of a clock counting down to three p.m. To the moment my father will either let me die, or help these terrorists kill hundreds of innocent people.

I can't let it come to that.

"Who are you?"

"Philosophically?" Sebastián laughs. "Or are you asking for my National Identification Number?"

"You're not cartel." I shrug. "Silvana, maybe. But not you."

He holds out his arms and lets his rifle hang across his chest, showing off his uniform and his gun. "Do I not look the part?"

"You don't *sound* the part. You're not after money, and you don't relish violence."

He laughs again. "I bet you're no fun to play poker with."

We arrive at a small cluster of banana trees, each bent by a massive ring of fruit bunches so heavy they hang just feet from the ground. Several of the bunches have gaps, where someone's already picked the fruit.

Sebastián studies the clusters, then breaks off two bananas. He holds them out, letting me choose.

"You're an activist, aren't you?" I select the ripest, but it's still greener than any I've ever seen in a store. "You'll pick up a gun if you have to, but you'd rather fight with words."

He breaks open his banana and it's perfectly ripe on the inside, in spite of the green peel. "What would you fight with, Genesis Valencia?"

Every weapon at my disposal. But I can't show him that.

"If I have to fight, I've made a mistake somewhere along the way," I say as I peel my banana.

"That's because you're privileged. If you wind up somewhere you shouldn't be in life, it's because *you* took a wrong turn. For most of us, someone else is behind the wheel."

"I didn't put myself here." I spread my arms to take in the jungle and the entire hostage situation. "Someone else is driving this time. *You're* driving. You've been watching me since the night I got to Colombia."

"And how did that happen, Genesis? How did you wind up in Cartagena?"

"I—" I stare at him, stunned.

"*That* was your wrong turn." He breaks off the end of his banana. "You could be in the Bahamas right now."

"How the hell did you know that?"

Sebastián just watches me, biting into the fruit.

"Nico?" My grandmother would have told him as soon as I agreed to come visit, so he could help her get the house ready. "Is he in on this?"

Sebastián shrugs. "We all play a part. Whether we know it or not."

"And my dad's part? I told you, you can't just fly a bomb into—"

"And I told *you* we don't want a plane."

"But that's the fastest—" My mouth snaps shut as I think it through. Planes are the fastest way into the United States, though airports do have a lot of security and vigilant customs inspections. "You want a ship."

His smile is grim. Like he's reluctantly proud of me. "I told Silvana you'd figure it out."

Blood rushes to my head as I fight panic. "What port?" I demand. "Where is Silvana sending her bombs?"

He gives me a bleak shrug. "What does that matter?"

"Sebastián, we can stop her." I stand straighter, and we're almost eye to eye. "I *know* this isn't what you want. You don't have to kill people to send a message."

He drops his banana peel on the ground and crosses his

arms over his chest. "You have a better idea?"

I fight through exhaustion and hunger, grasping for a clear thought. I've never felt so desperate or out of my element. "I know cash isn't what you're after, but money can do a lot of good. A *lot* of money can do even more. You could start a foundation to help disenfranchised farmers get a new start. Or establish scholarships for their kids. Or fund a series of free clinics. Or build houses for the poor." Before he died, my uncle worked for a non-profit that did all of those things.

"Those are Band-Aids for bullet wounds, Genesis. Until the US stops interfering, Colombia's problems will persist."

"Okay, then take out a bunch of ads, to educate the American public." I feel like an auctioneer, trying to sell him all the right words before time runs out. "Or back a US politician dedicated to your cause. My dad does that all the time, for issues he thinks are important."

"So, your father throws money at problems?" Sebastián's laugh is harsh and bitter. "That's no surprise."

"He's trying to help," I insist.

"He's the *problem*, Genesis!" Sebastián stands, and I push myself to my feet in front of him. "The gap between the rich and the poor is getting bigger all over the world. Wealth and entitlement create inequalities, not fix them." Anger flashes in his eyes, and I step back, distancing myself from his clenched fists.

"Is that why you killed his brother?"

Sebastián's fists release suddenly. "We need to get back."

"Tell me!" I demand. "He was my uncle. I deserve to know!"

"You . . . ?" His voice is soft, but his gaze is hard. "All *you* care about is what *you* deserve. Because you're part of the problem too."

18 HOURS EARLIER

MADDIE

"I hear another stream." Luke faces the direction of running water like a hunting dog on point. "That's our cue for a break."

"No, it's too early for lunch, and I'm not tired yet." I stand straighter to make my lie more convincing. I don't have time to be tired.

"We've been walking for three hours." Luke adjusts the straps on his pack, and his shoulders sag. "We have to take water where we can find it, Maddie."

I know he's right. And the only way we can boil water is to empty more soup cans.

I don't realize how hungry I am until I pop the top from my beef stew, and my stomach growls.

When our refilled cans are sitting on the attachable grill over the camp stove, I notice Luke watching me with a cryptic smile. "What?"

"I have a surprise."

I fake a gasp. "How could you *possibly* improve on luke-warm soup and boiling water?"

He pulls a clear plastic bag from his backpack. Clumped up in the bottom are four soft, white poufs.

"You have *marshmallows?*"

He shrugs. "This is all that's left from camping with my parents. Will it upset your glucose level?"

"Not if I just have one." Right now, I want a marshmallow so badly that I don't give one single shit about my blood sugar level. Which is easy to say, as long as I still have insulin in my pump.

Luke reaches behind the log he's sitting on and pulls out two sticks he must have trimmed while I was getting water. He impales a marshmallow on the end of each stick, and when he hands one to me, our pinkies brush.

We hold our marshmallows over the fire, and Luke's goes up in flames almost instantly. I laugh as he grins, then blows it out.

I roast mine slowly, savoring the brief break from pain, grief, and misery.

He pulls his burnt marshmallow from the stick. "Come on, we have to eat them at the same time."

"Is that a Boy Scout thing?"

"No, that's just how my parents do it. So they can share the experience." He shrugs, and for once, his cheeks don't flush. "It's just more fun that way."

I lower my marshmallow until it catches fire. He watches

me blow it out. "Ready?" I ask, and he nods. "Okay, but you have to eat the whole thing at once. That's how Ryan and I used to do it."

Luke gives me a solemn nod. Then we count to three and each shove a charred marshmallow into our mouths.

"That's the best thing I've ever tasted," he moans around a mouthful of sugar goo.

"Right?" I agree, though that might have as much to do with how he's watching me as with the sweet surprise.

His eyes close, and I watch him chew. He looks truly at ease and confident for the first time since he gave me the other half of his sandwich on the beach at Cabo.

The bag crinkles when I pick it up, and his eyes fly open. "No, we have to save them for tonight!"

"We don't even know where we'll be by then. We could be rescued. Or we could be captured. Or we could be . . ." *Dead.*

"We'll be fine, and having something to look forward to will get us through the day, even if that something is just a brick of processed sugar."

"But I *really* want that other marshmallow."

Luke eyes me suspiciously. "Give me the bag, Maddie."

Instead, I grin and deliberately tuck it behind my back. He reaches out, but I lean to block his arm. He can't take the marshmallows if he's too shy to touch me.

Luke's eyes narrow. He lunges. I squeal, and we fall onto the ground, the log shielding us from the camp stove. His elbow lands on my hair, his face inches from mine. He's cute, for a Boy Scout gamer, and the flash of heat in his eyes has nothing to do with the firelight flickering on the side of his face.

Then Luke freezes, and suddenly seems *very* aware that he's lying half on top of me, his left knee between my thighs. His chest pressed against mine.

"I'm s-sorry . . ." he stammers, lifting himself. "I didn't mean to—"

I pull him down, his hesitancy melting until our lips meet.

My eyes close and we both relax into the kiss. For a few minutes, there is no jungle. There are no kidnappers and no hostages. There are no spiders, snakes, or caimans. There is no grief, and no pain.

For a few minutes, there is only Luke and me, and the sweet, shared taste of marshmallow.

17 HOURS EARLIER

GENESIS

"Gin!" Domenica says as she lays her cards on my straw mat. I've lost four games in a row, and no one will play poker with me anymore because I won all of Domenica's breath mints and all of Rog's rolling papers. Which are no good without anything to roll.

Hiking through the jungle sucked, but boredom is its own special kind of hell.

Álvaro cranks up the radio his group is listening to at the next campfire.

"Thanks for joining us. It's eleven a.m. here in Miami . . ." Neda's voice rings out loud and clear.

I look up as Holden finally stops trying to suck Penelope's soul out through her mouth.

"This morning, we have confirmation that a small group of the missing hikers were actually out of camp on a sightseeing tour during the kidnapping. They made it out of the jungle overnight and have reported their fellow hikers missing. Among those Americans still unaccounted for are a husband and wife from Texas, four young backpackers from San Diego, and a high school dropout from Indiana. You can hear more about that on just about any news channel. Seriously, they're playing it over and over," Neda continues. "But what *we* have for you today on South Florida's Power 85 FM is an exclusive interview with the parent of one of the Miami Six, the local teens and my personal friends who were brutally kidnapped at gunpoint yesterday from a Colombian army bunkhouse. Stay tuned . . ."

Neda has found her calling, and after all the years she's spent pining for a career in modeling, I'm surprised that it's radio.

Thinking about Neda makes me miss my dad. I don't care if he's nagging me to try that disgusting protein powder his trainer got him hooked on or trying to talk me into going to his alma mater. I just want to hear his voice.

When the show comes back on the air, Neda teases the exclusive interview, then shares several short, funny stories about the Miami Six, no doubt intended to cement her personal connection to the crisis. She tells the world how Penelope can do a back tuck on a four-inch wide balance beam, but won't walk over a street grate because she's afraid it'll collapse and dump her into the sewer. How Holden handed out gourmet muffins to the poor, without mention-ing that his community service was court-ordered.

"And Genesis . . ." Neda's voice breaks with emotion, and my eyes water. "Genesis is my best friend, and if it weren't for her, I'd still be out there like everyone else, only crippled by my recent injury. She's the one who arranged for me to be airlifted out of the jungle, and . . ." Her voice cracks again, and the DJ suggests another break.

But I can't stop thinking about what she said. *Nico* is the one who got Neda out of the jungle. I just paid for her ride. Like my father, I threw money at the problem, even when the problem was one of my best friends.

Indiana takes my hand and intertwines his fingers with mine.

Neda comes back on the air, and I hold my breath as she introduces Amanda Goh. Penelope looks close to tears, and I let go of Indiana's hand to go comfort her. But then Holden puts his arm around her, and I remember that she chose him over our friendship.

"*Please* give our daughter back to us," Mrs. Goh begs over the radio, her voice half choked with tears. "We've raised just over a million dollars." Probably donated by people who remember watching Penelope Goh take Olympic silver on the uneven bars. She's an American hero, and her fans will do anything to bring her home.

Penelope presses the heels of her hands to her eyes to hold back tears. She's been doing that since she failed to place in her very first gymnastics meet, when she was six.

"One million for the little acrobat!" Silvana stands near the fire pit closest to the headquarters tent, her arms raised in victory.

Wait. I practically offered to write Sebastián a blank check, and she's ready to celebrate over a mere million?

"We'll send it wherever you want," Mrs. Goh adds. "However you want it. Just please call. Please tell us how to get Penelope back."

"*What?*" Silvana spins around with a look so furious I catch my breath.

The radio goes to another commercial break, but no one's listening anymore because Silvana is on the warpath.

She marches across the clearing, and men move out of her way. "Why doesn't she know where to send the money, Sebastián?" Silvana demands. "Why haven't you called in the ransoms?"

MADDIE

Luke holds a branch out of the path for me, but won't make eye contact. He hasn't looked directly at me or said a word since we packed up after lunch.

Since we kissed.

He seemed like he was into it, but now I'm afraid I ruined everything. I need to fix it. But I have no idea how.

"Hey." I nudge his shoulder. "What's up with you?"

Luke stiffens, and I want to take it all back. Obviously the direct approach was a mistake.

But then static crackles from the two-way radio clipped to his waist, and we both stop, frozen. Staring at each other in tense silence while we wait.

The static fades into nothing, but Luke is still looking right at me. "Why did you kiss me, Maddie?"

I'm not sure how to answer that. I've never made the first move before. I should have known better, after Benard. After Sebastián. Kissing hasn't turned out well for me so far, and I don't want to mess things up with Luke.

But he's looking at me like his whole life is riding on whatever I say next, and that's terrifying in a completely different way than having a gun pointed at my head.

"Um . . . It was a thank you. For the marshmallow. And for hiking through the jungle with me. For burying my brother. For hitting Moisés with a rock."

"That was just a thank you?" He sounds wounded. Does he want me to tell him that he's funny and sweet? That I saw him looking down at me with the stream gurgling, the fire crackling, and the birds chirping all around us, and I just wanted to touch him? That I hadn't given it any real thought?

And suddenly I understand my mistake.

"That came out wrong. It wasn't *just* a thank you."

Luke scruffs his cap over his curls and his focus drops to his feet. "You know I like you. You *have* to know that. Right?"

"I . . . yeah, I guess." I shrug. "I mean, you're here."

"Maddie, I'm here because you need help, and because combining our skill sets gives us a better chance of surviving the jungle than we'd have on our own. But you don't *owe* me anything. Especially not . . . that." His flush extends down his neck and beneath his collar. "That's not what I wanted."

"You didn't want me to kiss you?" The thought makes my throat feel raw.

"That's not what I meant." He shifts his pack on his shoulders and finally looks at me again. "I'm just saying I don't expect anything from you. I don't need any incentive to be here."

My cheeks flame and I close my eyes. Is that what he thinks I was doing? Manipulating him to keep him around? Like I'm no different than Genesis.

Is he right?

I replay the memory of our kiss, filling each ambiguous moment with self-doubt.

No. My eyes fly open. *I don't use people.*

"I'm not trying to bribe you, Luke." I swipe at my damp eyes with both hands. I can't handle any more complications right now. This is life and death. I need to focus. "If that's what you think, I don't even want you here."

"Whoa, Maddie, I never said that." Luke reaches for me, but I back away from him. "I just don't want you to kiss me unless you mean it. And you don't mean it."

"Don't put words in my mouth! You don't know what I mean!" *I don't even know what I mean.* "All I know is that everything was miserable. Then you gave me a marshmallow and made me laugh, and everything was a little less miserable." I swipe both hands over my face again, hoping he won't notice how damp my eyes are. "But you're right. Everything is *really* hard right now, and I shouldn't have complicated that by kissing you." I turn and continue down the trail. "Don't worry. It won't happen again."

"That's not what I . . ." Luke sounds like I just punched him, and the blow hurts me too.

"Look, let's just forget it ever happened, okay?" I say as he jogs to catch up with me. "I never kissed you."

His hurt expression hardens into anger. "Good. Because I never wanted you to."

I push guilt to the back of my mind. He doesn't mean that, but he *should* mean it. If I've learned anything from Genesis, it's that anger is much more productive than pain.

16.5 HOURS EARLIER

GENESIS

"Sebastián?" Silvana demands. "Start talking."

The entire base camp goes still. Óscar turns off the radio, leaving nothing to fill the silence but croaks and hoots from the jungle, and I swallow my disappointment. I'm *desperate* for news from Miami as my father's deadline draws closer.

"I don't answer to you," Sebastián says, and we all turn to watch the tense volley of power. "When my boss tells me to make the demands, I'll make the demands."

"No money, no distribution channel," Silvana growls. "That was the deal."

"And maybe it still would be, if you actually *had* a distribution channel." Sebastián points in my direction without looking at me. "So far all you have is one-third of the leverage that was supposed to make Hernán Valencia cooperate."

"She's plenty," Silvana snaps. "Hernán still has three and a half hours, and he *will* respond by the deadline. And so would the others, if you'd called in the ransoms. Wainwright *alone* is worth a fortune! Make the calls, Sebastián."

Sebastián shrugs. "You can tell Moreno that he doesn't get his money until Hernán agrees—"

"*¡Cállate!*" Silvana cuts him off with a glance at me. But finding out she works for Gael Moreno, head of the infamous Moreno cartel, is no real surprise.

The part I can't quite wrap my head around is that Silvana and her boss aren't behind the plan to ship bombs to the United States. They're just in this for money.

The bombs are all Sebastián.

16 HOURS EARLIER

MADDIE

"Hey, Tim, what's your ETA?" a staticky voice calls from the two-way radio clipped to Luke's waistband.

I freeze, clutching a thin branch to help keep myself from sliding downhill. Luke goes still on my right, his eyes wide.

We're so close to the beach we can hear the waves crash over the shore.

"They can't hear us if we don't push the button, right?" I whisper.

"Right." His voice is so soft I can hardly hear him. He hasn't come within two feet of me since our fight, and I don't know how to safely breach the gulf between us. Or even if I should. "But if they're close enough for us to pick up their signal through the dense vegetation, they might be able to hear us stomping around out here. Depending upon the range."

I let go of the branch with exaggerated caution, just in case.

"I'm about half an hour out," Tim replies through the static and there's something about his voice.

"I don't think they're the kidnappers," I say, and Luke shushes me with one finger pressed against his lips. "They sound American. Maybe they can help us."

Luke pulls the radio from his belt. His thumb hovers over the button on the side. "Should I say something?"

I stare at the radio, frozen in fear. They might be dangerous even if they're not with the kidnappers. But they might end up saving our lives.

"They could move out of range any second," Luke reminds me.

Finally I nod. "Say something."

Luke brings the radio up to his mouth.

"Have you guys seen Moisés?" that first staticky voice asks.

Adrenaline shoots through me. I snatch the radio from Luke's hand before his thumb can press the button. He stares at me, surprised. "What—?"

"They're working for Silvana and Sebastián," I whisper.

He frowns. "But they sound American."

"I know," I murmur. Why would Americans be mixed up in a kidnapping in the middle of the Colombian jungle?

"Haven't seen him since yesterday morning," the other voice calls over the radio. "Why?"

"Silvana sent him on an errand yesterday, and he never came back."

"Silvana's thugs are her own problem," Tim says. "I'll be there as soon as I can."

The radio goes silent.

I stare at Luke. "What the *hell* is going on out here?"

15·25 HOURS EARLIER

GENESIS

A long, slim afternoon shadow falls over me, and I look up
to find Silvana heading my way with a folding metal chair
under one arm. In her free hand, she carries a half-empty
bottle of *aguardiente* and a plastic shot glass.

She unfolds the chair next to my stump and takes a seat.
"Okay, *princesa*." She pours a shot, then sets the bottle on
the ground between her feet. "You and I are going to have a
nice, civilized chat."

"Stop calling me that."

"*¿Por qué?*" She offers me the shot, and when I shake
my head, she drinks it herself, then follows it with a swig of
water. "Only your *papi* can call you *princesa*?"

I hold her gaze. Like any predator, if she sees weakness,
she will pounce. "How do you know my dad?"

"We go *way* back. Professionally and personally." Her
raised brows imply things I don't even want to think about.

"You're lying." My dad recognized her on the phone, but
that doesn't mean they were ever *involved*.

Silvana turns sideways in her chair to face me, one arm stretched out over the metal back. "He takes his coffee with cardamom and *canela*, like his *mami* always made it. He sleeps in satin boxers. And he's a very generous man, when he's happy." She leans forward, eyeing me in the flicker of the nearest fire pit, and cruelty shines in her dark eyes. She's tuned in to my pain like a dog on the scent of prey. "I know how to make him very, very happy."

A sour lump rises in my throat. I'm going to be sick.

Silvana pours another shot and holds it out to me. "Change your mind?"

I take the glass, and she laughs when I throw it back in a single gulp. "What do you want?"

"I want you to convince your *papi* that resuming our business relationship will be beneficial for everyone involved. Particularly for *you*."

"*Resuming?*" I want to call her a liar again, but she wouldn't be so confident in her verbal arsenal if she were shooting blanks.

Yet I know better than anyone that the truth can be twisted. Their business dealings could have been perfectly innocent.

"Until nine months ago, your father shipped our product all over the world."

"Your product?" I stare at Silvana, waiting for the punch line.

"Snow." She frowns. "You know—dust. Blow. *Cocaína*."

I roll my eyes. "I know what it is. I just don't believe you."

I have no illusion that my father is a saint. In international shipping, as in any business, palms have to be greased and sometimes votes have to be bought. But there are lines he would never cross. "My dad would *never* work with you or with Gael Moreno." I stand and grab my bag.

"Oh, *niña*. Do you *truly* believe your father built a multi-*billion* dollar shipping company in under two decades because he's a brilliant businessman? Or because he poured his heart and soul into the company? What he poured into Genesis Shipping is *drug money*. We gave him the means to expand early in his career. To invest in advancements. To buy out competitors. We did that because he knows who to pay off in customs and how to take the product off our narco subs and load it onto his ships in the middle of the gulf, without being seen. I laughed when you were born, and he renamed his dirty empire!" Her smile is a bitter parody of joy, mocking my pain. "Genesis Shipping is a tribute to his only child. The one thing in the world that he loves more than the company itself."

Numb, I shake my head. "Bullshit. My father worked for everything he has. He *deserves* all of it." Everything he's given me.

"Yes, he works *very* hard, *niña*." Silvana's laughter bruises me all the way into my soul. "Until nine months ago, your father was the most successful drug trafficker in the world."

MADDIE

I stare through the tree line, so relieved to see the crystalline Caribbean coast that I can practically taste the salt water. I want to fall to my knees in the sand, but we can't just stroll down the beach like tourists. We have to follow the shore from the cover of the jungle so we'll see anyone on the beach before they see us.

Because we're within radio range of Silvana's men.

As we pick our way through yet more dense vegetation, I have to bite my tongue to keep from channeling Neda.

The beach is *right there*. My legs ache for the faster, easier pace of packed sand. My gaze keeps sliding back to the rifle. If I could think of a plausible excuse to take it from Luke, I would.

I need to be ready the moment we find Julian.

Luke pulls his cell phone from his pocket and angles it toward the beach. I check the screen. Still no signal.

"Hey, Shawn?" Tim's voice calls over the radio, and Luke and I freeze in a thick patch of undergrowth. "I'm not going to make it back in time to help load the subs."

"Subs?" I mouth silently to Luke.

He shrugs, staring at the radio. He still hardly looks at me.

"Got it." Shawn's response is shot through with static. "We'll . . . without you. Hey, have . . . from Moisés yet? Silvana's furious."

"Not a word." The signal from Tim is much stronger.

Shawn unleashes a static-riddled stream of curses, but Luke and I share a relieved smile.

"What's going on over there?" Tim asks.

". . . lost two of the VIPs," Shawn says. "The boy's confirmed KIA . . . sister . . . off a cliff . . . hasn't washed up yet. Moisés . . . off the grid too."

Luke frowns. "Moisés must have managed to untie himself."

"Then why don't they know where he is?" I shake my head, though the answer seems obvious. He's afraid to go back to Silvana until he catches us. Or they haven't yet looked for him at the bunkhouse.

"The static means Shawn's farther away, right?" I whisper, and Luke nods.

"So they're down to one VIP?" Tim whistles over the static. "God help us all when the boss finds out."

In the silence that follows, Luke looks up from the radio to stare at me in astonished confusion. "You're a VIP."

Well, *that's* a first. "Let me know if you find the velvet rope section of the jungle."

"What do you think it means?" he asks as we continue

on a covered path parallel to the beach, and I'm so glad he's talking to me after hours of near silence that I don't even care how morbid the topic is.

"They were probably hoping for triple the ransom from my uncle, for me, Ryan, and Genesis. But why would they care about finding my body?"

"Maybe they think your uncle will pay to get it back," Luke says softly. "You know. For a proper burial."

The bastards want to ransom my corpse. Does that mean they plan to dig my brother up?

My eyes close as the horrific scene plays out in my head.

I *won't* let that happen.

I open my eyes, fresh fury burning in my gut. I failed Ryan in life, but I will *damn well* have his back now.

14 HOURS EARLIER

GENESIS

Silvana's heartless laughter drowns out everything but the roar of my pulse in my ears.

Across the clearing, Indiana stands. He can see that something is wrong, but I shake my head, telling him to stay back. I don't want him to hear any of this.

Drug trafficker.

My father quit working for Moreno nine months ago.

Uncle David died nine months ago.

There are no coincidences.

My voice is an angry whisper. "Did my dad stop working for you because you killed his brother, or was it the other way around?"

"Brother . . . ?" Silvana laughs again, but this time the humor doesn't reach her eyes. She's not going to answer my question. No one wants to talk about what happened to my uncle.

"Sit, *princesa*." She pulls me down onto the stump again, and my bag hits the dirt at my feet. "You want to talk to your daddy? *Vale*, I'm going to give you ten seconds to convince your father to ship Sebastián's product," she says as she takes the clunky satellite phone from her pocket.

Her watch reads two thirty. My dad still has thirty minutes left until the deadline, but she clearly thinks he needs a nudge.

I swallow the lump in my throat. "I'm not going to ask him to help you kill people. That's not going to solve the world's problems."

Silvana grabs my chin, and I pretend her grip doesn't hurt. "Don't mistake me for one of Sebastián's bleeding hearts, *niña*. I don't give a shit about Colombia's problems. I'm here to collect ransoms and secure distribution, so you can talk your father into cooperating, or we can let him listen over the phone while Álvaro takes you apart piece by piece."

She lets me go, and my focus strays to Álvaro, who's sharpening his machete with a large rock.

The stump I'm sitting on suddenly feels unsteady. All I can hear is the metallic scrape of that rock across Álvaro's blade. All I can see is sunlight glinting off the sharp edge.

I fight to slow my breathing and when I tear my gaze from the machete, it's drawn to Indiana. He's leaning against a tree on the edge of the clearing, watching me. Ready to step in at the first sign that I need help, in spite of the personal risk.

If I tell my dad not to help Sebastián, I'll be sacrificing

Indiana and all the other hostages, along with myself. I have no right to do that. I don't *want* to do that. But I can't—

Silvana autodials a number, and my heart races while the phone rings. Once. Twice. "If you try to tell your *papi* where you are, I *will* slit your boyfriend's throat right in front of you."

"Hello?" my father says, and a sob explodes from my throat. "Silvana?"

She hands me the phone, and I grip it like a drowning man clutching a life raft. *"Papi?"*

"Genesis." He sounds so relieved. "Are you okay? Have they hurt you?"

"I . . ." The words freeze on my tongue.

"Listen, *princesa*, don't talk to them. Don't listen to them. Don't even look at them. Just sit tight and be smart. I'm going to get you out—"

"Don't do it, Dad." I swallow a sob and clear my throat. Then I suck in another breath and say the worst thing I've ever said to my father. The only thing that will work. "If you help them hurt those people, *I swear to God*, I'll slit my own throat right here in the jungle."

Silvana snatches the phone from me and slaps me across the face so hard that I land on the ground, two feet from the stump I was sitting on.

"Genesis!" my father shouts over the line.

Indiana lurches into motion, then freezes when Silvana

points her pistol at him. But his focus stays glued to me.

"We both know your *princesa* won't do that," she spits into the phone as I bring my hand to my burning left cheek. "Álvaro's here, Hernán, and he's *itching* to show Genesis what you've been shielding her from, up in that ivory tower."

This is why my father is so paranoid and protective. This is why I had to take Krav Maga and learn to shoot. This is why he wouldn't let me come to Colombia.

Why my uncle was murdered. Why I was kidnapped. Why Ryan was shot.

And my mom . . . ?

I hear a thud, and my mother makes a strange sound. A hurting sound. Tears leak from the corners of my closed eyes. There's another thud, and she gasps. My whole body shakes.

The thuds go on, and she stops making noises. But I keep my eyes squeezed shut.

I am a good girl.

"This is your daddy's fault," the man says as his footsteps thump closer.

My father shouts from the other end of the line, making threats I can't understand, with my heart hammering in my ears.

"I'm going to give you one more chance," Silvana says into the phone. "If I don't hear from you by midnight with the coordinates of your closest ship, you know what we'll do to her, Hernán." Silvana hangs the phone up and slides it into her pocket.

My father's furious shouting echoes in my head as she picks up her bottle and leaves me shaking on the ground, in the ruins of the delusion I've been living my whole life.

13.5 HOURS EARLIER

MADDIE

Another burst of static comes from the radio. "Hey, Shawn, can I get confirmation—"

I grab Luke's hand as more audio fuzz swallows the rest. "That's Julian." Chills run up my spine. I'll *never* forget his voice. "The man who shot Ryan."

Luke's hand goes stiff, and I swallow my disappointment. He still doesn't trust me. But then his fingers intertwine with mine, and I give his palm a grateful squeeze.

The minute I really need him, there he is.

"Um, just a sec . . ." Shawn's voice fades into more static while Luke and I stare at the radio. ". . . grab the list." The radio goes silent for a minute, then the static comes back. "Okay, I . . . Angeles, Chicago, DC, Memphis . . . York, and Miami. Did you get all those?"

"*Sí*," Julian says. "And Langley, Virginia."

"No, man, Sebastián said the boss scratched Langley from the list last week."

"Silvana . . . *very* clear," Julian insists, his accent thick and harsh with anger. "No Langley, no deal. You do *not* . . . anger Moreno."

"Okay . . . talk to Sebastián . . . get back to you," Shawn says, and the static ends.

I squeeze Luke's hand again, then let it go. "We are in *way* over our heads."

Luke nods. "Yeah, that's about the only part I understood."

"It sounds like Silvana works for the Moreno cartel. What's left of it, anyway." The Morenos were big news during a rash of drug raids a couple of years ago. "And whoever Sebastián's boss is, he isn't afraid to piss the cartel off."

"The cartel? So is this about cocaine?" Luke frowns. "The cities—are they some kind of distribution network?"

"But Langley?" My heart thuds in my ear while I try to figure out what's going on.

"Maybe CIA agents like to party hard."

"I don't know," I tell him. The only thing I'm sure of is that this is much bigger than what's happened to Genesis, Ryan, and me.

11 HOURS EARLIER

GENESIS

"He hasn't called." My foot won't stop bouncing. I grab Indiana's wrist and glance at his watch. "It's been three hours. He's not going to call." I'm not sure what I want my father to say, but I'm sure I want to hear from him.

Indiana scoots closer on the log and takes my hand. "He's going to call."

On the other side of our fire pit Penelope is running her fingers through Holden's blond waves while he naps with his head in her lap. Domenica and Rog are immersed in a game of chess on a set that's missing two pawns.

They have no idea what Silvana told my father. Or that the call I'm waiting on could get them killed.

Across the clearing, Óscar starts passing out soup cans and MREs to our captors for dinner.

I'm *so* tired. I want to lean on Indiana's shoulder, but I can't afford to look vulnerable. "I shouldn't have told him I'd kill myself. Now he thinks he'll lose me no matter what he does."

Indiana lets go of my hand and slides his arm around my waist. "There's no way your dad believes you'll really do it," he says into my hair.

"He does," I insist. "A Valencia never bluffs."

Indiana leans back and studies my eyes. "That's not true. I lost two sticks of gum and my last clean shirt playing poker with you this afternoon."

"Poker doesn't count." But I'm smiling now, and that seems to make him happy.

"Aren't they going to give us anything to eat?" Penelope asks.

I turn to see that Óscar is eating his dinner. The hostages were not served.

"Genesis," Sebastián calls from across his fire pit, and I tense at the sound of my own name. "*Ven acá.*"

I stand, and Indiana stands with me, so close I can't see anyone else. "You don't have to go. You could just stay here." He slides one hand into my hair and his lips brush my cheek. "With me."

I want to kiss him, and I don't care who's watching. But Sebastián was right—he's calling plenty of shots. "I'll be right back." I can feel everyone watching as I cross the base camp. Domenica and Penelope look curious, but Holden's glare feels like a knife in my back.

Sebastián and his men sit on logs and handmade stools, but he gestures for me to sit on the mat at his feet. "Are you hungry?" he asks as he scoops up a bite of canned ravioli.

Lunch was six hours ago, so of course I'm starving. But I

know better than to admit it.

"You can eat as soon as you get your dad to cooperate." He takes a bite and speaks around it. "Time's running out."

"I'm not going to ask my dad to help you *kill* people. Why are you doing this? I thought you wanted to make things better!"

"We *are* making things better. The world is no different than a gangrenous limb, Genesis. You have to cut out the rot to save healthy flesh." Sebastián glances at Silvana. "She's telling the truth. Your father is not the man you think he is."

"He's the rot," the American to his left says.

"Shawn," Sebastián snaps. But the American only shrugs.

"My dad never forced anyone to get high." I'm clinging to that certainty because I don't know how else to defend my father. I don't even know if I should. "People make their own choices and pay for their own mistakes."

Shawn looks disappointed. "The apple and the tree. She's going to take root *right under him.*"

My face burns. "And where are *you* taking root?" I demand. "How is blowing people up any better than shipping cocaine?"

Fervor burns in Shawn's eyes like some kind of mania. "The American sense of entitlement and ruthless capitalist agenda has preyed upon the disenfranchised—both here and in the States—for *decades*. We're going to destroy our country's symbols of greed and excess. We're going to open peoples' *eyes!*"

I turn away in disgust, but Sebastián grabs my arm.

"You don't recognize the problem because it's been staring at you *en el espejo* every day of your life. But just because you can't see it doesn't mean it isn't there. You *reek* of waste and destruction."

I pull free, but he's still talking. "You may not be hungry, but your friends are. *None* of you eat until you convince your dad to cooperate."

"It's seven hours until the deadline," I remind him. "I think they'll survive."

"Make sure they know why they're going hungry, *princesa!*" Silvana shouts as I return to the hostages' fire pit.

"What does that mean?" Holden demands, but I march right past him. They're not truly trying to starve us; they're trying to manipulate me with social pressure. "What did you do this time?"

"Nothing." I sink onto the log next to Indiana again, and I can feel Holden glaring at me, but I block him out. "They're not going to feed us until I talk my dad into cooperating," I whisper.

"No one can blame you for that," he insists. "Just tell them what's going on. It's not like anyone *wants* terrorists to set off bombs in the States."

But it doesn't seem fair to tell them that I've already chosen the lives of hundreds of strangers over theirs. Over all of ours.

"Holden doesn't consider anyone else's well-being his responsibility, and right now Penelope would follow him off a high dive into a pool full of venomous snakes if he so much as smiled at her."

Indiana gives me a crooked smile. "So all we have to do is convince everyone that we're actually on a hunger strike."

"And that it was Holden's idea," I add with a laugh.

10.5 HOURS EARLIER

MADDIE

"One rifle and five shells won't be much of a threat to a drug cartel, but in case you have to pick this up, you need to know how to use it. They'll know right away if you don't."

I study the rifle as Luke ejects the chambered round. "Don't I just take aim and pull the trigger?"

"Kind of." He bends to pick up the ejected bullet. "This is like the one I learned on, except it has an automatic and a semiautomatic mode. I've switched it to single fire, because—again—we only have five bullets."

I take the rifle from him, and it's heavier than I expected. I thought it would make me feel strong, but it makes me feel small and awkward. "How do I hold it?"

"Like this." Luke positions the back of the stock against my shoulder, then guides my left hand to cup the grip around the back of the rifle's long barrel. "This is called the handgrip."

When he moves into place behind me, his chest brushes my back, and I want to lean into him. To just . . . close the space between us and let that gesture say the things I don't know how to tell him. Because I can't trust my mouth not to mess this up again.

"It's unloaded, but you should get in the habit of keeping your finger off the trigger unless you're ready to fire," he says, and I can feel his breath on my neck. "Now aim at that tree."

"That one?" I let go of the handgrip to point, and Luke guides my hand back into place. He's confident with the rifle. His hands are steady.

"Yes. Keep both hands on the gun." He lifts it a little higher against my shoulder, and he's pressed so closely against me now that I can feel every breath he takes. "Now line up the rear sight and the front sight and make sure they're right over what you want to shoot."

"What do I want to shoot?"

"See that knothole?" His breath brushes my ear, and I nod, afraid that if I speak, everything I'm thinking will fall out. I need this lesson. This gun and those five shells are the only chance I'll get to avenge Ryan. But the closer I get to Luke, the less I want to drag him into this.

Luke readjusts my grip on the rifle, and his hip presses against mine. He lifts the barrel a little higher, and a cord of muscle stands out from his arm. I blink and force my focus back to the tree.

"Line the sights up and squeeze the trigger. Gently."

I squeeze. The trigger clicks. Luke pushes the rifle up by the barrel and shoves the stock into my shoulder.

"Hey!" Startled, I drop the gun.

Luke catches it with one hand.

"What was that for?" All thoughts of kissing him are gone.

"I was simulating kickback," Luke says. "For an authentic experience. The first time you fire a rifle, it might knock you back a couple of steps, if your stance isn't right. You have to be prepared. Which does *not* include dropping the gun."

"Well, you could have warned me!"

"Sorry." He tries to hide a grin.

"What's so funny?"

"You just looked so surprised."

It's hard to be anything but tired and terrified, knowing that the Moreno cartel is involved in my cousin's kidnapping and my brother's murder, but Luke's smile is contagious. And he's finally stopped putting distance between us.

"Are you ready?" he asks, still grinning.

"Yeah."

Luke picks up my backpack and hands it to me. "Let's do it." His face flushes over the accidental innuendo. "That's not what I meant," he says, and I can't stifle a laugh.

I like that I don't have to wonder what he's thinking or feeling. He isn't playing games. He isn't trying to get me drunk. He isn't hiding a beautiful French girlfriend.

He isn't hiding *anything*. Every thought he has falls right out of his mouth, and that's actually kind of refreshing. And funny.

With a warm jolt of surprise, I realize I *really* want to kiss Luke again.

10 HOURS EARLIER

GENESIS

Across the fire pit, Holden is whispering with Penelope, Domenica, and Rog. I can only hear every other word, but that's more than enough to lift the mystery from his escape plan.

Wait until everyone's asleep. Disable the guards on duty. Run.

His plan is disastrously simplistic and dangerous, but I can't blame them for considering it. We have to do *something*. And my plan has failed.

"He's going to get them killed," Indiana says as he sinks onto the mat next to me and hands me a bottle of water.

"I don't know." I unscrew the lid and drink until my stomach feels a little less empty. "Maybe Holden's onto something."

"No," Indiana says. "He's not."

I set the bottle down and turn to face him fully. "Silvana is going to let Álvaro chop me into pieces so my dad can hear me scream over the phone," I tell him.

Indiana's jaw clenches. He takes my hand. "Genesis, I won't—"

"You can't stop it. And my dad won't be able to stand it. He'll cave, and a lot of people will die. Then he'll go to prison. But if I run, Silvana will have no way to convince my dad to cooperate."

"Holden's plan doesn't sound any smarter when it comes out of your mouth, G." He rubs my knuckle with his thumb. "We won't all make it out of here if we try to run, and the terrorists will still have their bombs. They *will* find another way into the US. If you run, you'll only be delaying the inevitable."

"Damn it." I give him a small shove, but his chest is tantalizingly unyielding. "Why do you have to poke holes in my plan?"

He laughs. "It's Holden's plan, and you were never going to go through with it."

"How do you know that?"

Indiana leans in, and I'm caught in his hazel gaze. "I know because you are the moon, not the tide." His lips brush the corner of my mouth with each syllable, and anticipation blazes through me. I've never wanted anything in my life like I want to kiss him. "You don't roll with the flow, Genesis, you *create the current*. And Holden is nothing but a boat bobbing on the waves."

Indiana takes my hand. His lips meet mine, and his other hand slides into my hair. His tongue traces my lower lip. I groan and my arms wind around his neck.

His kiss trails along my jaw toward my ear, and I let my head fall back. "Why did you wait so long?" I whisper.

"Because you should never rush a good thing," he murmurs against my skin. "And no matter what is going on around us, this is a *very* good thing."

9.5 HOURS EARLIER

MADDIE

The radio spits static again, and this time we hardly glance at it. It's been doing that for the past couple of hours, and though the indication of how close we must be to Silvana's base camp was exhilarating at first, now it's a terrifying and exhausting reminder of just how dangerous my quest for revenge really is.

We could both die tomorrow.

"Hey, Maddie," Luke calls as he comes back from the stream with fresh water. "I have a surprise, while we wait for this to boil."

Luke takes Moisés's knife and splits two bananas along the inner curve, still in their peel. He sets each one on the grill, then pries the fruit open and stuffs them with bits torn from our last two giant marshmallows.

Then he pulls a quarter of a bar of milk chocolate from his backpack. The label reads, "Godiva."

"You have *chocolate*?" I stare at the candy as if it were

a mirage sure to disappear any second. "Where did you get that?"

"I found it in a tent when I was searching for supplies, before you got back to the bunkhouse."

I smack him on the shoulder. "Why didn't you tell me?"

"You can't eat much of it anyway, so I was saving it for a special occasion." He unfolds the wrapper and begins breaking the bar into chunks, which he wedges between the halves of both bananas, alternating with the bits of marshmallow. "My mom calls these banana s'mores. My dad calls them bonfire banana boats." He shrugs. "I just eat them."

Luke pushes more twigs into the camp stove, then sits back and smiles at me. "You're supposed to set them in cradles made of aluminum foil, but we make do with what we have."

Within minutes, the banana peels blacken. The chocolate is shiny and melted, and the marshmallow bits are gooey. The aroma is *amazing*.

Luke carefully pulls the banana boats from the grill, touching only the ends, and balances each on top of one of our empty cans, since we have no plates. We blow on them to help them cool. "Normally, we would scoop out bites with plastic spoons, but since we have no actual utensils . . ." He shrugs and pulls Moisés's multi-tool from his pocket. "We'll have to make do with this." He flips out one of the tools and shows me a shallow metal spoon.

I frown. "That would have come in handy for our soup."

"Yeah, but I forgot I had it."

We take turns eating, blowing on each steaming spoon-ful, and when we get down to the last bite, I scoop it up and feed it to him.

Luke looks at me as if I've just offered him the entire world. He smiles, and I'm mesmerized by a smear of choco-late on his lower lip.

I lean toward him, and his mouth opens. "Dibs on the last of the chocolate," I whisper as I wipe the smear away. Then I suck my thumb clean.

Luke's groan follows me as I head back to the stream for more water.

GENESIS

"I don't know what to do," I admit as the crackling fire pit sends sparks up into the night, and the confession feels even more disappointing knowing that Indiana thinks of me as the moon. As a force of nature capable of bending the entire world to my will.

I haven't felt so frustrated and powerless since I was a kid.

Since the night my mother died.

Indiana threads his fingers between mine and kisses my knuckles.

Under normal circumstances, I'd call a campfire and a beautiful boy I actually like the perfect spring break combination. Even if Holden does shoot bitter glances at us every time Penelope looks away. But the fact that we're sitting twenty feet from a dozen terrorists and a tent full of bombs paints somewhat of a bleak filter over an otherwise exquisite moment.

"There's a way out of this," Indiana insists. "We just haven't thought of it yet."

"You're right about running. The problem isn't that they have me, it's that they have explosives," I whisper with a glance at the green tent. *"That's* what we need to take away from them. No explosives, no terrorism, right?" My hand tightens around his as the solution finally becomes clear. "I have to detonate the bombs."

Indiana shakes his head. "G, that's suicide. Even if you survive the explosion, they'll kill you."

I exhale slowly. Then I scoot closer to whisper. "What are the alternatives?" Other than following through on my threat to my father. "I'm going to die either way. At least this way, I'll have taken their arsenal with me."

"Genesis . . ." Indiana whispers, and for the first time since he saw me kneel on the edge of that cliff, I see fear in his eyes.

Fear for me.

"This is the only way we can stop them."

Finally he leans closer until his cheek brushes mine, and that ghost of a touch makes me shiver. "I'm in."

I pull back until I can see his eyes, and I wish we were anywhere else in the world. I wish I'd dumped Holden on the beach in Tayrona, and never followed Nico into the jungle, but the thing I can't wish, even now, is that I'd never come to Colombia.

If I hadn't come to Colombia, I would never have met Indiana.

If I hadn't come, Silvana might have used my grandmother as a pawn against my father.

Indiana leans in for a kiss, then whispers into my ear, "I knew the moment I saw you dancing on the beach that you would light up the night. I just didn't think you'd take that so literally." He pulls back and holds my gaze. "But what the hell? At least we'll go out with a bang."

But the thought of him dying because he followed me into the jungle makes me feel like Álvaro is already cutting me open.

"You . . ." I slide one hand behind his neck and pull him close for another kiss. "I need you to take advantage of the explosion to get everyone else out of here."

"G, this is a two-pronged operation. They've moved some of their stuff to the beach, but the rest of it is in that tent." He runs his hand over my shoulder and down my arm. "Even the moon can't be two places at once. You need help."

"I'm not going to let you—"

Indiana swallows my argument with a kiss. "This isn't your call, G." Another kiss. "I make my own decisions."

"You're supposed to make out when you're *done* arguing," I whisper against his earlobe.

"We are done arguing." He drops a series of kisses along my jaw until he finds my mouth again. "You lost."

I *never* lose. But I know when to change tactics.

"Okay," I say when we're both breathing heavily. "We'll have to do it tonight, before my dad calls back. But we have to get into that tent first. We need to know what kind of explosives we're dealing with."

And while he works on that obstacle to our plan, I'll figure out how to keep him out of the line of fire. . . .

9 HOURS EARLIER

MADDIE

I lift my foot, and the wet earth beneath me makes a sucking sound. "It's too wet to sleep on the ground."

Since we stopped for water—and banana boats—the beach has gradually narrowed until patches of sand alternate with a scraggly, marshy coastline that reminds me of the swamps of Southern Florida.

"I know," Luke says. "We're going to have to sleep in one of these trees."

"*In* a tree?" I look up, but none of the branches are tangled or close together enough to hold one sleeping human, much less two.

"Well, hanging from the tree, at least." He puts his rifle on the ground and begins unbuckling a bundle I'd assumed was a second sleeping bag, which we couldn't fit in our one-man tent.

The material is actually a bright blue hammock.

"Should I be worried about snakes, or some other arboreal predator up there?"

"I don't think so. This'll be like a tent, just in a tree, and we've slept together with no—" He chokes on his own words, and I try to hide my laugh. "I mean . . . Not that we've slept together. We've just slept in close proximity. Together. Damn it."

I laugh harder, and he tosses his hands into the air, giving up.

"Excuse me while I stick my head in the ocean and take a deep breath."

"You better not. We're in this together."

Luke's smile is the brightest thing I've seen since the sun went down.

I hold the flashlight while he ties each end of the hammock to a different thick branch. Then I watch, fascinated, while he saws small branches from the same tree with Moisés's multi-tool, leaving two-inch "hooks" from which to hang our backpacks.

I climb into the hammock and Luke climbs in after me, then pulls a sheet of mosquito netting over us. We can see through it, of course—what little there is to see in the dark— but the netting feels like a boundary between us and the rest of the jungle.

We are alone, suspended in our cocoon.

The curve of the hammock rolls us toward the center, gravity closing the distance between us, so I settle into the arc of Luke's arm with my head on his shoulder and my arm over his chest. I can feel his heartbeat through his shirt.

Every breath he takes makes me more aware of how much of him I'm touching.

How much of him is touching me.

"Luke?" I whisper, because I'm right next to his ear, and the dark seems made for soft voices.

"Yeah?"

I prop myself up on my elbow so I can kind of see his face in the dark. "I'm going to kiss you, but I don't want to imply gratitude of any kind. This will be an ungrateful kiss. The most thankless of kisses. Purely recreational. Okay?"

"That's quite a disclaimer," he says, and I can hear the smile in his voice. "Do I need to sign something?"

"Shut up." I lean down and kiss him. Just a touch of my mouth to his, until I know—

Luke kisses me back, and his moan sends a warm ache through me.

He rises onto one elbow and slides his other hand down my back. We're both breathing hard, and suddenly the one-man hammock seems built for two after all.

"Hey, Maddie?" Luke says against my cheek.

"If you ask me how many experience points I think that kiss was worth, I'm going to knock out all your hit points with one blow," I warn him.

Luke laughs, and his hand trails down my hair and over my back. "I was just going to ask if you want to do that again."

I really, really do.

7 HOURS EARLIER

GENESIS

Around nine p.m.—three hours before the deadline—I look up from the chessboard to see Silvana, Sebastián, and one of the American guys who spends most of his time in the green tent head down the footpath toward the beach, from which we'd been hearing odd metallic pounding sounds for the past hour. They each carried a flashlight and a closed cardboard box. The five captors who haven't gone down to the beach will be leaderless for at least the next half hour, by my guess, based on previous trips.

This is my best chance to sneak into the green tent.

"Hey," I lean over the board and whisper to Indiana. "I need you to get the guards' attention while I slip into the tent. And I'll need a heads-up, if anyone else tries to go in."

He glances around the clearing, then gives me a heated smile. "I'd rather sneak in there with you. But I've got you covered."

I move to the fire pit closest to the military tent and pretend to be gathering empty containers. Indiana heads toward one of the open-sided tents across the campsite, and casually lifts Óscar's guitar from the tent pole where he hangs it to keep it out of the rain. Indiana sits on a stump with the guitar, and when he plays the first chord, I'm so surprised by his obvious skill that I almost forget why he's playing in the first place.

"¡Alto!" Óscar shouts.

Indiana plays a few chords. Everyone turns to look, including the guards. Then he starts singing.

His voice is clear, mellow, captivating.

Almost reluctantly, I take four slow, quiet steps to my left and slide through the entrance into the military tent. I have no idea how long they'll let him play, so I assume I'll have no more than a minute before I'm missed.

It takes the first five seconds for my eyes to adjust to the lower light level.

I scan the two closest folding tables, where scraps of wire, rolls of electrical tape, and the guts of some electronic device I can't identify are spread out. Definitely bomb-making materials.

A third table stands at the rear of the tent, and I search the ground and every surface I pass as I make my way back, adrenaline firing in my veins.

Then the table comes into focus. Two rows of cell phones stand upright, like toy soldiers lined up for battle.

I lean forward for a closer look and see that each one is taped to a small, square package, connected to the phone with thin wires.

My heart racing, I pick one up, and am surprised by how much it weighs. The package on the back is soft, like clay, and the words stamped on its paper wrapper read, "C-4 High Explosive."

I've seen enough action movies to know what C-4 is and to understand that they're using the cell phones as triggers. One call to the phone will detonate the C-4 it's strapped to. But . . .

No.

I squint in the dark for a closer look at the phone in my hand. The screen is cracked in the corner, *just like Maddie's.* I bend to look at the others. Second from the left, a block of C-4 is taped to a phone still in the purple designer case I gave Penelope for her birthday.

The terrorists have turned *our* cell phones into bombs.

My palm slick with sweat, I carefully set Maddie's phone back on the table. Each improvised device is no taller or wider than the phone it's taped to, and no more than two inches thick.

In the movies, a brick of C-4 that size will blow open a safe. It *might* demolish a whole room. These bombs won't teach the United States much of a lesson.

And even if they would, there's no reason they need to be assembled in the jungle and not on US soil.

A piece of this puzzle is missing.

"*¡Baja eso!*"

Outside, Óscar shouts in Spanish for Indiana to put down the guitar.

"*No hablo español,*" Indiana replies. The he starts singing again to a chorus of laughter. But I know his time is up, and so is mine.

I scan the rows of phones until I find mine, then carefully tuck it into the waistband of my shorts. I'm not sure what I'm going to do with it yet, but I am *not* letting them use my phone to kill people.

"*Put it down!*" Óscar shouts from outside, and I flinch so hard the bomb falls from my waistband onto the floor. My heart jumps into my throat.

I'm about to be blown up by my own cell phone.

But nothing happens. C-4 must be very stable.

Pulse racing, I pick up the bomb and slide it deeper into my waistband this time. On my way back to the tent entrance, I notice a box of phones that haven't been made into bombs, and suddenly I understand how the explosives are supposed to work. The unaltered phones will be used to call the bomb-phones, which will trigger the explosion.

Holden's is on top of the pile. The Eminem quote on the back of the case is a dead giveaway.

I snatch it and slide it into my pocket.

I peek between the tent flaps to make sure no one's watching before I rejoin the other hostages.

When he sees me emerge from the tent, Indiana stands and gives a deep bow. The hostages all clap, except for Holden. Óscar snatches his guitar and shoves Indiana toward the others with the barrel of his rifle.

My hands are still shaking by the time I slip back into

the circle around the fire pit. Indiana sits down next to me and takes my hand. He has no idea that I am dressed like a suicide bomber, and I can't tell him without drawing attention.

Terrified, I glance around to see if anyone saw me, but the guards are gathered around a fire making tea, teasing Óscar in Spanish about the fact that Indiana is a better musician. Pen and Holden are whispering to each other on the other side of our pit.

Rog is watching us. Watching *me*.

But he only gives me a smile and a small nod, then retreats to the edge of the clearing to lean against his favorite tree trunk.

"Genesis." Domenica scoots closer to me as I subtly tug my shirt down, terrified that my stolen bomb will be discovered. "What did you find in there?" Her last few words carry no sound, so I have to read them in the shape of her lips.

She saw me.

6 HOURS EARLIER

MADDIE

I sit up straight, suddenly wide-awake, and the hammock sways beneath me. "Luke! Did you hear that?"

He mumbles something unintelligible, so I shake him.

A second bang echoes toward us. Luke sits up, disoriented, and nearly turns the hammock over before he realizes where we are. "What was that?"

Before I can answer, we hear a third bang, and now he's awake. "Where did that come from?" I ask, staring into the dark jungle. "Can you tell?"

He turns toward the sound, digging his phone from his pocket, then pulls up the compass app. "West." When he closes the app, I see the time on his home screen. It's not quite ten p.m. We only slept for half an hour.

His phone has no cell service, and its power is down to 3 percent.

"Come on!" I toss back the mosquito netting and turn on the flashlight. "If it came from the west, it has to be Silvana and her men."

Luke grabs the flashlight and turns it off again. "We can't hike at night, Maddie. If we use the light, they'll see us coming from a mile away."

"Okay, then we'll walk on the beach, but stick close to the tree line so we can hide again if we need to. Let's go!"

Climbing down a tree with no light is far from easy, and I tumble at least a third of the way to the ground. But then I'm up again, pulling on Luke's arm as soon as his boots hit the jungle floor. "Leave the hammock. We'll come back for it."

"Maddie . . ."

"We're *so* close, Luke." To Genesis. To my insulin. To Ryan's murderer. "But if you want to stay . . ." He'll be safer here in the tree.

Luke groans. "Come on."

We head west along the beach, and a few steps later, we hear another bang. I pull Luke to a halt in the sand, with the sharp metallic impact still ringing in my ears. "What *is* that?"

"I don't know," he whispers. "But it sounded close. Maybe just around that bend."

We stare at the moonlit curve in the coast, where a thick patch of jungle hugs the shore. The banging, like a hammer hitting metal, echoes toward us again. "Come on."

We pick our way through the brush as carefully and quietly as we can in the dark, and I pray that we don't run into a snake or a caiman. Within minutes, we hear voices shouting orders, then I see a flash of light through the foliage.

I put a hand on Luke's arm, and he stops, squinting, as he follows my gaze. "I can't tell what they're doing," he whispers. "We have to get closer."

The noise covers the sound of our approach, but my heart still hammers in my throat as we walk, hunched over, toward the edge of the jungle.

At the tree line, Luke pulls me back from a sudden two-foot drop into stagnant water, lit by a bright battery-powered utility light hung from a tree.

There is no beach here. There is only a scraggly stretch of marshy inlets, fingers of water reaching into the jungle.

Overhead, vines stretch from tree to tree creating a dark nest of shadows cast by that one bright light.

"Duck!" Luke whispers as he pulls me down behind a thick fern at the edge of the marsh.

Several men in jungle camo stand on top of what looks like an upside-down boat floating in the murky water. One shouts directions at the others while they work with hammers and what look like blowtorches.

I study the long floating object, and finally I realize that the inverted boat is being welded to another, larger boat, which is nearly submerged. "They're making some kind of submarine." And while some men are welding it together, others are loading it with . . .

"Is that cocaine?" I squint at the square packages, but I can't tell much in the dark.

"Some if it." Luke points at a man emerging from the jungle with an armload of smaller square bricks. "But *that* is plastic explosive."

"Whoa, *what?*" Why would they load drugs and explosives onto the same boat?

"*¡Venga! ¡Apurate!*" a man in camo shouts from the shore, and my throat suddenly feels tight.

"That's one of Silvana's men," I whisper to Luke, pointing him out. "If he's here, we must be close to their base camp." I turn to stare south, through the jungle, and adrenaline fires through me. "Genesis is around here somewhere."

And so is Julian.

GENESIS

". . . and it has to be soon!" Holden leans around Penelope to whisper fiercely to Domenica.

He jumps, startled, when I lower myself onto the mat next to him, careful not to bump the bomb tucked into my waistband. My biggest fear in the world at the moment is accidentally pressing a button on the trigger phone.

"Get scared and change your mind?" Holden demands softly.

Indiana drops onto a pile of dried palm leaves on my right, turning our cluster into a tight circle, and Holden puffs up like a dog with his hackles raised.

"Actually, I'm here to propose an alternative to your heroic tuck-tail-and-run maneuver. Indiana and I know how to stop them." I toss a glance at the guard on patrol as he rounds the green tent headed our way. "But we need some help."

"You need *psychological* help. Domenica told us you snuck into the bomb tent," Penelope says, and I'm glad I haven't told anyone but Indiana about the plastic explosive beneath my shirt. Holden slides his hand into her grip, and she sits straighter. "Were you *trying* to get yourself killed?"

"I was doing recon. They have about a dozen small C-4 bombs in the tent—wired to *our* phones—but there must be more on the beach, because what they have here wouldn't knock down a house of cards."

"And you want to what?" Domenica whispers. "Cut the wires?"

"That would only be a temporary fix." Indiana's grin isn't so much excited as *committed*, and I want to kiss him again, right there.

"Oh shit." Pen covers her mouth with one hand, then speaks from behind it. "You want to detonate them."

The worst part about breaking up with Penelope is that one friendship-ending blowout can't suddenly make us strangers. She still knows me better than Holden ever did.

"There are several detonators in that tent. If we can get ahold of a few, we can use them to blow up whatever they've already taken to the beach."

"Genesis, that's *insane*," Holden snaps softly. "You'll just get everyone blown up!"

The guard on patrol eyes us as he marches past carrying his rifle, and I pick up Domenica's deck of cards.

"You're not going to die, because you're not going to be here," I whisper as I shuffle the deck. "You're going to get to run. All I'm asking is that you wait until I blow up whatever's down on the beach, and use that as your distraction. But I need you all to help me get down there without getting caught."

"Help you how?" Holden demands. "By drawing the attention of a bunch of armed terrorists?"

I roll my eyes at him. "You can't even hear your own hypocrisy, can you? You were perfectly willing to let *me* draw attention so you could enact *your* plan."

"My plan wasn't to blow up the jungle and everyone in it!" he hisses at a volume just below the crackle of the fire.

"I'm not—"

"Stop it!" Domenica snaps. "You sound like spoiled toddlers fighting for attention."

"She's right," Indiana says. "Everyone just calm down and let Genesis explain the plan."

"You mean the plan where she uses us to deflect notice while she—" Penelope turns on me, anger burning in her eyes. "How can we even be sure you'll go to the beach? For all we know, you'll take off into the jungle to save yourself and leave us here to die!"

"I would *never* leave you behind to pay for something I did!"

Penelope snorts and scoots closer to Holden. "Like you didn't leave me in Miami, to lie to your dad about this trip? Like you never left me dancing with Holden in some club, so he wouldn't walk in on one of your hookups?"

"Who the hell are *you* to talk about hiding a hookup?" I snap.

"Oh, so it's fine when you do it, but when I do it, it's unforgivable. Genesis does whatever Genesis wants, everyone else be damned. But not this time." Pen's angry gaze burns into me. "You can stay and blow yourself up if you want—"

"I'm not blowing up anything but the bombs." Unless something goes terribly, terribly wrong. But if Silvana and her men catch me, I might wish I'd blown myself up.

"—but we're leaving the first chance we get. So why don't you take your latest disposable boyfriend and go break him in on a patch of poison oak."

I can only stare at her, reeling from the unexpected blow.

"*Damn*, that was hot." Holden pulls her in for a kiss that's probably more for my benefit than hers. Not that I can tell for sure anymore.

I have to try one more time, even if she's still sucking on my ex's face. "Pen, if you guys run without a really good distraction, they'll shoot you. Or hack you to pieces. Holden's plan will get you *killed*."

She won't even stop making out with him long enough to look at me.

"Come on, G." Indiana takes my hand and we stand. "Those two don't have a handful of guts between them."

Holden finally pulls away from Penelope, looking disgustingly smug. "Sometimes being stupid *looks* like being brave."

"Maybe," Indiana concedes. "But cowardice always looks like what it is."

5 HOURS EARLIER

MADDIE

"If they're getting supply shipments from a boat there *has* to be a path leading to their base camp around here somewhere," Luke whispers as we fight our way along the edge of the jungle as quietly as we can in the dark.

"There it is!"

"The path?"

"No, the boat!" I grab Luke's arm and point north toward the beach. "We were right! It's small, though. It *may* hold six," I murmur, squinting at the small speedboat through the foliage. "But there are eight of us."

I hope.

Luke follows my line of sight to a dinged-up speedboat perched in the sand to the west of the homemade submarine, where a series of torches casts overlapping pools of light. Beyond the boat is a muddy, square blue tent, big enough to host a prom after-party. "There could be another one in there."

We pick our way toward the deserted beach carefully,

listening for voices and footsteps, then approach the tent from the far side, to reduce the chances of our footprints being seen. The front flaps are tied closed, but the rope is loose, and we're both small enough to duck under.

Inside, my flashlight beam highlights several long shapes draped by tarps, then settles on what we're looking for at the far end of the tent: another boat identical to the one on the beach.

"What if it doesn't work?" Luke squats to examine the hull. "I mean, why else would you keep a boat in a tent?"

"Because it's a spare? Half my neighbors have beat-up cars they never drive." I smooth loose strands of damp, frizzy hair back toward my ponytail, then stretch to relieve the strain from carrying a backpack for two days straight. "Maybe we should look for extra gas. Just in case." I swing the flashlight toward the closest unidentifiable shape and toss back one corner of the tarp.

My heart leaps into my throat. "Is that what I think it is?"

"Oh, *shit*." Luke pulls me back from a two-and-a half-foot-long metal cone lying on its side in a special wooden cradle. Next to it, still mostly covered by the tarp, is an identical cone. "Those look like warheads."

I take a deep breath, trying to slow my racing heart. Trying to think. The small bombs being loaded onto Moreno's submarines were bad enough, but this . . .

This is . . .

Bad.

"It's conventional." Luke leans closer to look at what's printed on the nearest warhead. "And I think this is Russian writing."

"Conventional? As opposed to the other, zanier kind of warhead?"

"As opposed to a nuke. Or a chemical warhead. Or a biological one."

"Why would they need to ship warheads? Can't they just . . . shoot them?"

"Because the warhead is just the tip. Without the missile, it's a bomb, but not a projectile."

"Did you learn that from the Boy Scouts?"

"Nope. Call of Duty." He circles the tent to the two other tarp-draped lumps and pulls back the material to expose two more warheads in each bundle. "*Shit.* These look *old.* Maybe . . . Cold War era? I wonder how they're planning to detonate them." Luke sounds almost as interested as he sounds scared. "Without the missiles, they'll have to have something to provide the initial blast needed to trigger the real explosion."

Terror burns up from my stomach. "Simple English, Luke. What does that mean?"

"They need a small bomb to set off each of the big bombs."

"How big is big?" I take a deep breath and release it slowly. Then I look up at Luke. He's fifteen. If *he* can deal with this, I can too. "How much damage can these do?"

"Unfortunately, the specifications and explosive potential

of Cold War–era Russian missiles don't fall within my arguably extensive collection of trivial knowledge, Maddie."

"Acknowledged."

"But, best guess?" He turns to me in the dark tent, his face shrouded in shadow. "I think there's enough fire power here to make any decent-sized city look like an active war zone. Think Syria. Iraq. Afghanistan." The grim set of his jaw confirms the gruesome potential. "This is enough to kill *thousands.*"

GENESIS

Indiana and I reclaim grass mats on our side of the fire pit, where the blaze itself blocks our view of Holden and Penelope.

Across the clearing, Sebastián and his men are playing poker for cigarettes, while Silvana and the rest of the Moreno henchmen pass around a bottle of *aguardiente*. They glance our way every few minutes, but the only captors who've kept a truly close eye on us since we got to the base camp are the guards on patrol duty, who don't seem to care what we do, as long as we follow orders and don't leave the clearing.

Indiana takes my hand as we sit. "Well, it may be just you and me, G."

"Maybe not." Rog and Domenica are embroiled in a whispered discussion near the edge of the clearing, and they keep glancing at us, then at Pen and Holden. "They could still side with us." But they need to decide soon. Now-ish.

If Holden tries to run, the guards will be much more vigilant—maybe even vindictive—and I won't get a chance to sneak down to the beach.

"We need a plan B." I rub my temples, fighting a headache brought on by hunger, stress, and exhaustion.

Indiana opens his arms, and I scoot back until my spine is pressed against his chest, his mouth inches from my right ear. "Plan A will still work. I'll be your distraction." He runs his hands down my arms, then settles them at my waist—until his fingers brush the C-4 packet, and he recoils. "I almost forgot about that," he whispers. "G, you're *wearing* your plan B. It's big enough to provide a distraction, but too small to do much damage, if we set it off out in the jungle."

"That's brilliant." I twist in his arms and pull him down for a grateful, almost hopeful kiss. "So, all we have to do is figure out how to get this thing into the jungle before Holden makes his move and ruins our chances."

"Which means we need to get going."

"Five more minutes." I lean my head back against his collarbone and pull his arms tighter around me. "I need a little more of this first."

Indiana chuckles. "It's kind of ridiculous, isn't it? We're worried that your ex will *stop* us from blowing ourselves up. Hell of a spring break finale, huh?"

"Well, when you say it like *that* . . ." I can't help but laugh at the morbid absurdity. "The only thing better than a memorable entrance is a memorable exit." But he's not going to make one. He's going to slip into the jungle unnoticed, with the rest of the hostages.

I'm going to make sure of that.

I turn to sit facing him, practically in his lap, and we are eye to eye. The position is intimate, but the eye contact is *personal*. I feel like he can see every thought I have, and for the first time in my life—and maybe the last—I'm willing to let that happen.

When I can't wait any longer, I lean in and kiss him. Slowly, at first. Gently. But he slides one hand behind my head, deepening the angle, and I give him everything I have. Everything I am.

I might have minutes to live, and I have nothing to lose. This could be my last kiss.

"You know, we might survive this," I whisper when I finally pull away.

Indiana leans his forehead against mine. "Then why did that feel more like the end of something than the beginning?"

"Sorry to interrupt," Domenica says as she drops onto a mat of leaves to my left.

Reluctantly, I start to pull away from Indiana, but he holds on to me until I give in and lay my head on his shoulder, careful to keep space between him and the phone trigger. He's not ready to let go, and I'm not ready to make him.

"Change your mind about escaping with Holden?" he asks.

"I'm still trying to decide. He doesn't even know how to get back to the bunkhouse for sure." Domenica glances over her shoulder at Holden and Penelope, who are now blatantly watching us. "So, what would you need me to do, exactly?"

Indiana lets me go, and I angle myself away from the guards, then lift the tail of my shirt so she can see the explosives tucked into my waistband. Too late, I realize that Pen and Holden can see it too.

Domenica gasps. "What are you going to do with that?"

"Since Pen and Holden won't help, I'm going to set this off in the jungle, to distract the guards while we blow up the rest of the explosives," I explain. "There's another phone in my pocket. I'm going to use it to call the one strapped to C-4."

"You're going to blow up *those* explosives?" She points to the tent. "That'll kill us all!"

"There's nothing in there but C-4. No point in blowing that up," I assure her.

"We figure they've made something bigger," Indiana whispers, "maybe pressure cooker or backpack bombs, and we're guessing they're on the beach. But G can't get into the jungle without a distraction, and I've already played the only card I have." He glances at the pole where Óscar's guitar no longer hangs.

"So you want me to, what? Make a scene?"

I nod. "Preferably without getting hurt."

Domenica closes her eyes for a second, as if she's thinking. Or praying. Then she opens them and nods. "I'm in. When do you want to do this?"

"Yesterday," Indiana says. "But we'll have to settle for now."

MADDIE

The path to some sort of base camp is easy to see from the beach, but we take a route parallel to it, to keep from being seen, stepping carefully in pools of moonlight. About a quarter mile inland, we glimpse torchlight shining through the vegetation.

Luke tugs me behind a tall tangle of underbrush, and I scan the base camp between the branches.

"There she is." Relief eases part of the tension I've been carrying for two days. Genesis sits on a grass mat in front of the nearest fire pit, between Indiana and Domenica, with her back to the trail leading to the beach. To the boats that will get us out of here.

Does she know that a means of escape is just a ten-minute hike away? Have they let the hostages leave camp at all?

"I have to talk to her. I have to tell her about the boats." I turn to Luke. "Any ideas?"

"Well, if we had something to write with—or on—we could wad up a message and throw it at her. Or shoot it to her through a bamboo shoot. Like a spitball."

"We don't have anything to write with or on."

Luke shrugs. "That's why it was a hypothetical. I'm assuming neither of you knows Morse code?"

"A solid assumption."

"Well, then, short of just shouting at her, I'm out of ideas."

"I—" *Wait.* "You're a genius. And not just a math genius. Like, a *real* genius." I kiss him on the cheek, then stand, but he pulls me back down.

"Do *not* start shouting. You'll get us caught."

"Only one of us," I tell him.

"No, Maddie, listen to me." He takes me by both arms and stares right into my eyes in the dark. "I'm a genius. You just said so. And I'm telling you this is a *very bad* plan. Why don't we just go make out in our tree hammock again? That was safe, and fun!"

"There's a tree in this plan too, but you're going to be in it by yourself. Find one nearby, where you can still see the camp, but won't be seen."

"Maddie, *no.*" Luke crosses his arms over his backpack straps.

"There's no other way." I'm talking fast, because I have to do this before I chicken out. Just like with the cliff. "I'll tell them about the boats, and we'll make a break for it the first chance we get. You just stay ready and follow us." I glance at the rifle. "With the gun. Just in case."

"No!" Luke whispers fiercely. "We're in this together. We stay *together.*"

He starts to say something else, but I cut him off with

a kiss—the only reliable way I've found to shut him up. "Mmmm, see? There's making out in this plan too."

"That was *highly* manipulative."

"Yeah, well, sometimes a girl has to play dirty. Two minutes. Find some place to hide, or I'm giving us both up. But I really need you to be my backup, Luke."

"*Damn it*, Maddie," he mumbles. And that's how I know I've won.

4 HOURS EARLIER

GENESIS

"Are you ready? It needs to be now!" I whisper, and Domenica gives me a shaky nod. "Have you ever actually had a seizure?"

"I used to get them as a kid. My parents would never let me go anywhere by myself, so I swore that when I grew up, I'd grab my backpack and . . ." Domenica blinks, and her eyes seem to refocus. "Never mind. I'm ready." She stands, and Indiana and I start a game of war so we won't be obviously watching her. But she only makes it a few steps before—

"Oh my God, Genesis."

I look up to see Domenica staring over my shoulder.

I turn, and my cards land on the ground all around me. I forget all about the bomb pressed against my stomach.

Maddie stands on the edge of the clearing.

I stand and blink, expecting her to disappear like a mirage. But she's still there. "Maddie?" She's covered in grime, and her eyes look a little glazed. She's in shock.

How did she get here? How is she still *alive*?

"*Dios mío*," Silvana mutters from somewhere behind me. "Grab her!"

Footsteps stomp past me, and Óscar seizes Maddie's arm. Rifles swing her way.

"No!" I shout. "Let her go! I'll take care of her." The rifles swing my way, and I step back with my hands up, suddenly hyperaware that I'm still wearing a bomb, which would *definitely* blow up if it were shot. "Please. Just let me see if she's okay."

"Let her go!" Sebastián runs past us all and shoves several rifles away from Maddie. He pulls her from Óscar's grip. "*¿Estás bien?*" he asks as he looks her over.

Maddie nods slowly, and he turns to me. "*Dale*. Come get her."

My eyes water as I step forward.

"Wait," Silvana shouts. "Where did she come from?"

"She just stepped out of the jungle," Natalia says. "Out of nowhere."

"Are you alone?" Silvana demands, inches from my cousin's face. "Where's Moisés? And that kid with the cell phone?"

Maddie blinks, but her eyes don't come into focus.

"How did you find us?" Silvana practically shouts into her face. When Maddie doesn't answer, she turns to Sebastián. "Something's wrong. Why would she just give herself up like that?"

"Because she's clearly in shock and starving." I try to

take Maddie's arm, but Silvana points her pistol at me until I back away.

"Then how the hell did she find us?"

"Insulin." Maddie's so hoarse I can hardly hear her. She's looking right at me, but her focus is off. "You have my insulin."

And that's when I remember.

I frantically pat my shorts pockets until I feel the small vial. "She came back for this," I say as I pull it from my pocket. "She had no choice."

Silvana grabs the vial before I can give it to Maddie. She squints as she reads the label. Then she rolls her eyes and gives it back to me. "Take care of her." She turns to Sebastián. "You watch them both. They're your problem."

I lead Maddie to a mat near the fire, and Sebastián follows us. "Look, she's clearly traumatized," I tell him. "She's no threat. Can you just let me get some insulin into her before you start interrogating her?"

He shrugs and sits on a tree stump several feet from our campfire. "Go ahead."

"Water," Maddie whispers as I lift her shirt to study her insulin pump. I have no idea how it works.

Sebastián frowns. "What did she say?"

"Can you get her some water? She's probably dehydrated." He starts to argue, and I turn on him. "Unless you want to ransom a corpse, go get her some damn water!"

Sebastián scowls at me, then grabs the nearest of his men by the arm. "¡Agua! ¡Ahora!"

While he shouts orders, I turn back to my cousin, her insulin vial in hand, and she looks at me. She *really* looks at me, with total clarity and focus.

Maddie's not in shock. But she's one hell of an actress.

"Genesis." Her voice is hardly a suggestion of sound. "There are six warheads and two boats on the beach. We have to get everybody out of here."

3 HOURS EARLIER

MADDIE

"Warheads?" Domenica whispers as she pours more water from a plastic jug into a bottle for me. She and Indiana have gathered close enough to listen as Genesis pretends to get me settled into the hostage situation, but Penelope and Holden just stare at me from across the campfire.

Rog seems to be watching everything from his seat beneath a tree on the edge of the clearing.

"Yes. Six of them." I move slowly as I change my insulin cartridge, clinging to my dehydrated-and-in-shock act to deflect suspicion. "Luke says they're conventional, so they're not leaking chemicals or biological hazards, but he thinks that's enough of a payload—"

"To kill thousands, if they hit the right targets," Indiana breathes from my cousin's left.

"Yeah."

"You found Luke?" Genesis asks as she unscrews the lid of the insulin vial for me. "Where is he?"

"Hiding in the jungle. Watching. Safe, for now." I

glance over my cousin's shoulder, and find Silvana watching us from one of the other campfires. "Genesis, they're making homemade submarines, out in the marsh. We saw them loading bricks of cocaine onto one, but some of the bricks looked different. I think they're bombs."

"Wait, I thought they wanted your dad to ship their bombs," Domenica whispers.

"*What?*" My hands freeze in the process of uncoiling the tubing for my insulin pump.

"That's why we're here, Maddie," Genesis says as she tucks my used medical waste into a pouch in my backpack. "They're using us as leverage to make my dad ship the bombs into the States."

She's holding something back. Something painful. I can see it in how tightly her lips are pressed together. But she won't tell me until she's ready, and I'm not going to waste time trying to make her.

We have to get out of here.

Indiana sits on a mat made of leaves and begins gathering up a scattered deck of cards. "Why load bombs onto submarines, if they think they're going to get ships?"

"Because a cargo ship can't deviate from its scheduled route or make unscheduled stops without looking suspicious and risking extra inspections." Genesis frowns as she thinks out loud. "That's why Silvana didn't ask my dad to send a ship here. She asked for coordinates of *where it will be.* They're going to send bombs out to the ship in their submarines. And from there, who knows where . . ."

"*I* know where. We heard a list of targets, over Moisés's radio," I say as I thread the tube through the lid of the vial. "Um . . . LA, New York, Chicago, DC, Memphis, and Miami. They're going to blow up *Miami*, Genesis." Our home. I feel sick at the thought of how many people might die. People we know. My *mother*. "We have to warn them."

"We're going to do better than that." Genesis lifts her shirt just high enough for me to see that there's a phone— *her* phone—tucked into her waistband.

"Where did you—" I squint, resisting the urge to bend for a closer look. Taped to her phone is a slim brick of a clay-like material with wires sticking out of that. "What *is* that?"

"C-4," she whispers. "They turned our phones into little bombs."

My cousin is wearing explosives like some kind of designer belt. Before I have a chance to process that realization, another one sinks in.

This is what Luke was talking about.

"They're detonators," I whisper. "Small bombs to set off the big bombs down on the beach."

"That's the plan," she says. "I'm going to use the extra phone to set this one off in the jungle." She pats a small lump in her pocket. "While the terrorists are trying to figure out what happened, I'll grab some more detonators from the tent, then run down to the beach and blow up the warheads," she explains. "But—"

"That *was* the plan when we thought they were IEDs," Indiana says, firelight flickering on the side of his face.

"Pressure cooker bombs. But warheads are *way* too big, G. They'll catch you before you can get far enough away to safely blow them up."

"No they won't, because we'll be on the water," Genesis says. "We can set the detonators on the warheads, then get in the boats and trigger the C-4 once we're far enough away."

"What about the men on the beach?" he asks.

"There aren't any right now," I whisper as I clip my new infusion set into place against my stomach. "They're all in the jungle, working on the submarine."

"But we still have to deal with the ones here," Domenica points out. "They won't all just run off and leave us unguarded when Gen's bomb goes off."

"No," Genesis says. "We'll have to fight. Are you in?"

Domenica hesitates for a second. Then she nods. "You still need a distraction, right? So you can plant that thing in the jungle?"

"Luke's right outside the camp. Let him plant it," I suggest. "The less time you're in the jungle, the smaller the chance they'll discover you missing."

Genesis looks hesitant. "He's just a kid, Maddie."

"He's *not* a kid." I can feel my face warm. "I wouldn't have gotten this far without him."

She frowns at me for a second, and I can practically see her internal debate. Finally she nods. "Okay. But I still need a distraction so I can get the detonator to him."

I give her a grim smile. "I've got that covered."

GENESIS

"*Tú. Y tú.* Boil more water." Sebastián points at Domenica and Indiana as he crosses the clearing toward us, and while she still has her back to him, Maddie flicks water at her own face and neck. "*Vamos.* Let's talk." He pulls Maddie up by one arm, and she stares at the ground, her gaze hardly focused. The water droplets glisten on her skin like sweat.

"Okay." She walks slowly and keeps pushing hair back from her face. Her hands are shaking and she stumbles with every other step.

I've seen her go into diabetic shock twice before, and this act looks so much like those episodes that I'm starting to wonder if she was faking then too.

She's halfway to Silvana's fire pit when her legs fold beneath her. And just like she predicted, half of our abductors descend on her like angels from on high, while the rest turn to watch the drama unfold.

They need her, and they're not going to let her die. Not after losing Ryan.

An ache resurfaces deep in my chest, but I force myself to focus. Grief is a waste of energy, but with any luck, blowing things up will be therapeutic.

When I'm sure all the guards are focused on Maddie, I slip into the jungle. "Luke!" I whisper as I walk, taking frequent glances back at the camp. I can't even see Maddie, because of the crowd gathered around her.

"Luke!"

Each second that slips by makes my palms a little sweatier. My throat a little tighter. I can't mess this up.

"Luke! Maddie sent me."

A twig snaps behind me, and I whirl around to see him holding the automatic rifle Maddie said they took from Moisés. His chin is stubbly and dirt streaks his arms. He looks like an extra from *Lord of the Flies*. A cute extra. I can kind of understand what Maddie sees in him.

"Genesis?"

"Yeah. Here." I pull the C-4 detonator from beneath my shirt and shove it at him. "Maddie said you could plant this in the jungle for us? Just put it at the base of a tree somewhere about half a mile out. Then come back here. I'll watch for you, and when I see you, I'll call the phone to detonate it."

"You'll . . . ?" He looks confused, but there's no time to explain about the other phone. The crowd around Maddie is already starting to dissipate. Óscar looks like he's taking a head count.

"When it goes off, run for the beach, and *make sure* Maddie gets in one of those boats. If I'm late, do *not* let her wait for me." I have to place detonators on the warheads in the beach tent. "Got it?"

"Yeah. Okay."

"Great. Go!"

He takes off at a run, clutching the C-4 in his left hand, and I hurry back to camp. I can see Indiana looking for me through the trees.

I'm three steps from the clearing when Óscar's hand wraps around my arm, and I jump, startled.

"Look who I found," he shouts as he hauls me back into camp. "Trying to escape."

MADDIE

Óscar drags Genesis back into camp, and my pulse spikes so hard that for a moment, I'm afraid I'll pass out for real.

My mind races. Is she still wearing the bomb? Did she find Luke? Have we lost our shot?

I stand, but Natalia pushes me back down on the folding chair and hands me a full-sugar soda, evidently the best they can do without juice or hard candy. "You said you needed sugar. So drink."

"What did I say would happen if you tried to escape?" Silvana demands as Óscar hauls Genesis closer.

The can shakes in my hand, and this time I'm not faking.

"You can't kill her." Indiana steps between Silvana and Genesis. His voice sounds strained, but his words carry loud and clear. "You need her."

"True." Silvana frowns, mocking Genesis as she pretends to consider the situation.

Genesis tries to pull her arm free, but Óscar only tightens his grip. "Silvana—"

"¡Cállate!" Silvana snaps at her. "You and your cousin represent not one, but *three* different ransoms. But *you* . . ." She grabs Holden by one arm, and her words drip with gleeful malice. "You only represent yourself."

She has no idea how right she is.

Silvana pulls Holden close and sneers in his face. "Your *mami* will pay whether you are dead or alive."

"No!" Penelope cries.

"Whoa!" Holden turns on Genesis, eyes wide with fear. "This is *her* fault! I didn't do a damn thing!"

Silvana nods to Álvaro, and he unsnaps a huge knife from his belt. My soda can hits the ground. My throat feels thick and swollen.

Penelope chokes back a sob but Genesis clenches her jaw shut.

Silvana throws Holden to the ground. He falls to his knees in the dirt, and Álvaro is on him in a second, his knife at Holden's throat.

"Please, don't do this." My cousin's voice is unsteady. "He hasn't broken any of your rules."

I've despised Holden since I caught him making out with another girl at Genesis's *quinceañera*, but he doesn't deserve to have his throat sliced open in the middle of the jungle.

"Yeah. This has nothing to do with me." Holden's voice shakes and his hands tremble.

Silvana shrugs. "Any last words?"

"*Please*," Genesis begs, fighting Óscar's grip, and her desperate plea makes my eyes water. "*I'm* the one you want to punish."

Silvana's eyes practically sparkle. "That's exactly what I'm doing."

2 HOURS EARLIER

GENESIS

"*¡Espérate!*" Sebastián shouts, and relief washes over me. Setting off bombs a thousand miles away is one thing, but he can't distance himself from the murder of someone his own age, right in front of his face.

He won't let this happen.

"Wainwright is old news," he says, and I frown, confused by his tactic. "*Ella no se preocupa por él.*"

Silvana turns to me, brows raised in mock surprise. "Then what is the new headline, *princesa?*"

"Him." Sebastián shoves Indiana down in the dirt next to Holden.

"Sebastián, no!" I twist my arm to break Óscar's grip and rush toward Indiana. "What are you doing?"

Óscar reaches for me again, but Sebastián waves him off. He presses his blade against Indiana's neck, and I freeze.

Indiana closes his eyes.

"No! Please!" I don't know what to do with my hands. I

want to pull Sebastián away from Indiana, but that'll make this worse.

"What *are* you doing, Sebastián?" Silvana's voice is a singsong taunt as she saunters closer for a better view.

"Genesis likes to call the shots," Sebastián says. "So let's let her call this one." He turns to me, and his gaze is cold and hard. His grin is dark and cruel.

Penelope sobs. "Please don't hurt Holden. Please. Please don't hurt him. Please—" she cries, until Domenica pulls her into a hug.

Rog wears a grim frown at the edge of the clearing, and Maddie looks frozen, afraid to move. But several of the gunmen come forward for a better view, eager for the show.

I wonder if they've seen this one before.

My eyes water, and I blink away tears. Looking weak won't help Indiana or Holden.

Think!

I've read Sebastián all wrong, and he wants me to know that. He wants me to know that he's in control here. That he's been manipulating me since before I even got on the plane—how else would he know how we got here?—and that he's tired of pretending otherwise.

He wants to show me *he* has all the power.

Fine.

"Just tell me what you want, and I'll do it."

"I want you to *choose*." He grins. "Which will you save? The old lover or the new?"

"Oh shit," Domenica says, horrified.

Silvana *laughs* as she paces in front of me. Studying my pain from all angles. "Who will it be, *princesa?*" She gestures to Holden, then to Indiana. "Which one will you save?"

"*Gen!*" Holden's voice is strained. His eyes plead with me. "Do something!"

"And you?" She squats at eye level with Indiana, where she brushes a strand of brown hair from his forehead. "Are you going to plead for your life?"

Indiana turns his head carefully, slowly, in spite of the knife at his throat, until he can look right into her eyes. "If you want to kill me, just do it. Don't put this on Genesis."

"*¡Éste es encantador!*" Silvana laughs as she stands and turns to me. "I can see the attraction. So who will it be?"

Indiana won't look at me. He doesn't want to make this any harder for me. Even now, he is above the drama.

Holden pleads with me silently. We're over, but I can't pretend that he means nothing to me. I can't watch while his neck is hacked open on the jungle floor.

"I can't." Tears blur my vision, and that's almost a mercy, because I can't stand this. I can't pick. I can't watch either of them die.

"You have ten seconds to decide, or we will kill them both." Sebastián holds his wrist up to stare at his watch.

"No." I can't breathe. I can't see through my tears.

"*Ocho* seconds . . . ," he taunts.

My legs fold beneath me and I land on my knees in the dirt. *"Please* don't." I wipe tears from my eyes and look up at Sebastián, who's watching my torture with a sadistic smile. "I'll do whatever you want."

"Five seconds," he says. "Do you want to lose them both?"

"No!"

"Three seconds!" Silvana is practically gleeful, and I can't think through the tangle of loyalty, guilt, and regret strangling me like a noose. "Which do you want to keep, the big mouth or the silver tongue?" She glances at her watch, then turns to me with excitement shining in her eyes. "Time's up, *princesa!* Make a decision! Who are we going to kill?"

"Genesis!" Holden's voice is a panicked squeak.

"I can't . . ." I bend over my knees, huddled around the hole in my heart. "I can't do it."

"Fine." Silvana turns to Sebastián. "Kill them both."

Panic pumps fire through my veins. "Wait!" I sit up straight and she turns to me with artificial surprise and anticipation. "Indiana. Save Indiana."

My own choice breaks me into a million pieces of remorse and regret. But I won't take it back.

"You *bitch!*" Holden shouts, and my chest feels like it's caving in.

"No!" Penelope sobs, and Domenica hugs her tighter.

Guilt is an abyss devouring me one shattered piece at a time.

Sebastián laughs so hard he sounds like he's choking. He steps back from Indiana and waves one hand at Álvaro. "Let Holden go."

He squats beside me as I stare at him in horror. "I didn't think you would do it!"

1·5 HOURS EARLIER

MADDIE

"Holden . . ." Genesis grabs his arm as he stomps past her, but he pulls free. "I knew she wouldn't kill you. You're the more valuable hostage. You were the safer bet."

She's lying, I can see it.

So can Holden.

"You deserve whatever you get out here," he spits. The hatred in his eyes is so absolute that it steals my breath. He retreats to the other side of the clearing and sinks onto a log with Penelope, who's still wiping tears from her face.

I make a show of getting up slowly while I sip my soda, careful to make brief eye contact with several of the guards so they can see that I'm feeling better. So I can gradually stop faking diabetic shock. And go to my cousin.

"Genesis." I squat next to her. "We need to—"

"I don't know how things got so screwed up between us," she says, and for a second, I think she's talking to me. Apologizing for all the times she was . . . well, herself. But then I realize she's still looking at Holden.

"Give him some time," Indiana says from her other side. "Eventually he'll understand."

"He already does," she says. "He's not going to get over that."

We need to make our move. But she's upset, and the girl with her finger on the trigger needs to have a steady hand. So I give Genesis some space and head over to check on Domenica and take the lay of the land.

Rog sits with his back against a tree, watching everything. His gaze finds me and lingers too long. As if he understands everything, now that, I assume, he's finally clearheaded.

Penelope and Holden are huddled close together, which is no real surprise, considering that Indiana is evidently the "new headline."

"Holden, we can't do that to her," Penelope whispers, and I freeze in my tracks. They haven't noticed me, but the guards will, so I bend to tie my shoe.

"She was going to let them *kill* me!" Holden growls. "She deserves what she gets. And we need a distraction— *now*." I can't see his face, but every muscle in his body is tense.

"I know, but—"

Holden grabs Penelope's arm so hard that she flinches. "You're either with me or with her, Pen."

"I'm with you. I told you. But . . ." She lowers her voice, and I stand, but I can't make myself walk away. "If you tell them she took it, they'll *kill* her."

I walk to my cousin as fast as I can without drawing

attention. "Genesis," I hiss as I kneel in front of her and Indiana. "Holden's going to tell them about the C-4."

She frowns. "He can't prove it. It's already in the jungle."

Holden is already up, heading for Sebastián.

"But what about the . . ." I glance at the bulge in her pocket, where the detonator phone is hidden.

"Shit." She glances around the clearing. "I have to blow it now."

But Holden is already talking to Sebastián. "There's no time. Give it to me."

"No, I—"

I take the phone from Genesis's pocket, then shove it into my waistband next to my insulin pump. "Trust me."

I stand, turn my back, and walk away.

"Genesis!" Sebastián aims his rifle at her chest. "Don't move."

GENESIS

I stand slowly, my hands in the air.

"Back off!" Sebastián shouts at Indiana. When I nod, Indiana reluctantly takes three steps back. "Óscar, *¡venga!*"

Óscar begins patting me down while Sebastián maintains his aim at my chest.

Silvana sticks her head out of the green tent. "*¿Aún más drama con la princesa?* What's going on this time?"

"Are you missing a detonator and a phone?" Sebastián demands as Óscar's hands trail down my sides.

Silvana disappears into the tent as Óscar pats my back pockets. "She's clean," he declares when he comes up empty.

"The hell she is," Holden shouts. "We saw it!" Rifles swing his way, and Penelope flinches. "Check her again!"

"She doesn't have anything," Óscar says. "The boy just wants revenge."

Silvana throws open the tent flap and charges toward me, her pistol drawn. "Where are they?"

I backpedal, my pulse racing. "I don't know what you're—"

"There's a brick and a phone missing." Silvana takes my chin and stares down into my eyes. "Lie to me, and I'll *kill every friend you have left.*"

1 HOUR EARLIER

MADDIE

Silvana shoves Genesis back by her chin and my cousin lands in the dirt. "Start talking." Silvana pulls her pistol on Domenica. "Or I will shoot her."

Domenica freezes, staring at the gun.

My pulse roars in my ears.

Indiana glances pointedly at my waist.

Now? I mouth.

He nods.

But what if Luke isn't back from planting the C-4 yet? What if he's still too close?

"Wait." Genesis pushes herself to her feet, hands held up, palms out. "Domenica has nothing to do with this."

I step behind Indiana and pull the phone from beneath my shirt. Which is when I remember that I don't have Genesis's number memorized. I don't have *anyone's* number memorized but hers isn't even in my favorites list.

Fear paralyzes me for a full second. Then I realize I'm

holding Holden's phone. The Eminem quote on the back of the case is a dead giveaway.

"I'm going to count to three, *princesa*, then I'm going to start shooting," Silvana warns, and the tension in the clearing is so thick that I'm afraid to move.

Domenica takes panicked, gasping breaths.

"Silvana. Point that at me," Genesis insists softly.

They made us disable our pass codes when they took our phones, so I tap the contacts icon. But my hands are shaking. I miss.

Silvana cocks her gun, and I jump. Penelope whimpers.

Desperate, I jab the contacts icon again, and the favorites menu opens. My cousin's name isn't there. *Damn* it.

"Last chance," Silvana says, and the phone trembles in my hand.

The third entry in Holden's favorites is "My Bitch." I tap it once. Twice. Over and over again.

Nothing happens.

I have no signal.

But I *saw* a guard on his phone earlier. I *know* there's reception.

Silvana's arm tenses on the edge of my vision. Genesis lunges as Silvana pulls the trigger, throwing her arm up. Gunfire explodes, and the shot goes wild.

I spin and hold the phone out from my body, too low to be seen.

One bar.

I almost cry.

I stab the call button once. Twice. Three times.

The call goes through.

For one terrifying moment, I can't move.

The jungle explodes into fire.

GENESIS

The ground shakes beneath me. I stumble away from Silvana. A pillar of flames and smoke rises over the treetops,
half a mile into the jungle.

Luke came through.

A low shaking moan comes from the edge of the campsite where Natalia lies, curled up. A thin strip of wood
protrudes from her left shoulder. Her pistol lies forgotten on
the ground.

"*¡Mierda!*" Sebastián shouts into the jungle, his face
purple with fury. The authorities are searching for us, and
we've just sent up a *huge* flare.

"*¡Vamos!*" Silvana shouts. But instead of pointing at the
jungle, she points toward the beach. "*¡Oculten el narco!
¡Evacúen!*"

Hide the narco? As in narco sub? Maddie said there are
several subs.

Gunmen run for the footpath to the shore. Óscar helps
Natalia stand, then bends for her pistol. Holden beats him
to it.

Another gunman pushes his way out of the military tent,
carrying the cardboard box of cell phones.

"Genesis!" Indiana shouts. I turn to look for him, but Sebastián steps into my path. He has Maddie clutched to his chest, his gun pressed to her temple. "You and Madalena are coming with me."

Maddie's face is streaked with tears. She's frozen in terror.

"Okay." I raise my hands, palms out. "It's okay, Maddie." But my focus is on Sebastián. "She's no threat. Let her go and aim the gun at me."

He actually laughs. "You tipped your hand with your boyfriend, *princesa*. The *only* way to control you is to point a weapon at someone you care about."

"Sebastián!" Silvana shouts. "*¡Vamos!*"

He turns for just a second.

"Duck!" I shout, and Maddie lets her legs fold, pulling him off balance. I spin and kick his hand. The pistol goes flying.

Maddie scrambles out of the way, and I spin into another kick. Sebastián catches my foot and shoves me back.

I fall in the dirt, and he's on me. He grabs a handful of my hair and slams my skull into the ground. My vision swims. My head falls to the side, and I see his pistol lying on a torn leaf mat.

Sebastián pulls his arm back, fist clenched. I buck him off and scramble for the gun. My hand closes around the barrel. Sebastián pulls me across the ground by my leg, skinning my back.

I grunt as I swing the butt of the pistol at his head.

He goes down hard.

MADDIE

I stare at Sebastián's unconscious body on the ground, stunned. I've never actually seen Genesis fight.

"Go down to the beach!" Genesis yells at me. "Now!"

But I can't go without . . .

Where's Luke?

"Luke!" I shout as I race past the green tent. Panic tightens around my chest. The jungle is on fire, I'm half deaf from the blast, and I have no idea where he is. "Luke!" Smoke stings my eyes. People are running. Shouting.

"Maddie!" Luke's suddenly beside me. Holding me. "Maddie." He's lost his cap, but he's whole and unburned. And still carrying the rifle. "The boats! Let's go." He takes my arm, but I pull away.

"No, we have to get a detonator. For the warheads. We're going to blow them up once we're on the water."

"But I'm supposed to—"

"Stand guard."

I turn and run around the corner of the tent, dodging men racing toward the beach path with supply boxes. I duck through the tent flap, and Luke reluctantly takes up a position at the entrance, facing the chaos. Rifle at the ready.

The inside of the tent is dark, and I fumble around for several seconds before Luke pulls open the tent flap. "Hurry!" he shouts.

For a second, the firelight from outside illuminates the inside of the tent.

It's empty.

The C-4 triggers are gone.

GENESIS

"Put it down," Óscar shouts, and I turn to see Holden aiming a pistol at him and Natalia. Óscar's rifle hangs at his back, temporarily out of reach.

"Get out of our way," Holden growls. Penelope stands next to him, eyes wide and terrified.

"G . . ." Indiana is suddenly at my side. "Are you okay?"

"Fine." I wrap my arms around him. He has a black eye and bloody knuckles, but he's okay too.

"Put the gun down," Óscar repeats, and I let Indiana go.

"Holden . . ." I take several slow steps toward him, and Indiana mirrors my careful approach.

"Stay back, Gen," Holden orders. His hand is steady, but his voice is not. "You had it coming."

"I know." His eyes are glassy. "Holden, give me the gun. Shooting people isn't like shooting big game."

"I'm not going to—" He glances at me and Indiana, and Óscar swings the rifle up.

"Holden!" Penelope shouts.

Holden turns back to Óscar and his hand twitches. The gun fires.

I fall backward. My ears ring. The gunshot echoes in my head and I can't hear anything else.

The gun falls from my hand.

A man lies on the floor next to my mother. His eyes are open. Blood swells from his chest.

I don't realize I'm screaming until my hearing comes back.

Óscar hits the ground on his back. The rifle lands across his stomach. He blinks once. Twice. Then his gaze loses focus.

Penelope screams.

"No!" Natalia collapses at Óscar's side, clutching her bloody shoulder.

Holden stares at them. He's breathing too fast. His eyes are wild and shiny, but they hold no guilt. No comprehension. Nothing.

"Holden!" Penelope reaches for him, and he turns on her. Still holding the gun. Something has cracked, deep inside him.

Indiana steps in front of Penelope. "Put the gun down. Slowly."

Holden blinks. Then he runs into the jungle, straight into the flames.

0.5 HOURS EARLIER

MADDIE

"There are no triggers!"

"What?" Luke shouts. He's still a little deaf from the blast.

"The C-4!" I shout. "It's all gone, and so are the rest of the cell phones!"

"Madalena," Silvana calls, and I look up to see her rifle aimed right at us, a psychotic smile turning up the corners of her mouth. "I see you got your strength back."

"Put the gun down, or I'll shoot you," Luke says, returning her aim.

Silvana laughs. "Put *your* gun down, or I shoot *Maddie*."

"She's bluffing," I tell him. "She needs Genesis and me alive to make my uncle cooperate."

"Oh, *niña*, he met our demands three hours ago," Silvana says. "The bombs are being loaded onto his ship *right now*. So tell your boyfriend to put down the gun before I blow pieces of you all over the jungle. Sebastián may still want you alive, but *I have no use for you.*"

Gunfire explodes. Silvana whirls around from the impact, and blood blooms from her right arm. Her rifle clatters to the ground. Genesis stands behind her, still holding a pistol, Indiana at her side.

Stunned, I stare at them, my ears ringing worse than ever. Then I pick up the rifle and aim it at Silvana's head. "For Ryan," I whisper as I position my finger on the trigger and my hand on the grip, just like Luke showed me.

Genesis lifts the rifle from my grip. "She's not worth it," she shouts. "Trust me." Then she slams the stock of the rifle into Silvana's forehead.

Silvana's skin splits open over her left brow. Her eyes close, and her head falls to the side.

"Get her to the boats," Genesis shouts at Luke.

Luke grabs my arm, but I pull free.

"No!" I shout. "I'm not leaving until I find Julian."

GENESIS

"Maddie, go with him!" I push her toward Luke. "Indiana and I will grab another detonator and be right behind you."

"The warheads are gone," my cousin says. "So is the C-4. They're loading it on your dad's ship right now."

"What? No!" My ears are ringing.

Luke runs one hand through his curls. "Silvana said he complied hours ago."

"*Damn* it!" I can't think. I turn to Indiana. "How could he comply?"

"How could he not?" Indiana pulls me into a hug. "He's your dad."

I turn back to the base camp, and find Rog escorting Penelope and Domenica toward the beach with a rifle slung across his chest. "He left me." Pen's face is stained with tears, and her eyes are puffy. "He just . . . left me."

"We need to get out of here before the rest of the terrorists get here," Rog says as they pass us.

"There are more?"

"There are *always* more."

"There are two boats on the beach," I tell him. "Get everyone on them. We'll be right there." Even if they've finished loading the bombs, the boat might still be within range.

I *have* to find a cell phone.

"Okay." I push hair back from my forehead and force myself to focus. "Go get the boats ready," I whisper to Luke. "We'll talk Maddie out of killing Julian and find a phone. Then we'll be right behind you."

"One of the boats is still in the tent on the beach," he says. "It'll take several of us to drag it into the water."

"Damn it." I turn to Indiana. "Will you go with him?"

"I'm *not* leaving you."

I spread my arms. "This is the safest place in the jungle. Everyone here is dead or unconscious. We'll find the phones and be right behind you, and we *need* the boats ready to go."

Luke gives Maddie a kiss on the forehead. "If I don't see you in five minutes, I'm coming back for you. Got it?"

Indiana pulls me close, and I *really* wish we had time to linger.

"We're almost out of this," I promise him. Then I tug him down, so I can whisper in his ear. "And when we are, I expect to be able to moan your *real name*."

Indiana groans into my hair. "Hell of a sendoff, G." He grins as Luke tugs him into the jungle, on the footpath toward the beach.

MADDIE

"Are you sure this is where you dropped the phone?" Genesis asks, sweeping torn straw mats aside with both hands.

"I don't know. Everything went crazy after the explosion. But it has to be around here somewhere. I was *right there* . . ."

"We don't have time for this, Maddie!" My dad's ship could already be out of range. "People are going to *die*."

"I know! I can't—" My hand brushes something hard, and I grab it. "Found it!" I sweep dirt from Holden's phone and press a button to wake it up. The screen is dim. "There's only five percent power."

"Then don't waste it." Genesis pulls me up by one arm. "Call your phone. They've turned it into one of the detonators."

My hands shake as I dial my number and press send, but . . . "There's no signal."

A twig crunches behind me, and Genesis and I spin toward the sound. Silvana stands with one hand pressed to her bloody forehead. The other aiming a pistol at us.

Fear spikes my pulse. Genesis should have let me kill her.

"Give me the phone," Silvana orders.

"Dial," Genesis says, her voice low and calm. "She got her ship, but she's in this for the money, and we're all she has left."

"You think your *papi* hasn't already paid? Give me the phone!" Silvana shouts, her accent thick, her words slurred from the concussion.

Genesis backs toward me, waving me toward the trees. I glance over my shoulder and aim for the footpath. We're just feet away. "Keep dialing," she whispers.

"Don't!" Silvana snaps. "If you want to live, give me the phone."

I press redial, but there's still no signal. "There's only three percent power!"

"Maddie?" Genesis whispers.

"Yeah?" My heart hammers against my sternum. My ears still echo from the explosion.

"Run."

NOW

GENESIS

Gunshots echo behind me.

I race through the jungle, swatting aside branches and jumping over exposed roots. Moonlight flashes through the canopy, glinting off the sweat on my skin and the blood splattered across my shirt, but the narrow trail is still shrouded in shadow.

I can't even see my boots as they beat the path.

"She's getting closer!" Maddie pants behind me.

I glance over my shoulder, and the movement throws me off balance. Maddie grabs my arm before I can fall, then she's in the lead, clutching the cell phone in one hand.

Footsteps pound behind us. Silvana huffs, as if each step drives more air from her lungs. But her pace is steady. She's strong and fast.

She's almost caught us.

"There it is!" Maddie points at a break in the jungle trail, and ahead, I see moonlight gleaming on dark water.

349

The beach. The boats.

We're almost free.

"Ow!" Maddie stumbles, then hops two steps, trying to grab her ankle without stopping. "I can't—"

"Yes you can!" I take her arm and haul her forward. "We're going to make it."

Maddie pulls me to a stop. I start to yell for her to go, but then I recognize the look in her eyes. Valencia stubbornness shines, even in the dark. "We *are* going to make it, but I can't run, so you have to get Silvana off the path. Take this." She slaps the phone into my palm. "Draw her into the jungle and press send as soon as you have a signal."

"I'm not going to leave—"

"Go!" she whispers fiercely as Silvana rounds the curve behind us. Then she ducks into the brush to hide, to the left of the path.

I make sure Silvana can see that I have the phone, then I take off into the jungle, to the right. I run with everything I have left, thrashing through the foliage to keep Silvana on my trail. Branches slap my face and tear at my clothes. Dirt gives way to sand beneath my feet, and I stumble, fighting to stay upright.

At the edge of the water, I see Luke run to Maddie and carry her into the boat. I hear music, and in the distance, I can see a cruise ship lit up like a party on all three levels. Help is *right there*. All we have to do is get to it.

There's a closer, smaller boat running dark in the water.

Headed north. My dad's cargo ship. It has to be.

The phone has one percent power and two signal bars.
I press redial.

The cruise ship explodes.

MADDIE

The night lights up like midday for a split second. An instant later, the boom echoes.

Then the shock wave hits us. The boat rocks violently. Luke and I fly into the dashboard, still clutching each other. He slams his shoulder against the steering wheel.

Indiana is thrown past us, into the windshield. He hits his head on the glass and crashes to the floor at my feet, eyes closed.

"No!" I kneel next to him, gripping the seat for balance as the boat rocks. I put one hand on Indiana's chest. It rises. He's still breathing. "Where are Penelope and Rog and Domenica?"

Luke points to the east, and I see the other speedboat barreling forward, parallel to the coast. Rocketing over wave after choppy wave.

They got away.

My cousin runs from the jungle onto the beach in a pool of torchlight. "Maddie—"

Silvana bursts from the brush and rams her from behind. Genesis hits the sand face-first. Silvana pounces.

"Go!" Genesis yells as she struggles to throw Silvana off.

Luke pulls himself up into the driver's seat and starts the engine.

"No!" I shout, but I can hardly hear my own voice.

"Go!" Genesis shouts again.

Silvana swings the pistol at her head. My cousin collapses on the sand.

"Genesis!"

"There's nothing we can do for her," Luke yells over the engine. Then he guns it. The boat shoots forward into the dark. Momentum throws me into the seat at my back.

Wind pummels my face through the cracked windshield, stealing my tears before they can fall. Ripping my screams from my throat. Indiana is bleeding onto the floor at my feet. I can't think. I can't see anything but flames on the water. I can't hear anything but the motor and the wind.

Then, it all stops.

The boat slows to a glide, and Luke kneels to take Indiana's pulse. He's holding a flare gun he must've found under one of the seats. "Maddie."

"We have to go back." I can still see the torches lit up on the beach, but they're as small as fireflies, and they flicker in the wind. I turn back to him, but I can't focus on his face through my tears, even with the moonlight. "I can't lose her, Luke." I sob, and my throat burns, but I can't stop crying. "I can't lose anyone else. I *can't*."

Pieces of the cruise ship float on the water. Some of them are still on fire.

He takes my hands. "If we go back, you'll lose me too.

And Indiana. If we go back, we *all* lose." His words sound thick, as if he's holding back tears. "That's not what Genesis wants."

He lets go of my left hand to swipe at his own eyes. Overhead, a helicopter beats the air, its searchlight probing the water. "She told me to get you out of here. And that's what I'm going to do."

Luke squeezes my hand. Then he stands and fires the flare into the sky.

LATER

GENESIS

I hear voices, but opening my eyes is a staggering effort. My eyelids are so heavy I wonder if they're taped shut.

Light floods my vision. Pain shoots through my skull.

I lift my hand to my temple, and the whole world spins around me. My temple feels oddly lumpy and damp. Sticky. My hand comes away bloody. My head feels like someone tried to scoop my brain out one tablespoon at a time.

I groan. The whole world is pain.

I sit up and feel something slick beneath me. I blink, and the surface finally comes into focus. I am on a sleeping bag, on a rough wooden floor. The walls around me are made of shoddily pieced-together boards. Daylight peeks in through the cracks.

A cabin.

From outside comes the devastatingly familiar chorus of birds, frogs, crickets, and . . . monkeys. I'm in the jungle. Still.

I never left. I may *never* leave.

My mouth is dry. My tongue feels swollen and clumsy. My throat aches. With every beat of my heart, a hammer seems to pound my head in echo.

"She's waking up," a voice says from another room, and I freeze. *Sebastián.* I remember him. But I can't remember how I got here. How I got hurt.

A shadow falls over me. My heart races, and the pounding in my skull matches its rhythm.

"Genesis?" The voice is older.

No. This makes no sense.

"Genesis, *niña*, do you remember what happened?"

My head spins.

"Uncle David?" He kneels next to me, and he looks *amazing*, for a dead man. I shake my head. The room tilts around me.

Who the hell did we bury?

"You've blown up half of my arsenal." He sounds impressed.

"I . . ." *What?* "Your . . . ?" The warheads. I blew up the warheads.

Oh, God. *I blew up a cruise ship.*

"Why—" My voice cracks. I lick my lips and start over. "Why were there warheads on a cruise ship?"

"Because smuggling is a creative endeavor, Genesis. Any cargo ship traveling from Colombia to the US is under suspicion, but the cruise liner . . . that was an experimental purchase, and the last one the DEA would think to check. There were *two thousand* people on that ship."

I'm breathing too fast. I'm going to pass out.

"Only half of them died." Uncle David shakes his head. "A humanitarian tragedy. But it says something about the culture of excess, does it not? All those rich people partying in the middle of the night. You really made a statement."

"No. I didn't know . . ."

He takes my chin, and his grip is hard. His brown eyes are not friendly or kind. This is not the uncle I remember. "All you had to do was sit still and wait to be rescued." A strand of graying hair falls over his forehead. "You could be at your grandmother's house right now, instead of bleeding on my floor."

Uncle David steps back and waves someone closer. Sebastián kneels next to me, holding a syringe. I flinch away, but he grabs my arm. His touch makes me sick.

He has two black eyes and a broken nose. Uncle David's knuckles are skinned and swollen.

"This wasn't the plan, Genesis," my uncle says. "Ryan . . ." His fists clench, and he turns away.

Ryan wasn't supposed to die. Maddie wasn't supposed to run away. I wasn't supposed to fight back.

Because Uncle David is *el jefe*. He's been the boss all along.

Sebastián slides the needle into my arm, but I hardly

feel the prick. My eye hurts. My head is in agony. But the real pain is deep, deep in my soul.

I am still in the jungle.

I am still a captive.

ACKNOWLEDGMENTS

100 Hours is a bit of a departure for me, and writing it was the most wonderful challenge. I'm privileged to have had the most wonderful support system in the world during the process. I hope I'm not forgetting anyone.

First, thanks go to my husband and my two awesome teenagers, for putting up with me during many long hours of research and revision. I know I'm not always easy to live with. I love you all.

Many, many thanks also to my amazing editor, Maria Barbo, for incredible dedication to this project and for spending so many after-hours hours indulging my every question and last-minute "let's brainstorm this" impulse. Genesis, Maddie, and I thank you.

Thanks also, as always, to my agent, Merrilee Heifetz, for making things happen. And for making me look good.

As usual, I owe a huge debt of gratitude to Rinda Elliot and Jennifer Lynn Barnes, for countless brainstorming sessions and hand-holding.

Thanks to CMSgt "Bear" Spitzer, USAF Ret., for indulging all of my research questions about the Colombian jungle.

Thanks also to Joshua Justice for answering so many questions about type 1 diabetes.

And a massive THANK-YOU to the HarperCollins production crew and art departments, for turning this story into a book. I can't tell you how happy I am to be working with you all!

DON'T MISS **99 LIES**, THE THRILLING CONCLUSION TO **100 HOURS!**

The elevator is too slow, and I can hear my uncle's footsteps thumping toward me. So I take off for the stairs at the end of the hall. Pushing the bar on the door sets off an alarm, but I'm only one floor up. I hit the midpoint landing before the door closes behind me, then I'm on the ground level racing toward the nearest exit. Which is the ER.

The TV mounted in the waiting room is tuned to a news station showing that picture of Holden walking out of the jungle. There's no volume, but I know what they're saying. Holden is a hero.

This is just more evidence that the world no longer makes sense, and I can't get out of here fast enough.

I bump into a man in a white lab coat on my way down the hall. "Sorry!" I call over my shoulder as I run, and the apology costs me my balance. My hip hits a cart standing in a doorway, and something clatters to the ground, but I can't stop to look.

Tears blur my vision, and by the time I burst through the ER doors into the parking lot, they're rolling down my face.

In my mother's car, I start the engine and suck in several deep breaths until I'm calm enough to be behind the wheel. Then I slam the gearshift into drive and pull onto the street. I have no idea where I'm going. As I change lanes and take turns, blinking to clear fresh tears from my eyes, all I can think about is that every single thing I thought I knew about my life has been a lie.